# Dante crossed the yard, stomped up the steps, grabbed Marlena's arms, and shook her.

"What in the hell were you doing going into that house? You could have been killed."

Marlena straightened her shoulders. "I'm tired of being afraid. No one, absolutely no one is going to run me out of my own house." Her jaw flexed. "Not ever again."

He growled low in his throat. "But you should be scared," he said between clenched teeth.

The uncertainty in her eyes tore at him. His adrenaline was churning, his heart pounding, his blood racing. He'd never felt this kind of bone-deep terror before, and he didn't like it. Marlena could have died tonight, and he wouldn't have been able to stop it.

Unable to refrain, he jerked her to him. Her body trembled, her breath hitching, her gaze locking with his, questions brimming. He ignored the repercussions screaming in his head. The knowledge that she was forbidden. Instead, he dragged her into his arms, then claimed her mouth with his...

*n this page*
*for praise for Rita Herron...*

Also by Rita Herron

*Insatiable Desire*
*Dark Hunger*

# FORBIDDEN PASSION

## Rita Herron

FOREVER

NEW YORK   BOSTON

Copyright © 2010 by Rita Herron
Excerpt from *Insatiable Desire* copyright © 2009 by Rita Herron
Excerpt from *Dark Hunger* copyright © 2009 by Rita Herron

*Cover design by Diane Luger*
*Cover art by Franco Accornero*

Forever
Hachette Book Group
237 Park Avenue
New York, NY 10017
Visit our website at www.HachetteBookGroup.com.

Forever is an imprint of Grand Central Publishing. The Forever name and logo is a trademark of Hachette Book Group, Inc.

Printed in the United States of America

First Printing: April 2010

10 9 8 7 6 5 4 3 2 1

To:
Netti, one of my favorite booksellers!
Thanks for all your support!

# Acknowledgments

Thanks again to my editor Michele Bidelspach for her great insight and for making this a better book. Also, thanks to Dr. Lee Herron for sharing medical knowledge and for being the best husband ever!

# FORBIDDEN PASSION

# *Prologue*

Fire gave him power. It was his gift. His method of attack. His best defense.

It had also become his obsession.

Thirteen-year-old Dante Zertlav raised his fist to stare at his reddening fingertips. The urge to throw a fireball ripped through him, evil beckoning.

"Don't fight your dark side," Father Gio commanded. "Embrace it and you can rule the world."

Dante nodded. He'd known this day was coming, the final test for him and his band of demonic brothers. The elements were all here now, Storm and Lightfoot preparing for their own initiation.

So far, Dante had passed the initiation with flying colors. He'd tracked the animals, killed them with his bare hands. Done everything Father Gio had ordered, no matter how vile.

He'd learned long ago that disobeying Father Gio meant harsh punishments. Torture.

Being turned into the hunted instead.

But today, the last and final test would be to kill a human.

A sickening knot gripped his belly.

He didn't know if he could do it.

A maelstrom of ancient chants and sinister voices surrounded him as the other demons gathered. Smoke curled from the fire pit, and twigs and wood snapped and crackled, shooting flames against the inky sky.

Father Gio gestured through the woods, and Dante spotted a woman and a dark-haired little girl hunched by their own small campfire roasting marshmallows. A smaller blond girl sat swinging her bare feet into the gurgling creek water.

"Your assignment is to kill the youngest one, and offer her to Helzebar."

Dante stiffened. Although he'd been banned from attending school with mortals, he'd snuck by the schoolyards to watch. One memory struck him hard and had stuck with him.

A bully of a boy had chased a puppy into a storm drain, and this little blond had wriggled inside and rescued the animal. When she'd climbed out, she was filthy, her hair tangled, her knees scraped, but she'd scooped up the pudgy dog and sang to it like an angel.

Until that day, he'd only known demons and violence.

He'd been so enthralled that afternoon that he'd followed her home, had watched her mother laugh at the sight of the puppy. Then the little blond and her sister had played with the dog in a field of wildflowers until they'd both collapsed in a fit of giggles.

He'd envied their laughter. Their innocence.

Their happy family.

They had no idea demons lurked in the woods of Mysteria, Tennessee. No idea the demons had decided to hunt humans in their own backyards.

"Storm will take the oldest girl, Lightfoot, the woman."

Father Gio placed a clawlike hand on Dante's shoulder, drawing him back to the present. "But yours will be the biggest sacrifice for you are meant for great things."

Pride mushroomed in his chest. But anxiety tightened his breath at the same time. He had embraced the darkness within him, had enjoyed the hunt, the taste of the animals' blood, the screech of the kill.

He liked pleasing his master.

But something about taking this young girl's life felt...wrong, and needled at his conscience.

A conscience he thought he'd buried long ago.

Suddenly a roar of thunder rent the air, the collective hiss of the demons' war cries erupting, and Storm and Lightfoot charged toward their prey. The dark-haired girl cried out in terror.

"Run!" the mother cried as she shoved her daughters into the woods.

Both girls screamed as they stumbled over broken logs and brush in their haste to escape. But Storm and Lightfoot's human forms shimmered into monsters as they attacked.

Storm swept the mother up by her hair and flung her across the woods, her body bouncing off a boulder a few feet away. Blood spurted from her forehead as she tried to get up, but her leg was twisted, broken, and she collapsed with a sob as Storm jumped her again. Lightfoot caught the dark-haired girl and swept her up as if she was air itself.

The little blond ducked behind an overhang on the ridge, eyes widening in horror as she stared at the grisly scene.

Indecision ripped through Dante. If he disobeyed,

he would be ostracized from the only family he'd ever known.

How would he survive out here all alone? The demons would eat him alive...

Then the little girl spotted him. "Help me. Please help me."

Pain squeezed his lungs at her haunted whisper. She was so tiny, so young. How could he squash the life out of her?

He couldn't.

Tamping down the fire heating his fingers, he ran toward her, threw her over his back, then raced through the woods, adrenaline churning as the demons gave chase.

Behind him, the thunderous roar of the demons cheering Storm and Lightfoot rent the air, then Father Gio's voice commanding him to bring the girl back.

But the frail girl clung to him, burying her head against his shoulder, and protective instincts surged inside him. The fiery breath of one of the demons stung his back, but he flung fireballs at the demon, warding them off as he raced through the forest.

Finally he reached a clearing and spotted a dingy white church on top of the hill. He'd never been inside a church and wondered if lightning would strike him if he entered. But it was the only safe place for the girl, so he dashed up to the doorway, shoved it open, and slipped inside.

The scent of burning candles filled the air, and a rainbow of vibrant colors illuminated the room from the stained-glass window above the pulpit, a calm peacefulness enveloping the chapel.

The little girl whimpered, and he carried her to the front pew and placed her on it.

"Wh...o are y...ou?" she whispered.

"My name is Dante," he said softly. "What's your name?"

Her lip trembled. "Marlena..."

"You'll be safe here, Marlena. Just stay inside."

Tears streaked her face as she reached for him. "I'm scared...Don't leave me."

The wooden floor creaked, jerking his attention to the pulpit, and a priest wearing a long robe appeared from the back. His intense gaze pinned Dante, as if he could see into his black soul.

Regret and sorrow for all he'd done bled through Dante. But he didn't belong here, not in this holy place.

He cupped the little girl's face between his hands to quiet her. "You'll be all right now," he said, then lowered his head and pressed a kiss in her blond curls. She smelled of sweetness and innocence, things he'd never known. "The priest will take care of you."

Her lower lip quivered, tearing at him, but the earth shook and rumbled, the demons roared outside, and he knew he had to leave.

She was safer far away from him.

So he turned and fled through the doorway.

But as he stepped outside, the demons' angry chants echoed from the forest. He couldn't go back to Father Gio. He didn't belong with the demons.

He didn't want to be evil anymore.

But he wasn't good either, and he didn't belong with the humans.

He had to make his own path. Pay penitence for his sins before he lost his soul completely.

# Chapter One

Twenty Years Later

*Evil has no rules. It always wins.*

That creed had been beaten into Dante as a child. And when the portals from the underground to the Earth had opened on All Hallows' Eve three months ago, the pull of evil had grown stronger.

The very reason he'd returned to Mysteria. The reason he'd become sheriff.

His penance was to protect the town from his own kind.

And part of that job meant checking the underground tunnels where the demons thrived.

But as he strode through the tunnels, the darkness called to him like a siren begging him to her bed. Hard to resist.

The evil gave him great power in his hands, fueled his firestarter abilities.

It also threatened to turn him into a monster as it had his demon brothers years ago.

The scent of impending death and doom hovered in the dank air. Somewhere in the cavern, he detected a shape-shifter nearby. He heard the hiss of fangs snapping. The cry of an animal drawing its last breath.

Ever since the new lord of the underworld Zion had risen, Dante had noted more widespread chaos and violence across the States.

He'd heard that new demon factions had formed, making plans, honing their powers to please Zion, the most notorious leader of the underworld ever known. Some said Zion was a direct descendant of Satan.

Father Gio was probably working for him now.

Dante's gut tightened. He'd have to confront him eventually. Destroy him if he returned and began preying on the town.

Dante's cell phone buzzed, and he glanced at the number, his hand tightening around the phone. His deputy, Hobbs.

A man he didn't trust. Then again, he didn't trust anyone.

"Yeah?"

"Sheriff, that doctor lady named Marlena Bender phoned again to see if there were any leads on those missing blood vials from BloodCore."

Dante gritted his teeth. He'd seen the file on his desk and had been shocked to learn that she'd moved back to Mysteria.

Just as he had to face Father Gio, he had to face her. But not yet.

"I'll call her when I get time," Dante said. After all, a few missing vials of blood could wait.

The demons in the darkness posed a more imminent danger.

———

Marlena Bender forced herself to walk through the cemetery to her mother and sister's graves. Gravel and dead leaves crunched beneath her shoes, the shadows of the ancient burial ground eerie in the waning moonlight. Dead flowers and faded plastic arrangements swayed and drooped beneath the elements, and dry parched grass bled between the rows of dirt-covered graves. A fresh mound a few rows over made her chest clench and stirred memories of the last time she'd stood here, burying her own family.

Images of the horrible night they'd died taunted her. Her mother and sister's screams echoed in her ears and suddenly a shimmering light sparkled in a hazy glow as if their spirits had appeared.

She blinked, shivering at the thought, the winter wind biting through her as it whipped leaves and twigs around her ankles. Moonlight glinted off the granite tombstones highlighting their names and the date their lives had ended.

*Beloved mother and sister—gone too soon.*

Lost to a horrible fate.

But she had survived. Not for the first time, she'd questioned *why* she'd been saved.

And the man—the boy—who had rescued her.

Just the thought of seeing Dante Zertlav made her chest clench with anxiety.

Although he'd saved her life, questions plagued her. What had he been doing in those woods? How had he been able to run so fast?

And who had attacked and killed her mother and sister?

Had they been monsters as she remembered, or had her childhood imagination simply played a trick on her mind as the doctors who'd treated her had suggested?

She'd wanted to talk to Dante back then to find out what he'd seen, but she'd been too traumatized, and her grandmother had whisked her out of town as if the devil had been on their tails.

She'd been shocked to learn that he was the sheriff when she'd moved back to Mysteria.

She'd phoned three times this week asking if he had leads on the missing blood vials.

Apparently he wasn't concerned.

But she was.

The missing vials held blood samples from violent criminals, individuals who professed to have paranormal powers, and the mentally and criminally insane.

One day she hoped to find a genetic abnormality that could be altered to correct deviant behavior and deter violent tendencies.

Recently she'd noted disturbing markers in some samples that made her wonder if the monsters she'd thought she'd seen as a child were real, not figments of her childhood imagination.

That was one of the reasons she'd moved back to Mysteria. Her nightmares had grown more intense lately. She had to confront her past in order to move on.

She bent and spread the rose petals across her mother's grave, then her sister's. "I have to know the truth about who killed you."

And why the police had never found answers.

The ground suddenly felt as if it shifted beneath her, the dirt sucking at her feet as if the earth might literally suck her into the graves below.

She trembled. Mysteria was full of ghost stories, but she was a doctor, a scientist. She'd never believed in the paranormal.

Except for that day as a child...

But she was an adult now and she could face the truth. There had to be a logical explanation.

And what if her family's killers had remained in Mysteria all these years?

Had there been other unexplained deaths since?

She'd have to check and see...

Thunder began to rumble, thick black clouds swallowing the moon, and a raindrop splattered her cheek, mingling with the tears she didn't realize had fallen.

With a gloved hand, she swiped at the moisture, then turned and ran toward her car. Footsteps crunched leaves behind her, and she pivoted and scanned the distance, but the graveyard was empty. Twigs snapped on the opposite side and she jerked her head to the right. An ominous shadow floated behind a grave marker, then disappeared into the woods.

Suddenly sensing danger, she threw the car door open and collapsed inside, trembling. The shadow stood beneath the gnarled branches of a live oak, then spread his arms in a wide arc like some winged creature that had risen from the grave to attack.

God, she was seeing things again. It had to be a man. Or maybe some teenager trying to spook her.

Irritated that he'd succeeded, she started the engine and steered her Honda over the graveled drive, but the car suddenly lurched as if someone or something had pushed her forward.

Nerves on edge, she glanced in the rearview mirror, then over her shoulder, but didn't see a car—or a person. Nothing.

It's just the wind, she told herself.

But she felt the shove again and she accelerated, taking

the curvy mountain road toward her old homestead so fast that her tires squealed and she skimmed the guardrail twice before she turned up her drive.

A tiny sliver of moonlight fought through the storm clouds and painted the turrets and attic in sharp angles as her Victorian homestead came into view, the swaying branch of an oak clawing at the frost-coated window-pane. The wind roared, seeping through her bones as she grabbed her purse and computer bag, then walked up the pebbled drive toward the wrap-around porch.

An animal howled, and she looked up and spotted a lone wolf silhouetted at the top of the ridge. Fear slithered through her like a poison eating at her as she searched the woods. She'd avoided the forest for years.

But the thick trees and dark secrets surrounded her, whispering that evil hid in the shadows, waiting to prey.

*For God's sake, Marlena. You're a grown woman. You have to get a grip.*

Desperate to shake off her anxiety, she scrubbed a hand through her tangled hair, her keys jingling in her trembling hand as she climbed the porch steps.

She would not give in to the fear. She hated the way it had paralyzed her when she was young.

Before that horrible day, she'd been a daredevil, had thought she was invincible.

But her naïveté had been shattered with her family's brutal murder.

The wind swirled her hair around her face, but a box on the floor in front of the door caught her eye.

A small silver gift box tied with a big red bow.

Surprised, she picked it up and examined it. There was

no card, no address, nothing on the outside to indicate whom it was from.

She unlocked the door and stepped inside, grateful for the blast of heat from the furnace. Yet the floors creaked, the windowpanes rattled, and the old pipes groaned like an aging person's bones popping.

Shivering, she flipped on a light and opened the box. Surprise flared inside her at the sight of a ring lying on top of the crumpled tissue paper.

Then her heart began to pound, and apprehension tightened her shoulder blades.

A tiny pearl was set in an antique white gold setting with two small diamond chips flanking the sides. She recognized the setting—the ring belonged to Jordie McEnroe, a young waitress at the diner.

Her hand trembled.

The ring was soaked in blood.

The phone in the sheriff's office was ringing as Dante entered. He glanced around the office for his deputy, then realized Hobbs had probably gone home for the night. Good. He wouldn't have to deal with the man now. Dante didn't want help, and Hobbs sure as hell didn't like working for him. He'd wanted the job as sheriff himself.

In three quick strides, he crossed the wooden floor and grabbed the handset. "Sheriff Zertlav."

A shaky breath rattled over the line. "Hello, who is this?"

A feminine voice finally squeaked out, "M...arlena Bender."

He scrubbed a hand over the back of his neck. Hell. He'd wanted to stall longer, but her voice had warbled as if something was wrong. "Listen, Dr. Bender, I know you called about that stolen blood and—"

"It's Marlena, Dante, so don't act like you don't know me. And I'm not calling about the blood this time," she continued, cutting him off. "I need you to come out to my house."

His gut tightened. Had the demons already found her? "What's wrong?"

"I just got home," she said, "and I found a gift...a box...on my doorstep."

"I don't understand."

"You will when you see it," Marlena said. "It's a woman's ring, and it's covered in blood."

Dante frowned. "Blood?"

"Yes, and it's fresh."

He made a disgusted sound as his mind churned with the possibilities. "Somebody's idea of a sick joke?"

"Maybe," Marlena said. "But it belongs to Jordie McEnroe, the young waitress at the diner. I just saw her yesterday and she was wearing it."

He rapped his knuckles on the desk, contemplating the situation. Why would someone leave Jordie's ring, covered in blood, on Marlena's doorstep?

"What if something's happened to her, Dante?" Worry laced Marlena's voice. "You have to check on her."

"I'll call the diner and see if she's there, then come to your place and pick up the ring." He paused. "And don't touch it. If there has been a crime, I'll need to dust it for prints."

"I know." Marlena sighed. "I just hope Jordie's all right."

"I'll be there soon."

A tense second passed. "Dante?"

He cleared his throat, tried to ignore the hint of emotion in her voice. "Yeah?"

"Don't you need my address?"

He couldn't admit that he already knew where she lived. That he'd followed her home as a child and watched her. That he'd checked out her house the first night he'd driven back into Mysteria.

"Yes, give it to me."

She quickly recited it, and he disconnected the call, then punched in the number for the diner. A quick glance at the clock told him it was 9:00 P.M. The dinner rush should be over.

Finally a woman answered. "Roadside Diner. Rosy speaking."

"This is Sheriff Zertlav. Can you tell me if Jordie McEnroe is there?"

"No, she didn't show up tonight," Rosy said. "And her mama is having a fit, too. It's just not like Jordie to blow off her shift."

An uneasy feeling slid up Dante's spine. "Give me her address and I'll check on her."

"You think something's wrong?" Rosy asked, suddenly panicked.

Dammit, he had a bad feeling. "No, just offering to ease Mrs. McEnroe's mind."

"Awww, Sheriff, you're a sweetheart. I know she'll appreciate that."

A bitter chuckle escaped him as he hung up. If she knew he was part demon, knew the things he'd done, she sure as hell wouldn't call him a sweetheart.

Dark shadows flickered off the tall, thick trees as he

drove from Main Street toward the mountains. The roads grew curvy, more narrow, the shadows thicker, the silence more ominous. Five miles around the mountain, and he spun up the graveled drive toward Marlena's.

The hundred-year-old blue Victorian house sat atop a hill, the paint slightly weathered, the sharp turrets and angles reminding him of an old haunted house.

Throwing the SUV into park, he climbed out, pulling his bomber jacket around him to battle the brittle wind as he walked up to the porch. The steps creaked as he climbed them, and the sound of a wolf howling from the woods made him twist his head and scan the edge of her property.

The trees shivered, but if there had been one nearby, it had disappeared.

Bracing himself to see Marlena again, and hoping like hell she'd turned into a geeky adult who would hold no temptation for him, he raised his fist and knocked.

But his lungs tightened when she opened the door.

She was even more beautiful than he could have imagined, a radiant full moon against a blinding sea of night.

From her heavy breasts to her narrow waist to hips that flared enticingly, she painted a picture of seduction. But she was the last woman on earth he could think about taking.

Gritting his teeth, he swallowed back guilt. But even as he fought it, the dark side of him emerged, lust heating his body.

Wavy, blond hair that looked like silk shimmered over her shoulders, and her frightened eyes were still the palest, oddest shade of green he'd ever seen.

He'd never forgotten those eyes. They had been luminous and trusting when she was a child. Now that she was a woman, they could suck a man in with their sensuality and promises.

But horror and sadness had filled them the day of the attack.

And that horror and sadness had taunted him day and night, reminding him of what he was.

She'd been made a homeless child because of his demon family. And if she knew the truth, she'd hate him.

He had washed his hands in her blood.

He was obsessed with it now. The thick, sticky crimson as it flowed from open wounds. The coppery metallic scent as it filled the air.

The tiny splatters that looked like artwork on the walls and his shirt.

Blood was the life force of the body. The river that swept a person along.

The heart and soul that gave life and took it away.

He lifted his fingers and stared at them now. Remembered the woman's body as she'd jerked and screamed and begged him to stop.

She had had to die.

So did the others.

It was the only way to stop them from becoming like him. A monster. A child of the devil.

A killer who stole lives for pure pleasure and worshipped the evil growing inside him. The evil that gave him strength.

Strength and a power he'd never possessed before.

But he'd had to set the woman on fire to throw off the cops. Couldn't let them know the real reason she'd had to die.

Besides, Zion had given him his orders. Make it look as if a firestarter had killed the girl.

And leave his trophy with the woman Marlena. The one who'd caused Dante to fail his initiation.

The woman who would have to die so Dante could find his way back to his father.

# Chapter Two

———

Marlena had dreamed of seeing Dante again for years. Only not like this. Not with a bloody ring from another girl in her hand, and the fear that someone else had been murdered.

Tension thrummed in the air as he stared at her, and for a moment, she literally couldn't breathe.

The boy who had saved her that day had been tall, big, strong, but he'd barely been a teenager.

Now he'd grown into a man.

One with thick dark black hair, and eyes so deep and brown they looked as if they'd never seen light. A hard intensity radiated from him, sending a frisson of fear through her. He looked as if he'd walked with the worst of mankind too long and was suffering for it.

Even his size was intimidating. He towered over her, his shoulders were broad like a linebacker's, his thighs thick and muscled.

And sexy. God, he was so sexy...

Her body actually trembled with the need to be near him. In her dreams, he was always the one who saved her just as he had when she was a child.

But his eyes held a warning, not a friendly welcome. And when she glanced at his hand where he gripped the door, she noticed dozens of scars on his skin. Burn scars.

His shirtsleeve rode up, revealing a dozen more rippling up his arm.

His gaze followed hers, and his jaw tightened. "You had something to show me?"

His gruff voice jerked her back to reality. She'd assumed they'd discuss the past, but apparently he didn't want to chitchat.

But she had questions, and eventually she'd force him to answer them.

She nodded. "Yes...in here."

Desperate to regain control, she led him to the pine table in the foyer where she'd dropped the box. "There it is."

Dante's jaw tightened as he slipped on plastic gloves, then used a pair of tweezers to pick up the ring and examine it. She wrapped her arms around herself as he brought it near his nose and sniffed.

"You're right, it's fresh blood. Human." He angled his head toward her. "You're sure this ring belonged to Jordie?"

She shrugged. "It's identical to the one she was wearing when I saw her. She told me it was a graduation present from her mother, that it had been passed down from her grandmother."

"I'll take it to the lab, have the blood analyzed, and the ring and box dusted for prints." He narrowed his eyes. "Did you touch it?"

"No, just the outside of the box."

"Was there a card or a note with the box?"

"No." She rubbed her arms with her hands. "There's no return address on it either, so it must have been hand delivered."

His frown deepened, and nerves skated through her. If someone had hurt Jordie, why would they leave the girl's bloody ring on *her* doorstep?

"You didn't see or hear anyone leaving as you drove up?"

She shook her head again. "I'm afraid not."

"So we don't know when it was left here?"

"I went to the lab this morning around eight and haven't been home since, so it could have been dropped off any time today."

He nodded, but anger radiated from his every pore. "What are you doing back here in Mysteria?"

His bluntness sounded almost like an accusation. "I work at BloodCore."

"Is that the only reason?"

Pain clenched her lungs. "I want to know what happened to my mother and sister," she said. "Why no one ever found their killers."

He stared at her for so long that her body trembled from the impact. "Don't, Marlena. Let it go."

"Why should I?" she said, her temper flaring,

The scar running down his neck into his shirt darkened as he tensed. "Because it's too dangerous."

His icy tone made her take a step back. "I can't. I've made it my life's work to understand deviant behavior. If I know who killed my family, maybe I can finally understand the reason and move on."

A sinister look settled in his eyes, one that made her wonder if this man was really the same boy who'd saved her years ago. If he was the hero she remembered.

Or if something had changed him.

"You treat psychiatric patients, Marlena. You know sometimes there is just evil."

She couldn't deny his comment, although his reference, or maybe acceptance, of evil bothered her. "You were there, Dante. I'd think you would want to know what happened, too."

He narrowed his eyes to menacing slits. "That was years ago. I'm sure the sheriff did his best to find the killer. I have a current case to investigate."

She crossed her arms. "Right. You need to see if Jordie is safe."

"Maybe one of your patients killed her and brought you his trophy?"

Guilt nagged at her as she considered that theory, but she couldn't accuse one of her patients without concrete evidence.

"I have Jordie's address," he continued. "She didn't show up for her evening work shift, so I'll drive out to her house and see if she's home."

Marlena reached for her coat. "I'll go with you."

A muscle ticked in his jaw. "No. I'll let you know what I find."

Marlena caught his arm just before he headed out the door. "I'm a doctor, Dante. If she's hurt, she might need medical treatment."

Hesitation flared in his expression, but he finally nodded.

She grabbed her coat and they rushed out to his SUV.

As he shifted gears, Marlena fastened her seatbelt and said a silent prayer that Jordie was all right.

❦

Dante clenched the steering wheel with a white-knuckled grip. Marlena had come back to Mysteria to find out what had happened to her family.

He couldn't let her discover the truth.

And he couldn't let her touch him again.

He was in deep shit here.

Just the brush of her fingers against his skin had sent a tingling rush through his system and aroused him to the point of pain.

Marlena Bender was off limits. Forbidden. A human he couldn't have.

But he wanted her with a vengeance.

Gritting his teeth, he forced himself to focus on the road as the wind battered the Jeep.

Marlena rubbed her temple as if massaging a headache, and he wished to hell he hadn't let her come with him. Her feminine scent was driving his blood wild with lust.

But if Jordie was alive and hurt, Marlena was right— she might need a doctor.

"I was surprised to find out that you were sheriff," Marlena said, breaking the tense silence stretching between them. "Although I guess I shouldn't have been surprised since you saved my life that day."

He grunted. She thought he was a fucking hero when he was only trying to make amends for his sins.

"I told you to leave the past alone," he muttered. "Nothing good can come of stirring up trouble."

"How can you say that?" Marlena asked. "Knowing who killed my family and putting them in jail would finally give me closure. And what if these guys have killed again? As sheriff, wouldn't you want to stop them?"

"Most likely they left the area a long time ago," Dante argued.

In fact, he knew they had gone on to hunt in other towns. But if they returned, he would track them down.

They weren't going to feed off the locals, not on his watch.

Marlena sighed. "I read the papers, Dante. I know there have been other unexplained deaths over the years."

He gritted his teeth. "That doesn't mean they're related to your family's death."

"I know that. But the nightmares...won't leave me alone. I have to do something."

Dammit. Her return could draw back the very demons who'd destroyed her life.

"Like I told you, it's dangerous," he growled. "If you start digging around and the killers find out, they might come after you, Marlena."

Fear turned her green eyes to dark emeralds. "I don't care," she said. "I have to know the truth. I've relived that attack for years."

This time he reached out and covered her hand with his. Instant lust shot through him. He liked his sex fast and furious. With Marlena it would be fast and furious and potent.

But then he might want her again and again...Slow and languid...

He might even want to wake up with her.

That was too dangerous.

"Let me handle things, okay?"

Her fingers tightened below his, curling up into his palm in a trusting gesture.

Hell, he was the last person she should trust.

"Why were you in the woods that day, Dante?" she asked softly.

There it was. The one question he'd feared she'd ask.

The one question he couldn't answer without exposing

the truth about what he was. And if that truth were revealed, the town would lynch him instead of allowing him to protect them.

"Dante?"

He abruptly released her hand. He had to break the connection and kill the desire thrumming through him. "I was camping downstream," he said. "When I heard the screams, I came running."

Thankfully, he found the dirt road leading to the cabin where Jordie lived and veered onto it. Ahead smoke billowed in a fog and curled upward.

Marlena tensed. "Look, something's on fire."

Dread balled in Dante's stomach as he broke through the clearing and spotted a smoking tree. Holy fuck. A woman's body was tied to it.

Marlena gasped as he threw the Jeep into Park.

He pressed his arm in front of her to stop her when she reached for the car door. "Stay here."

The scent of burning tree bark seeped into his pores the moment he stepped from his SUV. Slowly he moved toward the tall oak, his gaze zeroing in on the woman's body dangling from a low branch. Her skin was ashen where the flames had eaten it away, but he recognized her face. Jordie.

Marlena inched up behind him. "Oh, my God..."

Dante froze at the sound of her raspy sigh. Instincts honed, he pivoted and studied the periphery to make certain the killer wasn't lurking around watching.

The dead leaves covering the ground rustled in the hills, the bare branches swayed on the mountain, and whispers of death and evil echoed off the ridge.

Something was out there, but he couldn't be sure what

it was. A human or a demon? The killer or another predator?

Marlena's sob broke into the haze. "Poor Jordie... Who would do such a thing?"

Dante had witnessed gruesome murders, savage brutality, mutilated animals and humans before. But Marlena had left Mysteria to escape them.

The sight of tears on her face wrenched at him. He couldn't care about this woman. He had a job to do.

The fact that there had been other mysterious deaths and disappearances over the years gnawed at him. He knew they were demon-related, but the sheriff before him and the one before him had always found some plausible explanation. Wild animals. A drifter. A domestic dispute.

But he knew the truth.

He pulled her up against him and buried her head against his chest to shield her from the horror.

"Why would someone do this to Jordie?" Marlena whispered again.

The image of the bloody pearl ring flashed in Dante's head.

It wasn't a coincidence that Jordie had been sadistically murdered, and that the killer had left Marlena his trophy.

Dammit. The perp knew Marlena and wanted to lure her into his twisted game.

Which meant Marlena was in danger.

Marlena blinked rapidly to erase the horrible images in her mind. But her heart was pounding and all she could think was that it was too late. Too late for Jordie as it had been for her mother and sister.

That some sick twisted monster had brutalized the young waitress, and that he'd been at her house, on her porch.

That he'd left Jordie's ring for her to find. Jordie's ring all bloody...

Blood she could handle. She dealt with it every day. Samples of blood, but not fresh blood from a murder victim's body.

Especially a murdered woman that she knew. That she'd talked to almost every morning this past week when she'd stopped by the diner for coffee on her way to work.

"Marlena," Dante said gruffly. "I need to call in a crime unit and search Jordie's house." He coached her back to the SUV. "Wait inside the Jeep, and lock the doors. If you see or hear anything or anyone suspicious, just honk the horn, and I'll be right there."

She nodded against his chest, the cold wind coupled with shock chilling her all the way to her bones as he led her back to the car.

With one deft movement, he unlocked the glove compartment and removed a pistol, at the same time scanning the woods, the house, the property. He thought the killer might still be around.

"Do you know how to use a gun?" he asked.

She nodded, although she didn't know if she could actually shoot someone. But she glanced at Jordie's body again and self-preservation kicked in. "Yes."

"Good."

He pushed the .45 into her shaky hands, then closed the door, removed his own weapon, and headed toward the cabin.

He watched through the spiny trees from the top of the ridge, laughter bubbling from his throat.

The games had begun.

Marlena Bender had found the gift he'd left for her. And she'd done exactly as he'd expected.

Called Dante.

Zion's son would be a challenge, but the price would be worth it when he fell into Zion's hands.

Pleasing Zion was his ticket to eternal life. And he would live forever.

# Chapter Three

———

Dante entered the house with his gun drawn, visually sweeping the entryway and pausing to listen for an intruder.

But an eerie silence enveloped the place, along with the odor of bleach.

The killer had cleaned up after the crime. What exactly had he done to Jordie before he'd set her on fire?

Oddly, the inside of the front room looked undisturbed. Simple, worn furniture, magazines stacked neatly, a Diet Coke can on the counter along with an empty coffee cup and cereal bowl.

No sign of alcohol or indication Jordie had been entertaining.

He veered to the left to the bedroom and eased inside. An antique bed held an old-fashioned quilt, the dresser a small jewelry box and tray of perfumes, but the room was neat, no sign of a struggle or an intruder. Nothing to raise suspicion.

Except that the scent of bleach and cleaning chemicals grew stronger as he neared the bathroom, and he glanced at the tub. Without touching the tiled wall, he leaned forward to examine the drain. Blood rimmed the metal.

Blood had been on Jordie's ring. What exactly was the

cause of death? He'd have to ask the medical examiner to be thorough.

He mentally ticked away more questions as he strode back outside. A quick glance at his SUV, and he breathed a sigh of relief that Marlena was still safely inside.

Frowning, he walked back to the body and studied the crime scene again, searching for a clue to whether the killer was human or demonic before he called CSI.

His gaze skimmed over Jordie's body from head to toe, then he narrowed his eyes to study the plot of land surrounding the tree where ashes had fallen. Several pieces of charred bark lay on the ground.

The pieces lay in a pattern.

Anger roiled inside him—the bark had been arranged in the shape of a Satanic S.

Sweat beaded on his brow. The crime scene looked ritualistic, possibly a serial killer. One who was into devil worshipping.

Or maybe Satan himself was behind this murder.

⌐◆¬

Marlena's hands felt slick with perspiration as she eased the gun onto her lap. Thank God Dante had finally come out of that cabin.

She'd been terrified that the killer had been inside, waiting to ambush him.

And then the maniac who'd murdered Jordie might have come after her...

She inhaled sharply, struggling to calm her nerves as she watched him examine the crime scene. Something about the ground around Jordie's body was bothering him.

A coyote howled in the distance, and storm clouds

rumbled above, a streak of lightning flashing across the top of the mountain ridges.

Dante suddenly straightened and turned to study the forest again as if he suspected the killer was watching them. Then he unhooked his phone from his belt buckle and punched in a number.

She stared at Jordie's body, her chest aching. She'd felt helpless when her mother and sister had died.

Now she felt helpless again.

All her training and medical knowledge couldn't bring Jordie back or alleviate the suffering she'd endured.

But she would like to know who'd killed her, take a sample of the maniac's blood and study it.

Dante snapped his phone closed, then strode over to the SUV.

She depressed the window button and the glass slid down. "Did you find anything in her house?"

"The bathroom has been scrubbed with bleach. It might be part of the original murder scene."

Marlena forced herself to drag her gaze away from Jordie's charred body. "What were you looking at on the ground?"

"Pieces of bark were arranged in a pattern creating a Satanic S symbol."

Marlena frowned. "What does that mean?"

"That this is a ritualistic killing. That the killer may be a Satan worshipper." Dante paused, his steely eyes bleak. "That he's a serial killer and he's just getting started."

Marlena had studied profiles of famous serial killers. She'd also interviewed a couple in prison to study their behavior patterns and histories, ones who'd allowed her to use their blood for her research.

But none of their cases had hit this close to home.

"I can't believe this is happening, that Jordie is dead and the killer left me her ring."

Dante cleared his throat, then reached out and rubbed her arms. She hadn't realized she was shivering again, but his hands on her instantly warmed her.

"The fact that he did means he knows you."

Shock hit her, but she immediately realized he was right.

"I know this is tough, Marlena, but you're a psychiatrist. You work with the criminally insane. Do you have a patient who could have committed this kind of violence?"

Denial was her automatic response. "Dante, I'm bound by patient-doctor confidentiality. I can't reveal anything about my patients without their permission."

His mouth thinned in anger. "After what happened to your family, I can't believe you'd choose to protect some psycho rather than helping to find this killer."

Anger knotted her insides, and she pushed his hands away. "You don't have to remind me of the worst day of my life."

Dante glared at her. "Then tell me if you know someone who could have done this, Marlena, because he obviously intends to include you in his twisted game. And you know what that means."

"That he wants my help," Marlena said, falling back on her psychiatric training, "or that he wants to be caught."

"Maybe," Dante said in a hiss. "Or that he intends to target you as one of his victims."

~

Dante steeled himself against the fear in Marlena's eyes. Fear he'd put there with the truth.

But she couldn't walk around with blinders on, not here in Mysteria.

Dammit, maybe he should tell her everything. That demons roamed the world. That they might still be after her.

That they'd hurt her to punish him for defying them if he got too close to her.

"I'll study my patient list," Marlena said in a shaky voice. "If I discover any information or evidence regarding one of my patients that's relevant to Jordie's murder, I'll let you know."

Sirens wailed in the distance, cutting off any more conversation. Within seconds, the CSI team and Deputy Hobbs arrived, all of them jumping out and reacting to the sight of Jordie's burned body with disgust and shock.

He hated to call in the crime lab, wanted to track down this bastard and deal with him in his own way.

But he was the sheriff. He had to follow protocol to a point. This case was too brutal and violent not to have a crime unit search for forensics. If he didn't, his deputy and the locals would ask questions.

Questions he didn't want to have raised, much less to be forced to answer.

Like the fact that he sensed a demon had been here. He could smell the stench. But what kind of demon?

Hobbs glanced at Marlena. "What are you doing here, Dr. Bender?"

Marlena explained about finding Jordie's ring on her doorstep.

Hobbs shifted and dug the steel toe of his boot into the dirt. "Sounds like we've got a real sicko on our hands."

"Yeah, so let's get to work," Dante snapped.

Hobbs glared at him, but went to his squad car, retrieved crime scene tape, and began to stretch it in a wide radius around the tree and house. Dante grabbed his camera from the SUV. He wanted photos of the crime scene himself so he could study them.

A white van suddenly screeched up the graveled drive and stopped, and Dante cursed. Jebb Bates, the local reporter in Mysteria. Dante had been dodging his nosy questions for months.

"Dammit, keep him out of the crime scene, Hobbs. I don't want him contaminating evidence or interfering."

The deputy nodded and met Bates at the van. Bates tried to push past him, and Dante strode over to him, arms crossed. "This is an official crime scene," Dante growled.

Bates lurched forward to get a better look at the body, but Dante shoved him back. "If you cross it, I'll arrest you for interfering with an investigation."

"Listen, Sheriff," Bates said in a slimy voice. "The public has a right to know if a killer is on the loose. What happened to Jordie?"

Dante glared at him. "I can't release details until the family has been notified. How did you find out about this so quickly?"

"I have a scanner, it picks up police and 911 calls."

Dante silently cursed. The little fucker had better not get in the way.

If Dante decided to take things into his own hands, or if a demon showed up, he didn't want anyone around exposing the truth. "No pictures, Bates. No one in town needs to see the gruesome details, especially the victim's family." Besides, he would keep certain details private—he might be able to use them later to catch the killer.

"I'll hold off printing anything for now," Bates said with a nervous twitch of his right eye. "But I want the scoop when you get answers."

Dante nodded in agreement to appease him, although he had no intention of telling Bates anything. The son of a bitch had tried to dig up dirt on him when he'd first been elected. He'd even caught Bates snooping around his house.

Bates backed off but refused to leave the scene, and Dante began to snap photos of the crime scene, the way the body had been positioned, the burns, the Satanic S on the ground.

The CSI team divided up; two investigators inside the house, one on the exterior, and another at the site of the body. The medical examiner arrived and began to perform his initial exam. Dante went into the house and noticed the CSIs dusting for prints and searching for blood and other forensics. Hoping to find a lead on who Jordie might have met with or some of her friends, he checked her phone log.

Two calls from her mother the day before, but any record of other calls had been deleted. He'd have to request the records from the phone company. Next, he searched for a computer but didn't find one, then examined Jordie's purse. No cell phone or address book inside.

No car in the drive either. So where was her vehicle?

Questions ticked in his head, but he hoped CSI would find some evidence to lead him to the killer.

Knowing he had to inform Jordie's mother of her death, he returned to the deputy.

"I'm going to see Mrs. McEnroe," Dante said. "Stay here and guard the crime scene."

"Yes, sir," Hobbs said in a clipped tone.

Ignoring his surly attitude, Dante walked back to his SUV. Marlena looked pale and was huddled inside her jacket, so he climbed in and cranked up the heater.

"I'll drop you off, then I have to talk to Mrs. McEnroe."

Marlena touched his arm. "I'll go with you, Dante. I couldn't do anything for Jordie tonight, but maybe I can help her mother."

Dante didn't want her help. Didn't want her to be involved.

But he was out of his element in dealing with a grief-stricken mother, so he agreed.

But his hand tingled from her touch, so he pulled away from it and steered the vehicle onto the highway. The burn scars on his arms and hands mocked him.

Each time he used his power, a mark had been left. A scar to remind him of what he was.

A demon.

He had to protect his secrets.

# Chapter Four

———

Marlena felt the tension between her and Dante like a visible knife cutting into her skin.

Storm clouds thickened as they drove to the diner in town, thunder rumbling as they climbed out and walked up the pebbled sidewalk to the door. A neon sign flickered against the gray sky, blinking in the darkness and playing off Dante's chiseled face.

He opened the door and gestured for her to enter first, and she wondered if the anger in his eyes was for her or because of the murder scene they'd just witnessed.

The diner was virtually cleared out, with only a patron finishing dessert at a table in the back.

But the minute they entered, the room grew silent and Marlena felt the patron's eyes staring at Dante, an uneasy silence settling in the room.

Jordie's mother was wiping tables, the sound of dishes clanging echoing from the kitchen.

Dante cleared his throat. "Mrs. McEnroe."

The older woman glanced up from the table, her short brown hair curling around her chubby cheeks. She dropped the dishcloth on the table, then wiped her hands on her checked apron. "You want something to eat, Sheriff? We might have some of the special left. It's my chicken 'n dumplings."

"No, thanks," Dante said solemnly. "We need to talk."

Something about his tone must have alerted her to the seriousness of his visit, because her hands began to shake, and she sank into a wooden chair, her face paling. "It's about Jordie, ain't it?" A low cry escaped her. "Oh, God, no. When she didn't show up tonight, I was afraid something bad had happened." She clawed at her chest, and Marlena rushed to the table and began to stroke her back.

"Take a deep breath, Ms. McEnroe," Marlena said gently. "Let's go in the back."

"Tell me," she screeched. "Is my Jordie all right?"

Marlena helped her to stand. "Please, let's go to your office."

The woman nodded numbly, and Dante took one arm and Marlena the other and escorted her through a set of double doors through the kitchen, then into a small office crammed with books and a desk overflowing with papers.

Dante waited until Mrs. McEnroe was seated, then cleared his throat again. "Mrs. McEnroe, I'm sorry to have to inform you, but your daughter is dead."

"No...no...no..." She lurched up and jerked at his shirt, her plump body shaking as she began to cry. "No, it can't be so. Not my baby girl..."

Dante urged her to sit back down, and she sank into the chair like a rock. "I'm sorry," he said in a gruff tone.

She turned tear-stained eyes toward Dante. "Wh...at happened?"

"I'm afraid she was murdered," he said in a low voice. "And I need your help to find her killer."

"Murdered?" Age lines created deep grooves around

her mouth as she shook her head from side to side in denial. "How? Why? Who would want to kill my baby? Everyone loved Jordie."

Marlena stroked her back in an effort to soothe her.

Dante clenched his jaw. "That's what I'm going to find out, Mrs. McEnroe. I want to make sure this killer never hurts anyone else." Dante shifted and hooked his thumbs in his belt loops. "Was Jordie seeing anyone in town? Dating anyone that you know of?"

She wiped at her tears with a shaky hand. "I don't know. Not that she told me."

"Did she own a car?"

She nodded. "Jordie drove an old pickup that belonged to her daddy, God rest his soul."

"I need to look at it, as well as her computer."

"The truck's in the shop right now, put it in two days ago..." Her voice broke. "Jordie didn't have a computer."

Mrs. McEnroe pressed her hand against her chest again, and Marlena knelt beside her. "I'm so sorry. Is there anyone I can call? Family? A friend? Your doctor?"

"Dr. Joyner," she whispered. "Tell him to come." Her voice caught. "And Edith, next door. I need her."

Dante reached for his phone, while the woman slumped against Marlena, buried her head in her arms, and began to sob.

~

Dante braced himself against reacting to the woman's grief, but gave her time to vent her emotions. Finally, about half an hour later, the worst of her sobs had subsided.

"I have to go see Jordie," the woman whispered.

Marlena gave a brisk shake of her head, indicating she didn't think that was a good idea.

Dante had to agree. No one should see a loved one in the condition in which Jordie had been left.

"Mrs. McEnroe, you can't, not just yet," Dante said evenly. "She'll be transported to the morgue for an autopsy, and when she's released to the funeral home, we'll let you know."

A knock sounded at the door, and Marlena rushed to let the doctor in. Dr. Joyner, a white-haired robust man in his sixties, introduced himself and rushed to Mrs. McEnroe. She was huddled in shock, her body trembling. He took her vitals and immediately gave her a sedative. Within minutes, the neighbor arrived, and she began to comfort the distraught woman.

"Come on, sweetie," Edith said softly. "Let's get upstairs so you can lie down."

Mrs. McEnroe clung to her friend's hand and allowed her to assist her up the stairs.

The doctor turned to Dante, his bushy eyebrows furrowed. "This is awful, Sheriff. Who killed Jordie?"

"I don't know yet," Dante said. "I'm just beginning to investigate. We only found her body a couple of hours ago."

A weary expression made the age lines around his mouth deepen. "Her mother's heart isn't good. I hope she survives this shock."

"Did you know Jordie?" Dante asked.

Dr. Joyner shrugged. "Of course. I delivered the child." He rubbed his hand over his chin. "She was a good girl, Sheriff. A good one. And her mama worshipped her. Find out who did this and make them pay."

Dante gave a clipped nod, then glanced at Marlena.

She looked exhausted, the strain of the evening and the emotional upheaval wearing on her.

Dante laid a business card on the end table. "Tell her to call me if she thinks of anyone Jordie might have been involved with. I need to question all her friends, especially any men she dated."

Dr. Joyner mumbled agreement. "Let me know anything I can do to help."

Dante nodded, then he and Marlena walked to the door, stepped into the blustery cold night and headed to his SUV.

Thunder rumbled, and the first raindrop fell as he pulled onto the street. He hoped to hell the CSI team finished searching for forensics before the storm unloaded to contaminate the crime scene.

"Are you going home now?" Marlena asked.

Dante veered onto the curvy mountain road leading toward Marlena's. "No. I'm going to drive back out to Jordie's to make sure forensics covers everything before the bad weather sets in."

Marlena sighed wearily and ran a hand through her hair, drawing his gaze to the silky blond strands.

Strands that he wanted to touch. That he'd probably dream about tonight.

Dammit.

A bead of sweat trickled down his neck. "I need to talk to the medical examiner, too."

Thoughts of the ME and what his job entailed jerked him back to reality. The rumbling storm clouds and roaring wind reminded him that time was of the essence.

That the ME might not detect evidence of a demon attack. That he was on his own in that regard.

He had to be alert in case a new demon was in town. In case Father Gio and his minions had orchestrated this kill and intended to attack him and wreak havoc on the locals now he was back.

Marlena had lapsed into silence, and he pulled up the long winding road to her house. Fatigue and fear lined her face as he parked. The killer had been on her porch, had left her Jordie's bloody ring.

Would he come back tonight for Marlena?

—

The pain of Mrs. McEnroe's cries echoed in Marlena's head.

She understood grief, of having someone ripped from your arms too soon. Suddenly the fear and grief of her own family's loss welled inside her, and her throat thickened.

God help her. She'd moved back here to confront her past and get over her nightmares.

But a murderer had left his trophy for her, a reminder of how cruel life—and people—could be.

Her hand shook as she opened the car door, and Dante strode around to her side to help her. She wanted to lean on him, but she'd spent the last twenty years learning how to stand on her own, and she couldn't succumb to that need now.

She didn't want to get close to anyone ever again.

Instead she had to pour herself into her research work, find a way to help deter violent behavior so she could save others.

Maybe if she helped find Jordie's killer, it would atone for the fact that her family's murderers had never been caught.

Raindrops splattered her cheeks as she stepped from

the SUV and walked toward the house, but Dante placed a hand on her arm. "I'm going to check inside first."

Her heart stuttered. "You think the killer might have come back?"

His dark eyes met hers, a sharp warning glittering. "He knows where you live, Marlena. He probably knows you personally." His throat worked as he swallowed. "And for some reason, he's involved you in this crime, so you can't be too careful."

Fear slithered through her, and she gave a quick nod of understanding, then followed him up the porch. "Stay behind me," he ordered.

He withdrew his gun and held it at the ready as they entered. She flipped on a light in the foyer and crept behind him from room to room. Her heart hammered in her chest each time he paused to listen for an intruder.

The scent of the lavender candles she'd burned in her bath wafted through the house, and oddly she thought she detected the faint scent of the jasmine lotion her mother used to wear.

Lights flickered on and off upstairs and Dante gripped her arm. "Has it done that before?"

"Yes. I thought there might be a short circuit." Or that the house might be haunted, but she bit back the words. People had thought she was crazy when she'd talked about monsters as a little girl. She didn't want to admit that she thought her mother and sister's spirits still lingered in the house. That sometimes she felt her mother's hand on her shoulder just before she fell asleep.

That she heard her little sister's cries at night.

Dante inched up the steps, shadows flickering against the faded walls. The wooden floors creaked, the furnace groaned, and wind whistled through the eaves of the plastered walls.

When they reached the landing, she gestured to the right to her bedroom, the room originally intended as the guest suite. She hadn't been able to sleep in her old room, and certainly not in her mother's or sister's.

They checked each one, then he pointed to the door at the end of the hall.

"That's the attic," she said.

"It's locked?"

She nodded, then reached into her purse for her key and handed it to him. He unlocked the door, and slowly they crept up the stairs, the floor creaking, a whisper of cold air wafting through the stairwell.

At the top of the landing, her gaze searched the room. Barring the trunks of old clothes and household items stored inside, it was empty.

"It's clear," he said, then she sighed in relief and led the way down the stairs.

He stopped in the foyer. "Do you have a security system?"

"No. The house was built years ago."

"You should consider getting one," Dante suggested.

Exhaustion pulled at Marlena, and she ran her hand through her hair. "I'll think about it."

His dark gaze raked over her, and for a brief second, an odd look flickered in his eyes. It was almost as if he wanted to touch her, to say something more.

The air felt charged, electric. His masculine scent wafted toward her, arousing her desire. It had been a long time since she'd been held by a man or allowed anyone into her life.

Except for an occasional one night of sex . . .

Sex with Dante would be phenomenal. Intense. Passionate. Hot.

Her hand shook with the effort it took for her not to reach for him.

But a cold mask suddenly slid over his face, and he backed toward the door. "Call me if you need anything."

She needed him now. She didn't want to be alone. Not in the house with the painful memories, with the whisper of her mother's hand on her back, the torment of her sister's cries.

But the history they shared, that one night when he'd saved her, the questions regarding that attack stood between them.

And so did his warning. Asking about her family was dangerous.

But her resolve set in.

She didn't care. She had to know the truth, even if it killed her.

Dante hesitated before leaving Marlena's, and once again scanned the woods surrounding her house, assessing the situation.

Dammit. Marlena's home was too isolated. Anyone could park down the mountain road on one of the turnoffs, slip through the woods to her house without being seen or heard.

If anything happened to her...

No. She was safe in her locked house now. She had his number. She could call if she sensed danger.

Besides, he needed to put some distance between the two of them. Touching her hand had sent lightning bolts of need ripping through him. He couldn't imagine what would happen if he dared take it further.

And dammit, back there he'd wanted to take it a whole hell of a lot further.

Wrestling with control, he cranked the engine, shifted into gear, and drove back to Jordie's house.

By the time he arrived, the CSI team was finishing.

Dante tugged his leather bomber jacket around his shoulders and strode over to Hobbs and the medical examiner.

"Did you guys find anything?" Dante asked.

The CSI shrugged. "It's hard to tell. We took samples of the tree bark, the ground, the woman... We'll let you know once the lab processes everything."

"How about you, Doc?" Dante asked. "Was she sexually assaulted?"

"I won't know until I get her on the table, but I don't think so." He snapped off his gloves. "But even if he didn't rape her, he made her suffer."

Dante gritted his teeth. "I need cause of death, and to know if there are any distinguishing marks left by the killer."

Dr. Underwood narrowed his eyes. "You have something specific in mind?"

Dante considered the demons he'd met over the course of his lifetime. Considered Father Gio's methods of torture along with his band of brothers, the elements. And then there were factions of demons that swarmed the hills that he might not even know existed. But he couldn't elaborate, so he simply shrugged. "Just anything unusual."

"Was Jordie's mother able to help?" Deputy Hobbs asked.

Dante shook his head. "She claimed Jordie wasn't dating anyone. I'm going to examine her vehicle tomorrow."

A drop of sweat slid down his deputy's forehead. "Why do you think he sent his trophy to Dr. Bender?"

He had theories, but none he could share. "Maybe one of her patients is the killer."

Although that would be too obvious and easy, Dante thought. This killer was cunning, planned ahead, was sadistic and cruel.

And if he came after Marlena...

His gut twisted. The fucker would have to kill him first.

# Chapter Five

The early morning sun slashed through the sheer curtains in Marlena's room, blinding her but finally shining light on the dark shadows in the room that had haunted her all night.

That and the image of Dante.

For years, she'd been oblivious to the seductive powers of men she'd met. Yet Dante hadn't even tried to seduce her, and she'd dreamed of a passionate hot night in his big strong arms.

Reminding herself that she had a job to do, that studying violent behavior and treating patients had been her lifeline the past few years, and that a criminal was at large, she crawled from the bed and padded across the cold wooden floor to the shower.

The hot blast of water felt heavenly and helped to alleviate the tension in her muscles from lack of sleep. But forbidden images of Dante opening the door and stepping inside the shower taunted her.

Closing her eyes, she willed the images away as she soaped her body, but she could almost see his powerful body illuminated by the faint bathroom light, could almost feel his taut muscles flexing as he cradled her against his chest. Could almost smell the raw scent of his body emanating sexual prowess as if he had no control over his desires when it came to her.

*Good grief, Marlena. You've never lusted after a man like this.*

Flipping the water to cool, she rinsed, climbed from the shower, and dried off. She had work to do, and fantasizing about a man who didn't want her would get her nowhere.

A quick cup of coffee and a bagel later, she dressed, wrapped up in her long winter coat, gloves, and scarf, and hurried out to her Honda. The sedan cranked immediately, although with winter's arrival, she was tempted to buy an SUV with four-wheel drive to help maneuver the mountain roads when the ice and snow fell.

Gray skies clouded her property and the ancient trees shook, sending dried leaves raining to the ground. Mysteria Mental Hospital, the local psychiatric hospital where she worked, was only a few miles from her house. A concrete structure that looked like an old Gothic castle, it was situated on acres of land bracketed by thick woods and fencing near the river. It was isolated and had an eerie feel.

As soon as she arrived, Ruthie Mae Stanton, one of the psychiatric nurses, rushed toward her. "There's a patient in your office, Dr. Bender," Ruthie Mae said. "Gerald Daumer. I tried to calm him, but he's extremely agitated and insists he'll only speak with you."

"Of course." Marlena divided her time between her research and clinical work, seeing patients whenever possible, and recognized Daumer from her patient list. "I'll see him now."

Adopting her professional mask, she opened the door

and studied Gerald. He was rail-thin and pale, which made his thick wire-rimmed glasses look too large for his narrow face and pointed chin. He tugged at his goatee and paced in front of the window, his movements jerky.

"Hi, Gerald," she said in her most soothing voice. "What's going on today?"

He whirled around, pupils dilated, then began to pick at some invisible lint on his gray sweater.

"There's blood everywhere," he said in a shrill tone. "Blood on the floor, on the walls, on my bed." He threw his hands up in front of her face. "And when I look up, my hands are coated in it."

Marlena maintained a calm expression as she took a seat in her leather wing chair and urged him to sit down.

But he was too disturbed, bouncing up and down one minute, then pausing the next to straighten the magazines on the coffee table, placing them in an even line.

"Where were you when you saw this blood?" she asked cautiously.

Her words jerked him back from his obsession with the magazines, and he yanked at his hair again and resumed pacing. Gerald had been diagnosed with obsessive-compulsive disorder, but up until today, he hadn't exhibited signs of violence.

"I don't know…" His voice cracked, his agitation mounting as he pivoted, then rolled one hand into a fist and beat it against the side of his head three times as if he was trying to jar his brain.

"Sometimes I'm in a bed, sometimes a hotel. Different places." Knock, knock, knock, his fist hammered his temple again. "Then I hear that voice. A deep husky, ugly voice screaming at me to do bad things."

"What kind of things?"

"To kill the girls," he said. "Kill them and make them bleed."

"Gerald," Marlena said, once again interjecting a low, soothing tone. "Did you do something you need to tell me about? Did you hurt someone?"

He whirled on her, eyes wide and unfocused. "No...I don't know." He paced back to the window and shielded his eyes from the light shimmering through the blinds. "My head hurts, hurts, hurts. It won't stop. The voices, they tell me to do bad things. To kill the girls...I think it's the devil..."

"Did you do what the voice ordered?" she asked again.

He dropped to the floor in the middle of the room and began to pull at his hair again, yanking it viciously, then beating his head again as he rocked back and forth. "No...I don't know. I can't think. Have to stop the voices, have to stop them, get the devil out of my head..."

Marlena flipped the call button to request assistance, then rose and moved to stand beside him. "Gerald, we need to admit you and run some tests. I want to run a CAT scan and check for physical problems first. And we'll also run a full battery of psychological tests—"

"I'm not crazy! It's the devil in me! Don't you believe in evil, in demons, Dr. Bender?"

Marlena tensed, remembering her childhood. "I believe there are people with problems, impulses, and chemical imbalances that drive them to commit violent acts."

He grabbed her by the wrists, his nails digging into her skin. "Then make the evil voices go away. Please, I don't want to do what they say."

"I'm going to help you," she said softly. "I promise,

Gerald. Just relax and trust me. You need medication and rest."

The door opened and two orderlies entered, quickly assessing the situation. She gave them a nod. "He's ready, aren't you, Gerald?"

Gerald tightened his grip on her wrist. "Please don't leave me. I need you, Dr. Bender. I need you to make them stop."

"I'm not leaving you, Gerald, I promise. But first you have to calm down and let us run the tests."

The orderlies pried the man's hands from her wrists, and Marlena watched as they injected him with a sedative. Seconds later, he relaxed and allowed them to lead him from her office.

She left the room to consult Dr. Chambers, trying to shake off her unease. Oddly, Gerald was the second patient she'd seen in the last month who'd insisted that voices were ordering him to commit violent acts—though the first patient had been a woman, Prudence Puckett, a burn victim who'd suffered terrible childhood abuse.

Still, Gerald's rantings disturbed her. What if he had followed through on the voice's commands and killed someone? If she discovered he wasn't delusional, that he had committed a crime, she'd have to inform Dante.

But first she had to assess his medical condition and determine if he was just disturbed or truly violent and dangerous.

⤙

Dante inhaled the scent of death and chemicals as he entered the morgue, scents that stirred his dark side.

Death was inevitable.

He'd tasted the thrill of the kill when he'd destroyed a demon. Felt the life of subhumans slip through his fingertips as he'd forced them to take their last breath. And he'd enjoyed it.

But he only hunted evil. Those heinous souls who deserved his punishments. He'd made himself a crusader for the cause. It was the only way he knew to save his own soul.

Dr. Underwood met him at the front desk, pushing his goggles up as he removed latex gloves and tossed them into a bin. His limp seemed more pronounced today, his craggy face weary, his eyes, which were two different colors, racing back and forth.

"What have you found so far?" Dante asked.

"I had Jordie's dental records faxed over so I could confirm her identity. It's definitely a match..."

"What else?"

The thick vein in his neck pulsed. "You asked me to look for anything out of the ordinary."

Dante nodded. "What did you find?"

Dr. Underwood gestured toward a set of steel doors. "Follow me."

Dante did as he requested, stepping into the sterile room where Jordie lay on a steel gurney, her charred body draped with a sheet. Dr. Underwood had already made the Y incision and weighed organs. The acrid body odors, and the scent of burned flesh and blood, permeated the air, all reeking of death.

The doctor pointed at a jagged blood-red mark on Jordie's neck. "See that laceration?"

Dante leaned forward to study it, his pulse pounding. "It's made by some kind of tool with jagged edges." He paused, his breath tight as his mind processed the possibilities. "No...it's from teeth marks."

Dr. Underwood muttered a word of disgust. "Exactly. Looks like the maniac severed the carotid artery with his teeth."

Dante tensed. "So she bled out?"

The doctor grunted. "Yes. She was set on fire postmortem."

He ran his fingers over the dozens of photos of Marlena he'd clipped from the newspaper. That gorgeous silky hair of hers was so thick and lustrous he wanted to run his hands through it. Her eyes like clear emeralds. Her body...like a sex goddess.

And her brain...she was intelligent, strong, dedicated.

God. He wanted her with a vengeance. He had since the first time he'd laid eyes on her.

But she barely knew he existed.

Her work was all that she cared about. Her patients. Her damn research.

He'd read articles about her and her project at Blood-Core.

He disagreed with her theories.

But then the demon had possessed him, and he'd realized she was right. Evil was planted, embedded deep within the genetics of the body. Within the blood. The life force.

She thought she could find a cure.

But nothing could stop evil from growing.

He felt it running through his bloodstream now. The dark, primal, twisted urges. The hunger for death.

The need to kill.

The burning desire was already heating within him again. He was becoming a monster, his body changing just as the sinister thoughts consumed him.

He had power now, power in his hands and body.

His soul faded a little more each day.

Soon it would be nonexistent.

And he would serve only the Master.

# Chapter Six

———————————

Marlena buried herself in her work at the lab for the afternoon, desperate to distract herself from worrying about Jordie McEnroe's killer.

There was still no news on who had stolen the blood from her research project. She needed to collect more samples from the original subjects, but convincing them to participate and offer their specimens a second time when now her reputation—and confidentiality—had been compromised was difficult.

Dr. Edmund Raysen tapped on her office door and poked his head in. He was tall and thin, almost frail-looking, with pale skin, freckles, a mole on his chin, and eyes that twitched constantly. As coworkers, they'd had coffee to discuss projects before, but there had never been anything more than a healthy respect for each other's work and friendship between them.

"Hi, Marlena," Edmund said. "How's it going?"

She shrugged, not ready to divulge her concerns. "Fine. But I can't move ahead with the project until I find more subjects." She angled her head toward him. "How about your work?"

He made a dismissive sound. "You know cancer

research. You think you've found something, then you discover a deviation from the norm."

She nodded with a yawn. She knew her work bored others, but Edmund's monotone voice put her to sleep. "Thanks for stopping by," she said, too distracted by her own thoughts for chitchat.

"I was going for coffee. You want me to bring you some?"

Her cell phone buzzed, and she checked the caller ID. Mysteria Psychiatric Hospital, so she waved him off with a no thanks and quickly connected the call.

"Dr. Bender speaking."

"Dr. Bender, this is Ruthie Mae Stanton. Dr. Chambers wants you to come over immediately."

"What's wrong?"

"It's about Gerald Daumer. The doc will explain when you get here."

Marlena hit save to protect her work, then shut down her computer. "I'm leaving now."

She grabbed her purse and coat and raced to her car, battling the wind as she hurried toward the psych hospital. Had Gerald experienced a breakthrough? Had the tests come back? Or could he possibly have confessed to Jordie's murder?

Ruthie hurried up to her as she arrived, then beeped Dr. Chambers. He appeared within minutes, rubbing at his forehead, his thick brown eyebrows bunching together with his scowl. "We have a problem."

"What's wrong?"

"Gerald Daumer escaped," Dr. Chambers said. "Apparently one of the techs went in to draw blood, and Daumer went berserk. He attacked the tech and got away from security as well."

Marlena grimaced. "I don't understand. Gerald was never violent before." But he had been severely agitated and could have suffered a psychotic break. "Did you call the sheriff?"

"Yes, but he was out of the office. I explained the situation to his deputy, and he said they'd put out an APB for Gerald."

Marlena tensed. She hated to see Gerald hunted down like a wild animal, but he definitely needed to be found and treated before he hurt himself—or someone else.

And if he had killed Jordie, he had to be stopped before he killed again.

Dr. Chambers jammed his hands in the pockets of his jacket. "There's something you should see, Marlena. Something very disturbing. Follow me."

Her stomach twisted at his bleak tone, but she followed him to Daumer's room.

"I checked on him earlier," Chambers continued, "and he was nonresponsive. But I left a sketchpad beside his bed."

She wet her dry lips with her tongue as he handed her the pad, and she flipped the pages. Gerald had complained about voices in his head ordering him to kill girls and talked about blood splattering the walls and floor.

Page after page in the sketchpad depicted the violence and bloody scene he'd described. And in the middle of the crimson splatters lay a woman who'd been carved with a Satanic S.

~~

Dante studied the photos of the crime scene, focusing on the Satanic S on the ground. Had it been made by a mortal? A psychotic? A religious fanatic? A teenager rebelling against his parents by delving into the occult?

A bloodsucking demon?

A human who'd bitten into his victim's carotid artery—that was a first.

It was more likely he was dealing with a demonic force of some kind.

The lacerations didn't look like a werewolf's fangs. But they were similar to markings he'd seen inflicted by vampires, and also by other bloodsucking demons.

He licked his lips. Dammit, he'd controlled his dark side ever since he'd left Father Gio. But occasionally the scent of blood or thought of it on his tongue aroused him.

Marlena's face flashed in his mind, and disgust at himself filled him. He wished to hell she'd never come back to Mysteria. Now she was in the middle of his investigation, he couldn't avoid her. He had to stick close to her to protect her.

But seeing her, even thinking about her, stirred desires and fantasies that tempted him like the devil.

His pulse hammering, he headed out to his car. The bitter cold assaulted him as he climbed into the SUV and drove to the garage to examine Jordie's pickup truck, reminding him of the days and nights he'd spent living in the woods. Hiding out in caves or tunnels. Starving and alone and . . . fighting his own inner battle with evil.

Harry, a hefty guy in stained coveralls, wiped his hands on a grease rag as he approached.

Dante flashed his badge and introduced himself. "I need to take a look at Jordie McEnroe's truck."

The chunky man's face twisted into a grimace. "I heard about that little girl gettin' killed. She was a sweet thing. I hate it for her mama."

"Did you know her very well?"

Harry stuffed his grease rag in the pocket of his coveralls. "Me and my wife have both known her since she was knee-high. She babysat our younguns." He frowned. "You got any idea who done it, Sheriff?"

Dante had to treat everyone as a suspect, but Harry didn't strike him as demented or cunning enough to kill a woman in the manner in which Jordie had been murdered. "I'm working on it," Dante said. "Where's the truck?"

Harry spat chewing tobacco on the ground, then led him to the back parking lot. "There she is. I fixed her up, and had her all ready for Miss Jordie."

Dante crossed the distance to the Ford pickup, snapped on gloves and opened the driver's side. Jordie hadn't been driving the truck the night of the attack, so he didn't expect to find traces of the killer, but maybe some indication of her personal life.

A cheap perfume scent lingered on the seats. He found a spiral notebook inside, and he flipped the pages. A half-dozen listings of various courses in cosmetology, appointments at the Curl Up 'n Dye, a dentist appointment, lunch with her mother. Nothing significant or helpful.

He checked the glove compartment and back cab but found nothing suspicious, no leads.

As he headed back to his SUV, he called the phone company and requested they fax Jordie's phone records to his office. Then he punched in Jordie's mother's number.

A tired sigh echoed over the line. "Yes?"

"Mrs. McEnroe, did Jordie have a girlfriend she might have talked to or confided in?"

A hesitation, then Mrs. McEnroe sniffled. "Yeah, Sheila James. She works at the beauty shop, the Curl Up 'n Dye."

"Thanks."

"Please find him, Sheriff. I know it won't bring my baby back…" Her voice broke. "But I have to know he's in jail paying for what he did to my baby."

Dante swallowed. "I will." He had to.

It was only a matter of time before this killer murdered again.

Marlena's shoulders knotted as she gripped the steering wheel and maneuvered the mountain road up the ridge toward her house. The tall ridges rose above her, the jagged edges like sharp fingers reaching out to trap her inside.

Darkness bathed the old Victorian at the top of the hill, and a falcon soared above the angular roof. Once this house had represented a haven for her. As a child she used to climb up into the attic and stare out the dormer window. She'd pretended that she could climb all the way to the moon, and was intrigued by the animals and wildlife living in the midst of the dense woods.

Until that fatal day when she'd learned the dangers.

She hadn't felt safe since. Even now the house held sorrow, memories too difficult to forget, too painful to remember.

And now with Jordie's murder, she felt the evil like a pervading, invisible ghost clawing at her skin.

Fresh storm clouds robbed the moonlight, the signs of winter evident as the wind tossed dry leaves to the ground like crumbling ashes.

She tried to shake off her paranoia as she parked in the drive.

But her nerves were on edge, and worry over Gerald

Daumer nagged at her. She never should have left him. She should have stayed and supervised his tests, pushed him to talk more.

Now that he'd escaped, would he act on the violent thoughts in his head?

Sighing in frustration, she opened the car door and forced her feet forward. She'd come home to confront her past, and she wouldn't run from it or anything else again.

She was an adult, not a frightened child. A doctor, for God's sake. A rational woman of medicine and science. She wouldn't let the monsters in the closet chase her away.

Silently chastising herself, she tugged her coat around her neck, climbed the porch steps, and jammed the key into the door. But before she could turn the knob, the door screeched open. Then a cold blast of wind whipped past her, an acrid odor suffusing the air.

She stiffened and clenched the key in her hand. Hadn't she locked the door when she'd left this morning?

A quick glance revealed that her roll-top desk was open. Loose papers from her desk swirled across the floor, the curtains in the den flapping.

Panic shot through her. An intruder had been inside her house . . .

# Chapter Seven

Discomfort settled in Dante's chest as he entered the Curl Up 'n Dye. A half-dozen women who looked like aliens were huddled beneath hairdryers, some in curlers and others with aluminum-foil spikes in their hair. Noisy chattering and the buzz of the hairdryers filled the air along with the rancid odor of chemicals and thick volumes of hairspray.

The moment the women spotted him, the chitchat abruptly ceased, women shifted awkwardly, and nervous glances flitted between them.

A receptionist with flashy blue-blond hair sat behind a desk chewing gum. "Can I help you?"

"I'm looking for Sheila James."

She blew a bubble then snapped the gum back in her mouth. "Third station on the right."

Before he could go to her, a brunette with spiked hair in a bright orange dress with tattoos snaking down her arm leaned over and said something to the older woman in her chair, then sauntered toward him. "Sheriff, I'm Sheila. You came to talk to me about Jordie?"

He nodded. "You were friends?"

"Sure were." She grabbed a jacket on the hook by the door. "Let's step outside. I need a smoke."

He opened the door and gestured for her to go first, then they stepped onto the sidewalk. She whipped a pack of Marlboros from her pocket along with a lighter and lit up.

For a moment, he watched the tobacco ignite and begin to sizzle, mesmerized by the glow of the burning tip.

"Sheriff, do you know who killed Jordie?" Sheila asked, drawing him back to the job.

"Not yet. Maybe you can help. Was Jordie involved with anyone? Did she have a boyfriend or lover?"

Tears filled the young woman's eyes, but she swiped at them with the back of her hand. "No. Jordie had sworn off dating the past year. She was focusing on going back to school."

"Cosmetology school?" Dante asked.

"Yeah. She was a natural with color. Did better foils than me." Sheila tapped ashes on the ground and took another drag, then tilted her head back and watched smoke rings float into the air. "She was such a sugar. I can't believe this shit happened to her."

Dante clenched his jaw. Had the killer chosen her at random or was there a reason he'd picked Jordie?

"Did you ever notice anyone watching her? Maybe a man, someone she'd rebuffed?"

Sheila propped a spiked boot against the lamppost. "No, no one I can think of. Everyone liked Jordie. She was kind and trusting and friendly to a fault."

So trusting she'd been easy prey.

"Why?" Her forehead crinkled. "Do you think the killer was someone Jordie knew?"

He gave a noncommittal shrug. "That's what I'm trying to figure out. How the killer got close to her. There was no sign of a break-in, so I figure she must have let him into the house."

"That sounds like Jordie all right." More tears blurred her eyes. "She never met a stranger. I kept telling her to be careful, but if someone knocked, she would have probably answered the door. Hell, at the diner, she waited on everyone in town."

His phone buzzed at his belt and he checked the number. Marlena.

"Thanks, Sheila. If you think of anything else, give me a call."

He grabbed his phone and headed back to his SUV as he answered it. "Dante."

"It's Marlena."

A knot tightened his stomach at the warble in her voice. "What's wrong?"

Her breath rattled out. "Someone broke into my house."

Marlena's pulse was clamoring as she huddled inside the car.

"Are you sure?" Dante asked in a gruff tone.

"Yes," she said, her voice cracking. "I came home and the door was open. It looks as if someone's been inside."

"Where are you now?"

"I ran back to the car and locked myself inside."

"Good. Stay put. I'll be right there."

The line went dead as he disconnected the call, and she clutched her phone like a lifeline.

Why would someone break into her house? She had nothing valuable inside, nothing except her grandmother's

silver. Maybe it was just some teenagers or a vagrant looking for a warm place to escape the cold.

But the memory of the killer's trophy on her doorstep
taunted her. And Gerald Daumer had escaped today...

A noise rattled from the woods, and she glanced to the
left, searching the trees. The distinct snap of twigs breaking echoed in the tense silence. A vulture soared above the
treetops, its sinister squawk indicating it had found prey.

Another sound to her right made her jerk her head
toward the woods on the opposite side, and her breath
caught in her chest.

A shadow floated between the tall pines and oaks, then
hovered beneath the sweeping brown moss from the live
oaks. A coyote howled from the ridge, then the shadow
suddenly disappeared as if it had vanished into thin air.

Marlena pressed her fingers to her temple. Was she
imagining things, or had someone been in the woods
watching her?

The sound of a siren rent the air, and she heaved a
breath of relief at the sight of Dante's SUV screeching to a
stop behind her car.

His thick, wavy black hair brushed his shoulders and the
wind tossed it around his face when he climbed out. His
walk was powerful, intimidating, his scowl deep and harsh.

He withdrew his weapon and strode toward her car,
his intense brown eyes scanning the perimeter as he
approached, his shoulders rigid as if braced for an attack.
With one finger, he motioned for her to roll down the window and she complied.

"Are you all right?"

She nodded, feeling safer now he'd arrived, just as she
had as a child. She remembered how easily he'd picked

her up and run with her. How she'd burrowed against his chest and he'd hidden her face so she hadn't been forced to look at the people who'd killed her family.

He cocked his head to the side. "Stay here and keep the doors locked. I'll search the house and perimeter."

Nerves clawed at her as he strode toward the porch and inched his way inside.

---

Senses honed, Dante sniffed the acrid scent of another demon as he entered Marlena's house. A sulfuric odor permeated the air, and an odd tingling ripped through him as if someone was watching them.

A demon? A spirit?

Papers had been tossed onto the floor in front of the oak desk, the drawers open as if someone had been searching for something.

Bracing his gun at the ready, he sized up the space. A mystical sense hovered in the corners of the old house, and the floor creaked as he walked through the downstairs, searching the rooms. With a trained eye, he quickly noted the homey furnishings that he'd barely noticed the night he'd brought Marlena home—the antique armoire holding the TV, pine kitchen table with fresh flowers in a blue vase, crisp white cabinets—then inched upstairs to the bedrooms.

First to Marlena's room where a four-poster bed draped with a white lace canopy dominated the space. The white curtains flapped from the heat vent working to warm the old house. Heat speared him, and his cock hardened as an unbidden image of Marlena naked and sprawled on that bed flashed in his head, but he quickly banished it.

Being with Marlena could place her in danger.

Besides, she would hate him if she knew the truth about what he was.

The adjacent bathroom held blue and white towels and a shower and antique clawfoot tub. But both rooms were empty and seemed undisturbed.

He paused to listen for sounds from the other room, but only the whistling wind and creak of the furnace filled the air. He stepped back into the hallway, then inched to the room on the opposite side, a guest room with floral wallpaper that must have been Marlena's room as a child. Stuffed animals lined a white wicker bookcase, and a teddy bear with gauze wrapped around its leg sat on the bed.

Marlena must have played doctor as a child. As he descended the stairs, he noticed some of the papers on the floor were actually childhood drawings Marlena had made—drawings of the monsters she'd seen that day.

Ugly grotesque red and black creatures that spat fire and dripped blood from their jagged teeth and warped mouths. Creatures that stood over a woman and child and tore their hearts out with fierce claws, then drank their blood as if it was water.

The guilt that had haunted him for twenty years assaulted him like a fist in his gut.

Guilt he'd never expected to feel in his first years with Father Gio. Guilt he'd been taught to suppress.

The kind of guilt that made a man human, not a monster.

But he was both.

Remembering Marlena was waiting in her car, he jogged down the steps, praying those monsters hadn't resurfaced to kill Marlena as he'd been ordered to do.

Anxious to make sure she was safe, he rushed to the car and opened the door. "It's clear." He swallowed again, disturbed by his reaction to her. The slow burn of arousal heated his blood. Her scent enveloped him, the scent of an animal on the prowl recognizing its mate.

He'd never expected Marlena to make him feel like this, to have this instant attraction to her. This dark...lust.

This damn *need*...

The wind whistled shrilly, catching her shimmering hair and swirling it around her face, making her look almost ethereal. Reining in the fire in his fingertips and inwardly adjusting his body temperature, he cleared his throat. "Did you see anyone when you arrived?"

"No, but I saw a shadow in the woods."

"Then he's gone for now. Let's go inside," he said. "You can check and see if anything is missing."

She clutched her coat around her and rushed up the drive and porch steps. He followed, stowing his gun in his holster. Not that a gun would have been effective against a demon.

His hands would, though—they were lethal weapons, always ready.

She hesitated in the doorway, her gaze falling to the scattered childhood drawings, a shuttered expression slamming down over her face.

Her jaw set tight, she scooped them up and put them on the desk.

"Nothing appears to be disturbed in any of the rooms except this one," he said. "But you can check."

She gave a nod. "I don't know why anyone would search my desk."

"Do you have important work documents here?"

She shook her head. "In my laptop but nothing in that desk. My confidential files are locked in my office. And I don't have any valuables."

"Maybe you forgot to lock the door," he suggested.

"No," Marlena said. "Someone was here. I saw a silhouette of a man in the woods before you arrived. And the wind didn't open those drawers."

He conceded that point, but kept his suspicions to himself. A spirit of some kind was here, watching her. Watching him.

A spirit with sinister motives.

He'd felt it, smelled the foul odor of evil, the moment he'd entered the house.

"Did you see anything distinguishing?" Dante asked.

"No, it was too dark." She folded her arms. "Do you think it was the killer?"

Dante shrugged, but anxiety riddled him. "It's possible. Did you review your patient files and find anyone who fits the profile of the killer?"

Hesitation lit her eyes. "Actually, one of my patients escaped the mental institution today."

Alarm bells went off in his head. "Is he dangerous?"

"I'm not sure, but it's possible," she said.

Dante jammed his fists on his hips. "Why the hell didn't you call me?"

"Dr. Chambers phoned your office and told your deputy. He said he'd issue an APB for him."

Dante took her arm and forced her to look at him. "Sit down, Marlena, and tell me everything you know about this guy."

Marlena hesitated, then sighed. "His name is Gerald Daumer. He suffers from obsessive-compulsive disorder.

When he came in to see me, he was extremely agitated, ranting about voices ordering him to do bad things."

His interest was piqued. "Go on."

She stood, then paced by the fireplace, rubbing her hand up and down her shoulder bag.

"Marlena, what happened?"

"He kept talking about blood being on his hands, on the floor and walls," she said in a shaky voice. "I was concerned, but I couldn't be sure if he was delusional or if he was talking about something that had actually happened. When I pressed him for details, and asked him if he'd carried out the violent acts, he became even more agitated. Even incoherent."

She pushed her tangled hair from her face. "I had to sedate him. Then I ordered tests, a CAT scan, complete neurological workup, and bloodwork to determine if the problem was physical, a chemical imbalance, or psychological. I'd planned to question him further once he'd calmed down and I had the test results back, so I left for the lab."

Marlena shifted restlessly.

Dante had the insane urge to comfort her. But he clenched his hands into fists instead. "Then what happened?"

"At the lab, I received a call about his escape. When I reached the hospital, my coworker found sketches Mr. Daumer had made." She reached inside her bag and removed a sketchpad. "The drawings are ... disturbing."

He frowned, then pulled on gloves and reached for the pad.

His anger mounted as he flipped through the pages. The crude drawings depicted a female tied to a bed, blood splattering the sheets, the floor, and the walls.

The Satanic S the man had drawn was similar to the S formed by the burning bark.

Dammit, he had to find Gerald Daumer. He might be the killer.

The Seer bowed before Zion's throne, the fire blazing and heating her back. She had been assigned to track Dante and detect any obstacles that might stand in Zion's way.

Zion waved his massive hands. He was ready for the anarchy to begin.

He'd already commissioned his minions to spread the evil and escalate the attack on humanity. Soon he would join them on Earth to aid in the wars.

"You have seen my third son?"

The Seer lifted her head, her black eyes glinting with a streak of purple. "Yes."

"Have his brothers found him?"

"Not yet."

"Good. I will find a way to pit them against one another."

The Seer nodded, but her reluctance to share what she'd learned about his third son raised Zion's suspicions. "Tell me about Dante," he commanded.

"Master, I'm afraid he is not the man you thought. He has made it his life's work to protect the town."

"No!" Zion roared. "Dante is my hope. He is a fire-starter as I am. He has great powers."

"I'm sorry, Master, but he went rogue at his initiation years ago and refused to kill the girl he was assigned to hunt." Venom laced her voice "He has a weakness for women and children, and to this day enforces that code."

"Tell me about this girl—this woman," Zion said, seething.

"She is some kind of doctor and is obsessed with research into violent and aberrant behavior. Worse, Zion... she is Dante's soul mate, the one who has the power to restore his humanity."

Fury rolled off Zion in waves of shooting flames, crackling against the black walls of the cave. "Has my son mated with the woman yet?"

"Not yet," the Seer replied. "But, Master, if they copulate on the night of the Hunters moon, they will produce a child."

The Hunters Moon—that was only days away.

"This child cannot be created," Zion roared. "Not now. Not ever."

# Chapter Eight

Guilt plagued Marlena. "The police are looking for Gerald. I hope they can bring him in without hurting him."

Anger flashed in Dante's eyes. "How can you be concerned about him after the brutal way he killed Jordie McEnroe?"

Marlena sucked in a sharp breath at the animosity in his tone. With that scar running down his neck into his shirt he looked dangerous.

"We don't know for certain that he killed Jordie. I need to question him further."

Dante slapped one hand on top of the sketches. "This looks pretty damning to me."

"Fantasizing about doing something and actually committing a crime are two different things," Marlena said.

A muscle ticked in Dante's jaw. "True. But if this maniac hasn't killed, then he's going to."

"Not necessarily," Marlena argued. "There have been cases where people who witnessed a crime were so traumatized that they drew pictures of the crime scene, and other cases where they even confessed as if they had committed the act themselves."

"Which means Daumer might know who the killer is,"

Dante said in a harsh voice. "All the more reason to hunt him down and bring him in."

Marlena stiffened. "You say hunt as if he's an animal."

"Whoever killed Jordie is an animal," he said bluntly. "After what happened to your family, I'd think you of all people would want to see him punished, Marlena."

Marlena frowned. "If he's guilty, I do. But I just want him brought in alive so I can talk to him. I need to run tests on him as well, make a diagnosis so I can treat him."

"You want to use him as part of your research?" He shifted and made a sound of disgust. "You really think you can find a way to stop deviant behavior by altering blood and using genetics?"

Marlena arched a brow. "How did you know about my project?"

"I read the paper," Dante said icily.

Marlena swept a strand of hair from her cheek. "I do believe genetics plays a part in some people's tendency toward violent and aberrant behavior. Other behavior is learned. But yes, I think there may be genetic markers or chemical imbalances that cause some people to be more aggressive or to commit criminal acts."

A predatory look tinged his eyes, his thick brows set in a permanent frown. Yet she sensed he was shutting down.

She'd studied human behavior and body language, and Dante had secrets.

His offensive stance screamed of intimidation and power, and his guarded expression warned her not to probe too deeply.

That she wouldn't like the truth beneath his mask.

For a brief second, she flashed back to the day her family was murdered, to the way Dante had run so fast. To the fire that had erupted in the woods. She'd thought that the monsters had started the fire.

Dante had said he'd been camping in the woods that day, but he had come from the same area as the attackers.

He couldn't have been with them, could he?

No, that was ridiculous . . . he had saved her. He was the sheriff, not a killer.

She gathered the extra papers on the floor and glanced through them—odd, but they were scribbled notes about various research projects. Nothing specific or confidential, just a smattering of her suppositions and theories.

Why would the killer have been interested in them?

The need to protect Marlena warred with Dante's need to keep his distance. Marlena stacked the papers on her desk. Tension lined her beautiful face, but her defense of Gerald Daumer had irritated the hell out of him. If Daumer had killed Jordie, he deserved to suffer, not be pampered in some damn mental hospital.

Still, he sensed a demon had been in Marlena's house, and that the killer might come back for her.

He couldn't live with himself if she died at the hands of a demon, especially if this latest attack was from Father Gio or his band of brothers.

"I need to know where Daumer lives, where he worked, everything about him."

She nodded. "I'll get his file and send it over."

"No, I want to check his house tonight in case he went back there."

Marlena nodded. "I assumed your deputy already did that. Dr. Chambers gave him Gerald's address."

"I'll call Hobbs." Dante stepped aside to make the call.

"I haven't had time to go by the house," Hobbs said. "But I did issue an APB for him."

"Give me the address and I'll check out the house."

Hobbs recited the address and Dante quickly memorized the street name.

As soon as he ended the call, he phoned Judge Brannigan for a warrant. If he found evidence, he didn't want it to be thrown out in court.

If he allowed Daumer to live long enough to go to trial...

"Will you be all right here?" Dante asked.

Concern shadowed Marlena's eyes. "I'm going with you. If Gerald is home, I might be able to persuade him to turn himself in without anyone getting hurt."

He stared at her for a long moment, then finally conceded her point. "But you follow my lead. If we're right, he may be very dangerous."

Marlena lapsed into silence as they walked outside to his SUV. Dante's instincts rose and he scanned the property.

The scent of blood seeped from the woods, along with the acrid odor of charred wood and flesh, but he sniffed and recognized it as animal blood, so dismissed it.

A tense silence stretched between them as he drove down the mountain toward town. Her sweet, sultry scent filled the car, taunting him with her essence, and his primal needs erupted.

He wanted to soothe the worry from her brow. Protect her in case she was in danger.

He wanted to strip her and feel her bare skin against his, hear her sigh of pleasure as he stroked her body with his lips and tongue.

Hear her cry of orgasm as he claimed her.

A curse rolled through his head. He had to banish those thoughts. Marlena was the last woman in the world he could be with.

They stopped by the lab to drop off the sketchpad for analysis, then the judge's house for the warrant.

Judge Brannigan was in his late fifties, his hair thick and black, a cigar in his hand. His eyes were slanted, his chin bulbous, an icy coldness radiating from his scowling face. "You think you've got this guy?" he asked.

Dante avoided the man as much as possible. His job was his cover, and he had to be careful not to blow it. "We'll know more once I search his house."

Brannigan guffawed. "Put away this maniac, and you'll be the town hero."

Dante bit back a chuckle. Him a hero? Hardly. "Thanks for signing the warrant," he muttered.

Rain began to fall in heavy sheets, thunder booming, the wind beating at his SUV as he drove toward Daumer's. Dante flipped on the radio to listen to the weather report.

"Heavy storms are threatening the area with rains that could flood Stone Creek and Devil's Canyon and make conditions dangerous. Radar also indicates that the temperature is dropping and the rain might turn to sleet."

Dante slowed as water spewed from his tires and traffic crawled as he passed the new subdivision in town, turned onto a side road, drove by the mountain lodge the hunters used, then passed a series of cabins. Finally they arrived at the tiny clapboard house where Gerald lived.

"Stay behind me," he ordered Marlena as they climbed out and slogged through the rain to the front door. The house was run-down and old, the wood rotting, paint peeling off like dead, brittle skin.

Bracing his gun at the ready, he pushed Marlena behind him and pounded on the door. "Daumer, it's the sheriff. I have a warrant. Open up."

He ground his teeth while he waited, then pounded the door again, but no one responded. Raising his foot, he kicked at the frail wood until it splintered and snapped and the door burst open.

He held his hand up and gestured for Marlena to wait outside while he slowly inched inside and searched the premises.

Five minutes later, he returned, his expression grim as he signaled for her to follow him inside.

Instinct quickly kicked in as he assessed the house for details that would reveal more about Daumer. Signs of his obsessive-compulsive disorder showed in the neatly hung towels, the magazines lined on the table, the meticulously organized canned goods stacked in alphabetical order in the pantry.

Yet the man's bedroom seemed oddly disorderly, as if someone else lived in the room.

He pointed toward a large corkboard filling one wall, a board filled with dozens of articles about serial killers that had been cut from newspapers.

Photos of an arsonist who'd terrorized a small town in Tennessee lined another board along with photos of another man who'd brutally stabbed several women in Georgia. Another article detailed a group of Satan worshippers in a small mountain community who had given live offerings of females to Satan.

There were also articles about Marlena and her work at BloodCore.

"Oh, God," Marlena whispered.

"Don't tell me you're going to defend him now, Marlena."

Her face twisted with fear and concern. "No, I hate to say it, but this does look incriminating."

"Hell, Marlena, this maniac built a damn shrine showcasing his sick urges, a damn shrine to *you*." He gripped her by the wrists and shook her, determined that she see how much danger she was in.

"He killed once now, and he's going to do it again." Dante's voice hardened. "And the fucker's only getting started."

The sweet metallic taste of blood seeped through his fantasies. He dreamed about it, fed on it, craved it constantly.

He had ever since that night when the demon had been born inside him.

The monster had started to eat at him slowly. Whispering his name. Urging him to think evil thoughts. To commit heinous acts.

Eventually the pull had been too strong, too alluring, and he'd succumbed to it...

Tonight he intended to feed his bloodlust again.

Evening shadows danced across the room, the smell of the woman's fear palpable.

She slowly roused from her unconscious state where he'd tied her to the bed, perspiration dripping down her forehead into her eyes. "Please don't kill me. I promise I won't tell anyone what you did."

He laughed, then traced the knife blade across her bare breasts, smiling as her chest heaved and blood trickled between the heavy mounds.

"Please," she whispered. "My father has money. He'll pay to have me back alive."

"I don't want money," he growled. "I want to taste your death."

"I don't understand why you're doing this..." Her voice broke off into a sob and she twisted her head sideways, coughing as tears clogged her throat.

Excitement mounted inside him at the sound of her cries, and he used his knife to carve a Satanic S across her chest. His adrenaline churned as blood seeped out and trickled down her body.

She screamed and struggled against the ropes, her pain palpable. The bed creaked and groaned with her movements, the mattress dipping as he climbed above her.

"Someone help me!" she screamed. "Please help me!"

But her struggles and screams were futile. They were miles from town, deep in the mountains, safeguarded by the jutting ridges and cliffs.

Isolated from the world just as he'd cunningly planned it.

She jerked her head back to him, anger, terror, and pain blazing in her eyes. "What happened to you? You're a monster."

His mouth tightened in rage, and he bit into her carotid artery, smiling as her eyes widened in shock and she choked and gurgled.

Elation overwhelmed him as he watched her draw her last breath. His pulse clamored as he lowered his head and sipped her blood. Could hers possibly cleanse the evil from his own?

No. Bad blood ran through his veins now as it did hers.

He savored the euphoria of the kill. Nothing could stop him from enjoying another and another and another...

# Chapter Nine

—◄—

Marlena hated showing weakness. But more than that she hated the fear crawling through her. It had paralyzed her as a child.

She refused to let it do the same now.

She hated to think that Gerald Daumer would hurt her. But if he had butchered Jordie, he was seriously disturbed and desperate, and he might do anything, even kill her and Dante to escape.

Along with fear, guilt surfaced. Gerald had been her patient. She should have done more. Should have seen how sick he was and realized he was dangerous.

That shrine proved just how dangerous. She'd be a fool not to be cautious.

An image of her body burned and hanging from a tree like Jordie's flashed in her mind, Daumer's taunting laugh echoing in her head. "I told you I wanted to kill the girls…"

Her legs buckled, and she reached for the wall to steady herself, but Dante caught her and eased her to a chair.

"Are you all right?" Dante asked.

"Yes, of course." Marlena forced herself to breathe deeply, as she would instruct her own patients to do in therapy.

His disbelieving look indicated she hadn't covered her reaction very well.

He reached for his cell phone and punched in a number. "Hobbs, get a CSI unit over to Daumer's house. He isn't here but there's evidence we need to process."

Marlena was grateful to have his attention away from her, so she could compose herself. She couldn't rely on Dante or anyone else. And she certainly couldn't care about him— loving people meant losing them, and she didn't dare put herself in the position of feeling that kind of pain again.

As soon as Dante ended that call, he punched in another number. "This is Sheriff Zertlav. I want a security system installed in Dr. Marlena Bender's house ASAP."

Marlena gaped at him, then grabbed his arm. "Dante, what are you doing?"

He covered the mouthpiece with his hand. "Doing what you should have done when you moved back here. Making your house more secure."

Angry at his criticism, she shook her head. "I'm perfectly capable of arranging for a security system myself."

His brown eyes pierced her, but he didn't stop the call. Instead, he gave the person on the other end of the line her address.

Marlena folded her arms and glared at him. "You had no right to do that."

"I'm just trying to look out for your safety," Dante said bluntly.

"I can take care of myself, Dante."

He flicked his hand toward the grotesque shrine Gerald Daumer had built. "You have no idea what you're dealing with."

"I've dealt with psychotics and sociopaths before. I've

even interviewed serial killers." Although none of them had targeted her personally.

A muscle ticked in his jaw as he worked his mouth from side to side. He obviously thought she was foolish.

"They can't install the system for a couple of days," Dante said, ignoring her earlier comment. "So after the CSI team gets here to process this place, I'll take you home and stay with you tonight."

Unleashed anger tinged his words, but the heat in his eyes contradicted the anger. Was he being chivalrous or just doing his job?

But something else, something sexual rippled the air between them, a lust that stirred desires she hadn't acted on in years.

Still, silently she admitted that she didn't want to be alone.

She wanted him in her bed, holding her, loving her, making her forget the horror of Jordie's murder and this hideous shrine.

But she couldn't forget how they'd met. That death stood between them. That it was the only thing that had brought them together years ago, just as it was doing now.

---

Dante cut his gaze away from Marlena, desperate to break the spell she'd cast on him. No woman had ever turned him inside out like this, made him want to forget that he was a demon.

He didn't want to care if she lived or died, but he did, dammit.

Hands balling into fists, he spun back to the wall Daumer had created, methodically searching for some sign of how he'd chosen his victim. One killer chose all blonds. One chose prostitutes. One focused on women who reminded the killer of his dead mother.

With only one victim he couldn't yet determine a pattern.

Adrenaline churning, he searched desk drawers, the closet, beneath the mattress, every place he could imagine for a list of future targets, but came up with zilch.

"What are you looking for?" Marlena stood and studied the photographs and images in the shrine as well.

"For some pattern that might tell us who he'll choose next."

"I'll try to put together a profile," Marlena said.

Finally the CSI team arrived and began to process the house.

"Let's get his phone records, dust the place for prints, search for blood, any trace evidence you can find to help us nail this guy," Dante ordered.

Dante went into the bathroom, opened the medicine cabinet and found several razors. A check of the trash and he discovered a bloody one in the mess.

"He might have been suicidal." Marlena looked over his shoulder. "I didn't notice that he was a cutter, but he wore long sleeves, so the marks could have been hidden."

"Or he could have been practicing," Dante said. But he hadn't used a razor on Jordie; the lacerations on her neck had been inflicted by teeth.

That bothered him most and reeked of a demon attack. An hour later, he left CSI processing the house and shrine and drove Marlena home. His instincts urged him to go into the tunnels, to search for a demon who might share information, told him that every second counted.

But the killer might come after Marlena while he was gone.

Marlena remained silent, pensive, as they climbed the porch steps, but a determined look crossed her face and she paused at the door.

He caught her hand, heat sizzling between them at the touch. She was too damn tempting. Being close to her was testing him to the limits. "Let me check the house before you go in."

She conceded, handed him the key, and waited in the foyer while he combed through the house. Seconds later, his boots pounded as he descended the stairs.

"It's clear," Dante said. "You look exhausted, Marlena. Go to bed. I'll stay downstairs."

"That's not necessary, Dante. I'm fine."

His look hardened. "But Daumer might come back."

Fear flickered in Marlena's eyes for a brief second before she blinked and shook her head. "I appreciate the offer, but you searched the house and no one is here. If he does return, I'll call you."

He gripped her arms. "Listen to me. My job is to protect the town. You may think you can handle him, Marlena, but he may be even more dangerous than you think."

Marlena's face paled, but her lips tightened into a thin, stubborn line as she looked down at her arm where he held her. "I don't need a babysitter," she said, then shook off his grip. "Besides, I'm sure you have work to do. Shouldn't you be following up leads instead of coddling me?"

Her tone stung. He should be doing exactly that instead of worrying about her. But fuck. He couldn't help it.

"Go," she said, then gave his chest a slight shove. "The

best way you can protect the town and me is to find the killer, whether it's Daumer or someone else."

Or some *thing*, he wanted to say but bit back the words. She might have seen monsters as a child, but the adult Marlena thought she'd imagined them.

It was best if she continued to believe that and didn't probe to find the truth.

She sure as hell wouldn't like the answers if she did.

~———

Dante hissed. "Lock the doors tight, and call me if you need me."

His protective tone touched her deeply, yet once again, the thought of being alone with him in her house raised self-preservation instincts.

"Of course." She forced her hands to her sides to keep from reaching for him and begging him to stay.

His dark eyes locked with hers for a long, tension-filled moment, then he clenched his jaw, turned, and walked out.

Marlena locked the door, then leaned against the wooden frame, struggling for a breath. The wind rattled the windowpanes, the furnace growling. The day's trauma was wearing on her, resurrecting too many painful memories and questions.

Her sister and mother had been killed in a heinous way and now, twenty years later, the week after she'd returned, another young girl.

Somehow she felt responsible, as if her return might have started this violence. Too restless to sleep, she booted up her computer, then Googled the town's history and searched through archives of past crimes in Mysteria.

During the five years following her mother's and sister's murders, there had been at least five unexplained deaths. The reports blamed most of the deaths on attacks by wild animals, and one on a drifter passing through. After that, the crimes had tapered off.

Because the killer or killers had moved on?

Only now another girl had been murdered...

Her mind ticked back to the shrine Daumer had built, and she considered the general profiles of serial killers, usually young white males in their twenties with histories of childhood abuse or trauma.

The need to do something spiked her adrenaline, and she accessed the hospital files. She typed in Gerald Daumer's name and found the intake information from the counselor who'd assessed him when he'd been admitted.

*Gerald Daumer, 28 years old, parents deceased. Only child. Patient exhibits signs of obsessive-compulsive disorder and psychosis. Possibly suffering from psychotic break. Questions about his childhood triggered agitation, compulsive rocking motion, and manic-depression.*

*Patient admitted that he was claustrophobic, that he'd been punished severely as a child by being locked in a small closet for days, and that his mother was very religious.*

*Another notation: Watch for signs of violent behavior. Need to follow up...*

There was nothing that Marlena hadn't read before, and the intake information only confirmed that Gerald Daumer had been headed down a dangerous track. She wished she'd been able to delve deeper into his past, find out if he'd ever killed animals—a sign of a serial killer in the making. But his family was dead now, so that was impossible.

Maybe someone who'd attended school with him could shed some light on his past.

She searched his chart and frowned at the name of the school: School for Lost Souls, Eerie, Tennessee. Was it a Catholic school?

She searched for it online, but no such school existed in Eerie.

Her gaze flicked over the rest of his background information, and suddenly her breath hitched. Gerald claimed his parents were buried at the Cemetery for Lost Souls in Eerie.

Her heart racing, she punched in the name of the cemetery and the town, and thumbed her fingers while she waited on a link to appear. But again, there was no cemetery by that name.

Instead, several links to various myths and legends appeared. She clicked on the first link, perspiration beading on her neck as she skimmed the contents.

Cemetery for Lost Souls: a cemetery rumored to be haunted by lost souls, souls who traded their humanity for eternal life, souls who walked with Satan, souls who wanted vengeance for their death or other wrongs.

Suddenly she felt a hand press against her neck, a menacing grip that made her scream and jump up, battling for the hand to release her. The stench of sulfur swirled around her, and the door swung open and wind whipped through the room, sending a chill down her spine.

She spun around to face her attacker, but nothing was there. Still, she felt the presence of a menacing spirit just as she had at the cemetery and wondered if the legends about the lost souls could possibly be true.

All her life she'd been looking for answers to what had

happened to her family. To the reasons behind violent and criminal behavior. Searching for a medical or scientific reason.

Could there be another explanation—something supernatural and beyond medical reasoning?

No...she was a doctor. She believed in concrete evidence.

Still, the whisper of her mother's voice warning her to run whirled around her...

# Chapter Ten

Dante parked at his house, a modern structure sunk into the ground with solar windows and barricaded by the stone mountain surrounding him, a private lair that offered him protection from the elements and other demons.

As much as he hated leaving Marlena alone, finding Jordie's killer was the ticket to her safety. He needed to go underground and see if the demon world living beneath the town in the tunnels was responsible.

Not that he would be welcome.

But he refused to let that deter him. If anything, he hoped to convince the factions to form a truce, to agree not to hunt from the locals; then the town could live in peace.

They had the past few years while Father Gio had been away. But Father Gio would never agree to a truce.

As usual, the tunnels reeked of cold, evil, debauchery, death.

But he grasped his control with a determined hand. He had a creed, and he was determined to live by it or he'd become the kind of monster he abhorred.

Senses alert, he wove through a maze of corridors searching, listening for clues of demon activity, but the nightstalkers seemed to have disappeared somewhere in the crevices.

Or perhaps they were out hunting, out to do harm.

A stone door marked the entrance to the underground bar where the demons gathered. He'd stumbled on it another time when he'd been combing the chambers, but he hadn't been welcomed inside.

He didn't give a damn if he was welcome now.

Smoke created a hazy glow in the stone-walled room as he entered. Two torches provided the only light, and he glanced at the back room where the demons gathered for poker—and planning—and noticed it was empty. Save for the vampire bartender, Drake Mortimer, and a vixen trolling for a fuck, the bar was empty.

Another night and he might have responded to the siren's sultry look, but the only woman he wanted to sink his cock into was Marlena.

Dammit. The one woman he couldn't have...

He strode to the bar, took a seat, and ordered a shot of whiskey. "Where is everyone tonight?" Dante asked.

Drake's steely black hair gleamed against his pale white skin as he poured a shot glass full of bourbon and shoved it toward him. "I guess they sensed you might come. You have a way of clearing out the place, you know."

Dante traced a finger around the rim of the shot glass. "You heard about the local girl's murder?"

Drake's eyes slanted downward. "Yeah, but don't try to pin that murder on me. I only feed from animals, and—" he indicated a plastic bag of blood, "—occasionally the bloodbank."

Dante choked out a sarcastic laugh. "Any word down here about the killer?"

"No. But there's been rumblings about the new leader of the underworld stirring up trouble."

"What kind of trouble?"

"BlackPaw claims there's a new wolf pack moving in and one of his own was injured. There's also talk that the elements are gathering for something big. I don't know what yet, but it could rival another Katrina or a tsunami."

"No bloodletters or firestarters?"

"Not that I know of."

"Has Father Gio returned to the area?"

A long hesitation, then Mortimer shrugged, ripped open the bag of blood with his teeth, and poured it into a mug. "It's possible, but I have no clue where he's set up camp."

"If you hear anything let me know."

Mortimer glared at him. "I'm not a snitch, Zertlav."

Dante leaned into the man's bleached-white face with a snarl. "You want to keep this bar, have a place for the peaceful demons to hang out, then you'll do it, or I'll shut you down and expose the lot of you."

Mortimer hissed, his fangs slowly appearing. "You wouldn't do that."

Dante chuckled. "Damn right I would. Either those of us who want to exist in town form a truce not to feed from the locals or we become just as vile as the others."

A young woman wearing a gauzy black skirt, a dark blouse, and a shawl slipped into the bar, halting the conversation.

Her face was angled sideways, her hair forming a curtain across her cheek. Slowly she lifted her chin, and Dante's gaze zeroed in on the scarred flesh.

She had suffered third-degree burns. The scar was old, but the injury must have been extremely painful. Silently she walked toward him, then slid onto the barstool beside him with a coy smile.

His demon radar kicked in, and he sensed human blood flowed through her veins, yet the faint scent of something otherworldly radiated from her as well, as if she'd only recently come into her demonic side.

He'd never seen her here. How had she discovered the Dungeon?

"Hi," she said in a tentative tone. "My name is Prudence."

His lips curled into a half-smile. "Dante. What brought you here?"

She slid her hand to his thigh. "You."

He arched a brow. "Me?"

"Yeah," she said softly. Her hand moved across his leg, inching closer to his crotch, teasing him, triggering heat to flame inside him. "I followed you in the tunnels."

Man, his radar was off if he'd let a damn woman slip up on him unnoticed.

"How about a night together?" she whispered. "I'll do anything you want."

He downed the shot of whiskey, sensing her desperation and hunger. Most men in town probably ignored her, or turned away in revulsion. Oddly, her scar didn't bother him.

He had enough of his own: the ones on his back that he'd earned through punishment; the ones on various other parts of his body, battle scars; the ones on his hands and arm, the markings of each time he'd used his powers.

Did she know the clientele this bar catered to? Was she so lonely that she'd stoop to screwing anyone? Even a demon?

She rubbed her fingers across his waistband. "You can use those handcuffs on me."

That image taunted him. But instead of her face, he saw Marlena's. Sultry, erotic, beautiful Marlena.

The woman he wanted with a vengeance.

Hell, maybe indulging in a mindless fuck would relieve some tension and keep him from wanting her.

But the woman's hand on his leg did nothing to arouse him the way Marlena's simple touch on his arm did, and he stood with a curse and turned back to Mortimer.

"Remember what I said."

Mortimer glared at him with his fangs bared, but Dante didn't allow the vamp to faze him. He'd seen worse.

He'd almost been worse.

Nothing scared him now.

Except the thought of the demon attacking Marlena.

The nightmares plagued Marlena again. She tried to wake herself to escape them, but they trapped her inside the terrifying world of her childhood.

"Run," her mother screamed. "Run!"

Marlena heard the hideous whish of monsters attacking, saw them swoop down with claws and fangs extended, and worked her little legs as fast as she could, darting through the trees. She had to escape. Had to get away or they would eat her alive.

But she stumbled over a tree stump and fell into the dirt. Her knee scraped a rock and pain sliced through her. Weeds chewed at her legs and a snake hissed from the dirt beside her.

Her mother screamed again, and her sister cried out in pain as the monster snatched her up and sank his sharp teeth into her. Blood spewed from her sister's neck, and Marlena screamed in horror.

"Run!" her mother shouted, but the monster grabbed her and flung her against a rock, and she cried out.

Marlena sank her fingernails into the stone and tried to pull herself up, but terror immobilized her.

Then suddenly a teenage boy appeared out of nowhere, running like a streak of lightning.

She stared at him in shock, but he hauled her up, threw her over his shoulder, and began to run through the forest. One of the monsters chased her, his ugly head spitting something vile in a stream that made fire erupt behind them.

She buried her head, shaking and crying. She wanted her mommy and her sister. She didn't want to die...

Marlena jerked awake, her heart pounding. The house vibrated with the wind, floors and pipes creaking, windows rattling.

Perspiration soaked the bedclothes and her pajamas, and she threw off the bedding, stood, and shuffled to the den. She expected a storm to be raging outside, but when she slid the sheer curtain back from the window, the night was quiet. Still, the house trembled and vibrated, and the whisper of her mother's voice echoed through the eaves.

"Run, Marlena. Run."

Marlena choked back a cry as she felt a hand press against her back. Again, she turned and no one was there.

Or was there? Could her mother's spirit still be lingering in the house? Was she trying to give her some kind of warning? Was she here protecting her, or was there an evil spirit inside the house trying to drive her insane?

⌐

Gerald Daumer rocked himself back and forth beneath the giant oak tree outside Marlena's house, shivering as the cold engulfed him. He hated the cold.

A sob wrenched from deep inside him. He wanted to go home, but everyone was looking for him and would be watching his house. The doctors at that nuthouse. The cops.

The devil.

No, the devil had followed him here, had climbed inside his head and wouldn't go away. Just like he'd been inside Marlena's house earlier. In the attic.

*Go inside to Marlena. She left you in that crazy place. Make her pay for abandoning you.*

He covered his ears, pressing his hands tighter over them to silence the voices. They wanted him to do ugly things.

To hurt Marlena.

*It's her fault you're like this. You have to kill her.*

"No!" He beat at his head, over and over and over. "Leave me alone! I don't want to be evil."

But images suddenly bombarded him. Images of his hands tying Marlena to a tree. Lighting a match. Watching the flames ignite.

The bark of the tree caught ablaze, the crisp wood popping as it sizzled and burned, the erotic yellow and orange colors skipping up toward Marlena's feet.

The beauty of it mesmerized him.

Her screams pierced the night, the scent of burning wood and flesh swirling around him in a mind-numbing rush. Then the flames caught her hair and body, and the devil's voice finally quieted.

# Chapter Eleven

The next morning, Marlena tried to banish the thought of her nightmares and the fact that a killer had given her Jordie McEnroe's ring as she drew blood from the last subject of the morning. "Thank you, Miss Curtain. We'll be in touch."

The young woman nodded, tugged her purse over her shoulder, and exited the lab. Marlena labeled the blood sample and sighed. She'd conducted psychiatric evaluations on ten possible subjects for Dr. Sneed, the young genius of Neuropsychopharmacology, who'd transferred to Blood-Core to focus on the very research that had driven her own interest in the subject since childhood. Whereas she worked more of the clinical side of the study with her psychological exams and studies, he was the geneticist of the group.

At age twenty-three, he'd already published several papers in major medical journals and had earned a glowing reputation as a pioneer in his thinking. He had made strides toward proving that variation of genes of the serotonergic circuitry affected aggressive behavior. Yet other studies proved early-life experiences also played a part in aggression.

Marlena had been impressed, especially since his motives were altruistic. His sister had suffered a psychotic break as a result of a head injury and had struggled with drug and alcohol addiction as well as biopolar disorder ever since.

"How did that study turn out?" she asked him as he entered the lab.

"The preliminary results indicated that the frequencies of the S allele and the SS genotype were higher in the study group of violent suicide attempters."

"Have you had a chance to look at those blood samples from the two Valtrez men?" Both their samples had been lost in the stolen-blood incident but both men had agreed to a second sample. Vincent, an FBI agent, had been trying to find the person who'd stolen the blood, but so far they hadn't turned up a clue. Security cameras had been stopped and revealed nothing. And everyone at the lab had been questioned and had taken polygraphs. No one on the inside even remotely seemed suspicious, so they knew it had to be a break-in.

"Not yet, but I'll get to them."

Edmund Raysen loped in, quiet and awkward as usual, and Marlena's heart squeezed for him. Dr. Sneed already overshadowed him with his youth and accomplishments.

"Did you lose your glasses again, Edmund?" Marlena asked.

He gave a dismissive shrug and patted his pocket, then slipped the big, dark frames on, washed his hands, and loped back out.

Marlena's cell phone rang. Her heartbeat instantly accelerated as she saw Dante's number.

A second later, her stomach clenched. He wasn't calling for personal reasons—he was probably calling about Jordie's murder. Maybe he'd caught the killer...

She excused herself, then connected the call. "Marlena Bender."

"Marlena, I just wanted to call and see if you were all right."

Her heart fluttered again. "Yes, I'm fine. Any news?"

A pause. "The cause of death was not smoke inhalation nor was it a result of the fire."

Marlena tucked a strand of hair behind her ear. "What?"

"Jordie McEnroe bled to death."

Marlena frowned. "I don't understand."

Dante's breath rattled out. "The killer bit her neck and punctured her carotid artery."

Marlena sank into her chair. "Oh, God. How horrible."

"I'm going to organize a search party to search the mountains for Daumer."

She swallowed hard, the scene playing out in front of her like a horror novel. "Call me if you find him, Dante. I'd like to be there. Maybe I can help."

A heartbeat of silence. "All right."

"Dante?"

"What?"

"I'm going to talk to the sheriff who investigated my family's murder. I have to know what he did to find the killer."

A tense second passed, then Dante hissed. "Marlena, don't," Dante said in a gruff voice. "It's too dangerous."

"I don't care," she said. "I have to do this and no one can stop me."

Without waiting for a response, she ended the call. Her phone buzzed automatically, and she checked the number. Dante.

But she ignored it. She needed to get to the mental hospital to see patients, not listen to a lecture or another warning.

Then she would pay a visit to Sheriff Sam Larson and find out exactly what he had done to find her mother's and sister's killers.

———⟋———

Dante drove by the crime lab and spoke with the CSI in charge.

"Did you find anything at the McEnroe apartment? Fingerprints? Forensics?"

"We're still sorting through the prints. So far, the only ones we've identified belong to the girl and her mother."

"How about hairs or fibers?"

"We did find cat hairs," he said. "But we questioned the neighbors and one of them said the cat was a stray. The victim could have let the animal inside and fed it, but we didn't find the cat."

"Anything else?"

"Hair from the victim," the CSI said. "And a couple of short, dark, wiry hairs. We'll keep them on file. If you bring in a suspect, we can compare for a match."

"Any footprints?"

"No. This guy obviously knew what he was doing and covered his tracks."

Dante gave a clipped nod. Of course a demon wouldn't have fingerprints. He would also cover his tracks, especially if he had the ability to orb or fly.

A thin, balding CSI tech with red sideburns approached him. "I found something odd."

Dante checked the man's nametag: Horace Ford. "What is it, Ford?"

He crooked a thumb for Dante to follow him to the lab. When they arrived at his station, Ford indicated a computer printout. "The victim's blood type is AB positive. But when the killer bit her, he also left DNA in his saliva."

"DNA? That's good news."

Ford rubbed a hand over the top of his slick head. "Yeah, but that's what's so odd. The DNA is human, but there are also genetic markers that indicate an animal's DNA. In all my years of study, I've never seen anything like it."

Dante cursed beneath his breath. "You're sure? Maybe an animal smelled blood after the killer left and came up and licked her?"

Ford's look was skeptical. "I suppose that's possible, but I ran several tests and the properties appear to be from the same saliva." Ford leaned against the counter with his arms folded. "Tell me, Sheriff, what in the hell are we dealing with?"

"I don't know," Dante said matter-of-factly. "Let me know if you find anything else. And don't share this information with anyone, especially the press. We don't want to create panic."

Suspicion flared in Ford's eyes, but he nodded.

Unfortunately, the lab results had just confirmed his own fears, that the killer wasn't totally human. Now he just had to figure out what kind of demon he was.

Then he'd track him down and destroy him.

Marlena studied her newest patient, Prudence Puckett, a twenty-seven-year-old brunette who obviously suffered from low self-esteem triggered by childhood trauma. She'd also complained of hearing voices, which disturbed her even more. "Tell me about your childhood, Prudence."

Prudence touched the scar on her left cheek. "My mother threw a pot of hot water on me when I was ten."

Marlena swallowed, determined not to react. She couldn't imagine a mother hurting her own child in such a cruel manner.

"I'm sorry," she said gently. "That must have been very painful."

Prudence twisted her hands together. "She said I had the devil in me, that I was a bad girl and had to be punished."

"No child deserves that kind of punishment."

Prudence chewed on her bottom lip. "I played in her makeup. I just wanted to be pretty like her, but she said I'd never be pretty." Prudence angled her head sideways, then lowered her voice. "And she made sure of it."

Compassion swelled in Marlena's chest. "You're not ugly, Prudence," Marlena said softly. "You have beauty and strength inside you."

Prudence shook her head, her tone suddenly brittle. "I have bad thoughts, Dr. Bender. Evil thoughts about hurting others."

Marlena frowned. "Hurting others? Who do you want to hurt?"

Prudence looked down into her hands as if she was staring into a mirror. "Men," she whispered hoarsely. "The men who don't want me."

Marlena crossed one leg over the other. "Everyone gets rejected, Prudence."

Rage and years of self-consciousness racked the young woman's expression. "You don't," Prudence said shrilly. "You're beautiful and can have any man you want."

She pressed a hand over her chest, pounding it with her fist. "Men look at me like I'm some kind of freak. Some of them even pity me." Her voice broke. "But most of them turn their heads away as if it hurts their eyes to look at me."

Marlena let the bitter words settle before she responded. "Let's talk about your rage and anger toward these men."

Prudence pulled her scarf around her head, her heels clicking as she strode briskly toward the door. "I don't want to talk anymore. Talking does no good."

Marlena caught her before she exited, wanting to calm her before she left. "Prudence, promise me that you won't act on any of those feelings. That you won't hurt yourself or anyone else."

The glacial look of hatred in Prudence's eyes sent a frisson of fear along Marlena's spine. But Prudence didn't reply.

She rushed out the door, leaving the scent of her despair and rage lingering behind.

━━━━━◆━━━━━

Dante strode into his office, then the conference room to meet with the search party he'd organized. Six officers from the county and neighboring counties in all, each eager to help find the man who'd killed Jordie.

Dante knew they'd be at a disadvantage when they went out, that he couldn't share his demon theory, but they needed a manhunt now, and he had no friends to assist him.

"Any luck with Jordie's phone records?" Dobbs asked.

Dante shook his head. "Nothing stands out."

"How about Daumer's?"

"Just a couple of calls to BloodCore."

Dante tacked the photos of the crime scene, of Jordie's body, and of the shrine Daumer had built on the white-board in the room. "This is what we're dealing with, an obsessive-compulsive psychotic who will kill again if we don't stop him."

Rumblings of anger and outrage echoed through the room, and Dante held up his hand. "Listen, guys, we're not here to form a lynch mob; just bring in the guy."

In fact, he wanted him alive so he could question him, determine if he was working for someone else, a higher power.

If Father Gio was behind his crimes.

Dante turned to the county building planner, a pudgy man with a scruffy mustache named Hinkley, who'd brought maps of the area. "We can't possibly know where all the abandoned cabins and buildings in these mountains are," Dante said. "But this should give us a place to start."

With a red marker, the building planner stood and divided the area into quadrants. "There are some old chicken houses to the northeast," he said, then circled them. "Several old warehouses to the south. A group of cabins that were partially built by the river on the east, but the construction was brought to a halt when the builder discovered the land was a sacred Native American burial ground. He claims the land was haunted."

Dante didn't doubt it. He'd heard the spirits himself.

The door opened and, to his surprise, Sol BlackPaw entered, a gritty look in his eyes. BlackPaw was head of a werewolf clan and the last person he'd expected to show up. "I heard you need help," he said in a deep growl.

Dante nodded, narrowing his eyes in suspicion. Was he here to spy on them and make sure Dante didn't find the demon?

"Take a seat. We're having a briefing now."

The chair scraped the wooden floor as BlackPaw slid it back and sank his big bulk into it.

Hinkley tapped his knuckles on the map again to get their attention. "The fourth area to check would be these hills," he said. "There are rumors of old caves and tunnels in the area. Maybe some old mineshafts, but they're dangerous."

He and BlackPaw exchanged a knowing look. More dangerous than they realized. The underground tunnels provided safety for the demons.

"Legends say monsters roam those tunnels," the planner said with a sardonic laugh. "Don't know of many people who'd have the guts to go inside, but if Daumer is desperate, he might."

"It's a little far if he's traveling on foot," Dante pointed out, then gestured to the tunnels. "But I'll search those."

He gestured toward his deputy and the man beside him. "Let's travel in teams. You two search the chicken houses." He flicked his hand to the next two deputies. "Check out the old cabins."

The next deputy seated at the table drummed his fingers on the wooden surface. "I guess that means we check those warehouses."

"Right," Dante said. "And keep me posted if you find anything."

The deputies filed out, but BlackPaw remained seated, his big paws clasped on the table.

"What are you really doing here?" Dante asked.

BlackPaw grunted. "Mortimer said you've been asking about the underground."

Dante gritted his teeth. "Yeah. I'd like a truce, to keep the demons from feeding on the locals."

"My pack doesn't," BlackPaw said. "But there's talk about a new pack moving into town. There will be trouble."

"You think you can handle them?"

"We're preparing." He paused. "There's more. There's rumors about Zion creating an anarchy," BlackPaw said in a low voice. "He's ordered his minions to create chaos across the world and was responsible for sending the god of fear to Eerie to kill those women a few months ago. He was behind those attacks on the southern cities last month. Talk is the elements will surface as major players."

Dante cursed. So the elements would return—his old enemies. "Have you heard from Father Gio?"

"He's here, but lying low for now."

"Probably formulating a plan." Dante hesitated, studying BlackPaw. "Why are you telling me this?"

BlackPaw barked a laugh. "Don't get me wrong. I'm not the welcome wagon." He stood, his leather jacket crinkling as he moved. "But Mortimer and I and a few of the others have settled here, made cover lives in the town, and we'd like to keep it that way."

Without another word, he turned and strode out the door. Dante watched him go with a mixture of distrust and shock. He'd been on his own for so long he hadn't expected to have another demon on his side.

Then again, BlackPaw could have had a secret agenda for meeting with him.

For all he knew he was working with Father Gio, trying to throw him off by winning his trust.

But he didn't trust anyone. Trusting meant letting down your guard.

And that could get him killed.

# Chapter Twelve

Body tense, Dante checked his weapon, then strode out to his SUV. He spent the next three hours personally searching the mountains and caves.

The sun struggled to fight its way through the storm clouds, making sharp, ominous shadows splinter through the spiny leaves of the giant oaks. The scent of blood grew stronger, the acrid odor of death permeating the air in the wind from the west. He pivoted and hiked toward the source, the pungent odor of fresh blood so strong that his own dark hungers stirred. Just as he approached an overgrown cave, he spotted a hulking shadowy monster on the ridge, watching him, stalking him.

Dammit. It was a Gamosh-Ra, a lightning demon here in Mysteria. A string of expletives rolled off his tongue.

He was a demon hunter. He didn't like to be hunted.

And this one oozed with the need to feed.

Dante braced himself for battle. He didn't intend to be food for the demon.

He inhaled the pungent odor of blood from the cave and knew death lay inside.

Human or animal?

Squinting through the shadows, he spotted the enemy, a great, hulking mound of muscle and flesh that stood nearly three peds high. Charred black skin covered the mass, thick red blood seeping from gashes that he knew from experience were always bleeding.

Dante slowly approached from behind, his movements stealthy, the fire in his hands bursting to life. The foul, acidic odor of the demon's saliva filled the air.

"What are you doing here?" Dante growled. "Did Father Gio send you?"

The demon swung around, his eyes a bright white/yellow as if they were literally shards of lightning, his fists like great war hammers. "I smelled fresh flesh nearby."

The demon spewed a stream of acid toward Dante, but he dodged the stinging fluid, lifted his hand, and threw a fireball at him.

The Gamosh-Ra jumped aside, then charged, chunky fists ready for attack. Another stream of saliva shot from the demon's mouth, aimed at him.

Dante jumped aside, but wasn't quite fast enough. The scalding sting of the acid sizzled, scalding his arm, burning through his jacket all the way to his skin.

Rage shot through Dante, and heat seeped through his body in anticipation. He flexed his hands, smiling as his fingertips turned molten red and sizzled.

Dante jumped sideways again to avoid another scorching spray, then focused his power and hurled another fireball toward the ugly creature.

The demon howled, an inhuman sound, and stalked into the woods, growling, kicking down trees and shredding bushes with his teeth.

Fueled by the need to finish him off, Dante's super

speed kicked in, and he homed in on the target. The monster wouldn't escape.

His lips curled back over his teeth as he shot another fireball toward the demon. A tree burst into flames beside the monster and he pivoted, baring his own teeth to attack again. But Dante was faster this time.

Old instincts kicked in. The heat in his body, the absence of his soul at the moment, turned him into a predator, and he hurled more fire at the Gamosh-Ra, laughing as his scaly skin began to char and erupt into flames. The demon screamed and tried to spit out the fire, but the acid intensified the flames and the demon shook and dropped to the ground, glowing bright orange as flames consumed his hideous form, which disintegrated into ashes.

Even as adrenaline pumped through him from his victory, Dante knew the battle had just begun.

That demon hadn't killed Jordie. His type's MO didn't match.

The fight suddenly weakened him, as the use of his power always did.

Fuck. He needed to go home and rest, replenish his energy.

But he didn't have time to rest. He had to search that cave.

Mentally focusing to renew his strength, he slowly inched forward, senses honed. The inside smelled dank, musty, the metallic scent of blood so intense his mouth watered. He shone a flashlight at the crimson splatter on the walls, the dirt floor, the rocks.

Human blood. Another victim of Jordie's killer? Had the demon he'd just slaughtered taken a life?

No, he'd said he needed to feed. If he'd already had a human, he wouldn't have attacked him.

His head swirled with bloodlust just as his stomach convulsed, the hunger for blood mounting inside him, the need for vengeance for the innocent taken warring with his own dark desires.

If a human had been killed here tonight, where was the body?

Dizzy with the blood smell, he staggered outside, needing to ward off the succulent aroma. He'd have to send a crime scene unit out here. But first he had to look for a body.

He hiked away from the cave toward a sharp ridge in the distance, and another odor drifted to him, one he recognized.

One that fed his demonic side.

The scent of smoke.

Pausing to assess the situation, he scanned the trees and bushes. Smoke curled upward in a mesmerizing arc through the trees, teasing him with the alluring scent.

Gut clenching, he stilled. The smoke was in the woods near his house.

Adrenaline spurred him on, and he withdrew his Bowie knife and slashed tree branches aside, driven by the scent of burning wood and flesh as he jogged toward the source.

When he finally reached the clearing, he growled low in his throat. Dammit, another woman had been tied to a tree and set on fire, a Satanic S burning on the ground by her feet.

Marlena typed her notes on Prudence Puckett, disturbed by her behavior. She hoped the woman would return for therapy. She didn't want to let another patient get away from her.

Before she returned to the lab, she decided to visit the man who'd been sheriff when her family had been murdered.

A little research, and she learned he'd suffered a stroke and lived in a nursing home on the edge of town. The sun had set by the time she arrived, but she was pleasantly surprised to find that the facility resembled a series of hotel rooms with a common dining room and activity room for the residents.

Sam Larson lived in Unit 2B. She smoothed her skirt down, tucking a loose strand of hair back in the knot at the nape of her neck. More storm clouds dotted the horizon, and the temperature was dropping. She tugged her coat tighter around her and rang the doorbell.

Seconds later, a stoop-shouldered, white-haired woman with gnarled fingers answered the door. "May I help you?"

"I came to speak to Mr. Larson. Are you his wife?"

"Yes, my name is Donnelle." Age lines fanned beside her eyes. "Was he expecting you?"

"I'm the doctor who called earlier," Marlena explained. "Please, it's important."

Worry pinched the elderly woman's face. "I know who you are, Dr. Bender, and I don't want you to upset Sam. He suffered a stroke a while back, and sometimes his speech and memory are sketchy."

"I understand, and I'll try not to upset him," Marlena said. "But I'd still like to talk to him."

She gave Marlena a discerning look, then pursed her lips and gestured toward a small den, leaving Marlena to fend for herself. The room was painted a lemon yellow and somewhat bare of furniture, but looked homey compared to most nursing homes she'd visited.

Sam Larson sat hunched in a wheelchair with a blanket spread over his thin legs. What hair he had was white and patchy, liver spots dotted his arms and face, and he leaned to one side, obviously partially paralyzed. Her heart went out to him.

When he looked up at her though, his eyes looked keen, bright, as if his mind was still intact. At least for the moment.

"Hello, Sheriff Larson."

"My god…" His voice slurred, and he wiped spittle from the corner of his mouth with the back of a gnarled hand. "Are you who I think you are?"

"Yes, Marlena Bender," Marlena said, then slipped down into the wing chair nearest his wheelchair.

His chest rose on a wheezed breath. "Good God, child, I can't believe you came back to Mysteria."

Marlena folded her hands. "I had to, Sheriff." She explained about her life's research work, about her nightmares. "I studied the news clippings about the investigation into my mother's and sister's deaths. Did you have any suspects back then?"

His hand trembled as if he had palsy or Parkinson's as he lifted it to rub his forehead. Either that or she'd upset him. "I tried, but the trail went cold."

"There were other mysterious deaths in the following five years. Do you think those people were killed by the same killers who murdered my family?"

His eyes went vacant for a moment as if he was searching for a long-lost memory. "Animals, wild animals…they live in those mountains."

"What kind of wild animals? Did you see them? Were there witnesses to any of the other murders?"

"No...just heard the rumors," he stammered. "Talk about inhuman creatures."

"Just like I said," Marlena whispered. "Only everyone thought it was just my childhood imagination."

"Hate to say it, but so did I, at first," Larson mumbled. Again, his eyes glazed over as if he was lapsing into another time or place. Maybe into memories or nightmares of his own.

"What else can you tell me?" Marlena gently touched his hand, hoping to keep him talking. Was it possible that she hadn't imagined them, that the monsters had been real? And if they had been, had Dante seen them? He'd never admitted that he had. "Did you see any of these...creatures you heard about?"

A sudden coughing spell seized him, and his frail body shook and wavered. Marlena grabbed the oxygen tank that stood near at hand, pushed it over, and handed the mask to him.

Larson took it in an unsteady hand, pressed it to his mouth, and wheezed into it several times, then pushed it away for a second.

"And that boy...the one...you said...saved you?"

"Yes, Dante Zertlav."

He clutched her fingers tighter. "There's something strange about him," Larson mumbled. "Be careful."

Marlena's pulse pounded. "What do you mean?"

His grip tightened as he squeezed her fingers. "That one...he's not what he seems. He's dangerous."

He broke into another wheezing attack and pointed to the doorway where his wife stood glaring at Marlena. His expression was haunted. "Donnelle..." he whispered. "Donnelle..."

Marlena forced him to accept the oxygen again. "I'm sorry I upset you. I'll go now."

She turned and walked to the doorway, but the woman's condemning look sent a chill through her.

"Don't come back here, Dr. Bender," Donnelle said in an angry tone. "My husband doesn't need the kind of trouble you brought to this town."

Marlena frowned, confused and shocked by the woman's vehemence. She sounded as if she blamed Marlena for the deaths in Mysteria.

~

The shapeshifter demon morphed from Donnelle Larson's form back into the Black Shadow image as the Bender woman rushed to her car and drove away. He—well, Donnelle—had scared her shitless.

Good. He had enjoyed seeing the fear on her face. Zion would be proud.

From the other room, the old man coughed and wheezed for air, obviously distraught over seeing the image of his dead wife in his doorway.

Laughter bubbled from deep inside him. He had been sent years ago to torment the old man and drive him insane. He'd used Donnelle's form as well as other demonic images to terrorize the man into another stroke, but Larson had proven stronger than he'd first expected.

And he'd been lucid enough to communicate with the Bender woman.

The old man had to be dealt with now. He had to die so he wouldn't spill any more of what he'd seen over the years. His silence had saved the demons more than once.

His death would save them now.

# Chapter Thirteen

Dante had called the crime scene unit to the cave and they had arrived and were combing the area for forensics. Another team was searching the woods near the cave for the killer.

Dante cursed. Hell, the killer was probably long gone.

Unless he was hiding out somewhere watching them.

Dante pivoted, his gaze scanning the ridge above where he thought he had detected a shadow. Then the shadow morphed into a bat, its screech rending the air as it flapped its wings and flew overhead.

Not the killer. Drake Mortimer, probably going to report back to the vamps.

Dante scowled, the acrid odor of the body and smoke engulfing him as he studied the scene again. The Satanic S reminded him of his youth and the rituals he'd been taught. Satan had been their leader, their orders to follow his commands etched permanently in his brain. The creed, Father Gio had told him, a creed that was born in his soul, a life he had been born to lead.

The life of a demon. A killer. A man without mercy. Demonborn.

*You're evil,* the voice inside Dante's head whispered.

*Embrace it and follow your destiny and your powers will grow exponentially.*

Father Gio's words resurfaced as he stared at the girl's dead body. Yes, he was evil. And he recognized it now in the signature of this killer.

Only true evil could torture a woman this way and leave her exposed to the elements, her body crumbling to ashes, skin melted away, muscle and tissue exposed, bones poking through the black skin.

"Two victims in two days," Hobbs said in disgust.

Dante nodded. "He's hungry for the kill. He enjoys it. And he's going to escalate."

But what was his motive?

The thrill of the kill? Did he personally know the victims? Did he have something against women in general?

Or was this a sacrifice, a test, to please Zion?

He knelt and examined her neck, searching for the puncture marks he'd seen on Jordie's neck. There they were. Jagged teeth marks. Just as with his first victim, he'd bitten the woman's carotid artery and watched her bleed out. This time he's also carved an S into her chest with a jagged knife.

He'd changed his MO slightly.

Which meant he was escalating.

~

Marlena was so agitated by her visit with Sam Larson and his wife that she went back to the lab to drown herself in work. Work had cured her anxiety the past few years, had given her a purpose, had become her obsession.

She had to fall back on it now, or she'd give in to temptation and call Dante.

After the old sheriff's cryptic warning, she wasn't sure she wanted to talk to him just yet.

An hour later, she finished logging the results of her interviews for the day, her nerves on edge as she left BloodCore. Dr. Raysen and Dr. Sneed had left hours before, but she'd stayed, hoping to find something more specific about the blood samples. Two disturbed her the most—the samples from Vincent and Quinton Valtrez. Both law enforcement officers, brothers, and both with strange genetic abnormalities.

But what did they mean?

Perhaps she'd ask Sneed and Raysen to examine them tomorrow. Fatigue knotted her shoulders, and she glanced outside. Night had fallen, and the wind was picking up again. She needed to get home before the clouds unleashed the snow the newscaster had promised this morning.

Evening shadows danced across the parking lot as she rushed to her car, and she scanned the lot in case Gerald was watching. A car's lights shimmered on a side street, and she jumped into her car, locked the doors, started the engine, and sped onto the street. Tremors started deep inside her, and she checked the rearview mirror, then breathed a sigh of relief when she didn't spot anyone following.

Her tension mounted as she drove up the mountain to her house. She didn't like the fact that one of her patients might have killed a local girl. That he had left her ring on her doorstep.

A shiver ripped through her, and she cranked up the heater, but no amount of heat could erase the fear threatening to consume her.

The traffic was minimal on the winding road, the

isolation making her search the woods and trees as she chugged up the gravel drive. The wind whistled through the towering oaks and pines as she climbed from her car, dry leaves swirling around her feet, the hint of a brewing storm pervading the air.

Anxious to be inside by the fireplace, she tugged her coat around her and ran up the steps to her porch.

But her heart jumped to her throat when she spotted another small package on the floor. Just like the other, the box had a bright red bow. A quick glance told her there was no card, no address, nothing to indicate the sender.

She didn't have to open it to know that the killer had struck again. Her chest constricted, and she backed up against the porch and scanned her yard, terrified the killer was watching her.

Then she heard a noise from the house. Someone was inside.

---

Dante had checked in with the search party, and although they'd discovered evidence of vagrants and teenagers in a couple of cabins in the mountain, no one had found Daumer.

He took photographs of the latest victim's body to study later, searched for footprints around the scene, but the killer had obviously covered his trail.

Unless he possessed some kind of power that allowed him to walk through air, to orb, or to shapeshift into a creature that could fly. All were possibilities that he couldn't share with the others on the team.

His cell phone buzzed, and he grabbed the phone and checked the caller log. Marlena.

His pulse began to pound as he connected the call, beating even faster when he heard her irregular breathing.

"Dante . . . I think there's been another murder."

"There has been," Dante said. "I'm at the crime scene now."

"Oh, God . . ." She choked back a cry. "He may be at my house . . . inside."

Holy fuck. "Are you all right?"

"Yes." Her voice dropped to a whisper, "but I hear someone in the house."

"Do not go inside, Marlena. Get into your car and wait for me. I'll be right there." He rushed to tell the crime team where he was going, jogged to his car, and sped away.

Dammit, he should have posted someone to guard her house twenty-four-seven.

He should have stayed with her himself.

He flipped on his siren, barreling around a minivan crawling along the highway, swerved to avoid hitting an oncoming trucker. Precious minutes dragged by, his heart pounding.

Finally he veered onto the gravel drive to Marlena's. He checked the area as he raced up the drive and screeched to a stop outside her house. The wind whipped violently through the trees, the dark storm clouds nearly swallowing the waxing moon.

He scanned the front of the house, but he didn't spot Marlena. Dammit. He checked her car, but didn't see her there either. Where the hell was she?

Adrenaline surged through him as he cut the lights. Then he spotted the silhouette of a man climbing through the attic window. Cold fury bled through his veins.

Had the killer done something to Marlena?

The heat in his hands began to flare up, the itch to punish the man with a dose of his own medicine eating at him. One fireball. Two. He could send the man up in flames in seconds.

But Marlena might be inside, and he had to restrain himself. Had to hide his powers from the humans.

So he grabbed his gun, eased open the car door, and shouted at the intruder.

It was pitch-black and he couldn't see the man's face, but he suddenly vaulted down the roof and jumped off the house on the side nearest the woods.

Dante ran to the side of the house, expecting the man to be injured on the ground. He'd just jumped from a two-story house—he'd most likely broken a leg, if not both of them. He could catch the bastard now and end this.

By the time he reached the side, the bushes were empty and there was no body on the ground. Dammit. The intruder had disappeared into the woods.

How had he gotten away?

Channeling his night vision to search the woods, he spotted a figure running into the forest.

Marlena shouted his name, and he pivoted and saw her stumbling from the house, her hair disheveled, a fire poker in her hand. An image of the other women's bodies flashed into his head, and a dull ache suddenly shot through his chest. That could have been her...

His breath hitched as he raced to her. "Are you all right?"

"Yes, but he jumped out of the attic window," Marlena shouted.

"I know, dammit, I'm going after him."

⤙

Marlena paced inside the foyer, checking the windows and the darkness, her stomach knotted in a fist. Had Dante caught the intruder?

Had they fought? Was he all right?

The windows shook violently, the walls trembling with the wind, the furnace groaning. She glanced at the clock, counting the minutes. Outside, the storm clouds thickened and thunder rumbled.

Her gaze shot to that silver package and she thought about how the killer had tortured Jordie and shuddered. Whom had he killed now?

Would she recognize the trophy in that box?

God, she hoped not. Hoped that he hadn't killed someone else she knew.

That she hadn't failed again, and wouldn't have another death on her conscience.

Panic stole her breath, and she walked to the mantel, leaned against it, and forced herself to look at the photograph of her mother and sister, the one of the three of them at the local fair. Another photo of her and her sister wading in the creek. Another of them hunting Easter eggs at a church picnic.

The horrible memories had tormented her for so long that she'd forgotten to remember the pleasant ones. The way her mother used to sing when she baked blueberry pie. The sound of her voice reading Bible stories to her and her sister before bedtime.

The sight of her clutching the gold cross she always wore around her neck as if somehow that cross would protect her.

But it hadn't, and Marlena had turned inward after that. She's abandoned faith and turned to science and medicine.

Outside, leaves swirled, and a limb scraped the windowpane with an eerie screech. She raced back to the window and looked outside, searching the shadows and clenching her sweaty hands together.

Fear for Dante suddenly replaced thoughts of her lost family.

Sheriff Larson had warned her that Dante wasn't what he seemed, that he might be dangerous. Still, her heart pounded with worry.

What would she do if he didn't come back?

～

Clutching his gun with a white-knuckled grip, Dante ran through the thick copse of trees, jumping over broken stumps and fallen trees from the last winter storm that had swept through.

Ahead he heard the rustle of trees and bushes and increased his pace, racing past a dead coyote. An owl hooted above; the screech of birds and other animal life reverberating through the forest. The shadowy figure headed up the ridge, and Dante climbed the hill, jogging until he spotted the edge of the river. Rocks skittered beneath his boots and pinged into the creek bed below.

The shadow had reached the peak and catapulted itself over the edge into the river. Dante ran forward, skidding to a stop when he reached the cliff, then watched as the shadow disappeared into thin air. He waited for a splash of water, for him to resurface, but nothing.

A string of expletives exploded from his mouth. Dante was a powerful demon. A firestarter.

But this man—demon—had dived off a cliff and virtually disappeared.

What the hell was he dealing with?

Furious that he'd escaped, he turned and jogged back through the woods. As soon as he broke the clearing, he spotted Marlena leaning against the porch rail, looking pale and terrified.

He crossed the yard, stomped up the steps, grabbed her arms, and shook her. "What in the hell were you doing going into that house?"

Marlena gasped. "I thought it was probably Gerald, that I might be able to convince him to turn himself in."

"Good fucking lord," Dante shouted. "Whether it was Gerald or not, you could have been killed."

Marlena straightened her shoulders. "I'm tired of being afraid. No one, absolutely no one is going to run me out of my own house." Her jaw flexed. "Not ever again."

He growled low in his throat. He didn't know if she was brave or just plain stupid. "But you should be scared," he said between clenched teeth. "You should have trusted me and let me handle it."

The uncertainty in her eyes tore at him. His adrenaline was churning, his heart pounding, his blood racing. He'd never felt this kind of bone-deep terror before, and he didn't like it.

Marlena could have died tonight, and he wouldn't have been able to stop it.

Unable to refrain, he jerked her to him. Her body trembled, her breath hitching, her gaze locking with his, questions brimming.

He ignored the warnings of repercussions screaming in his head. The knowledge that she was forbidden.

Instead, he did what he'd wanted to do ever since she'd returned to Mysteria.

He dragged her into his arms, then claimed her mouth with his.

# Chapter Fourteen

Marlena's head spun with confusion, but her body burned
with desire as Dante kissed her. He'd been shouting at her,
angry, treating her as if she'd been rash, then suddenly
he'd yanked her against him and closed his lips over hers.

She should pull away.

She needed to protect herself.

But the past few hours had spiked her nerves, and having his arms around her felt so comforting that she clung
to him instead.

His muscles flexed and bunched beneath her fingers;
his mouth was bold and swept over hers in a demanding
lover's statement.

As if he had to have her.

No man had ever made her feel that way. Sex had
always been casual, slow...nice. Boring.

With Dante, it would be fast, intense, explosive...and
that terrified her.

His tongue pushed at the seam of her lips and she
moaned and parted them, erotic sensations pummeling
her as he ravaged her mouth with his own. One hand rose
to cup her face while the other jerked her hips into the
vee of his legs, pressing her heat against an erection that
bulged between her thighs.

Her hands rose to dig into his thick hair, her hips rotating to invite him closer, and he massaged her buttocks, groaning into her mouth. Her blood heated to a fever pitch, need and desire spiraled through her in a mind-numbing rush.

Scattered thoughts raced through her head. Another woman had died tonight. The killer had been in her house. She could have died.

Without knowing this...

Dante shoved her up against the porch wall, his big body smothering her, rubbing against her, taunting her with his strength and power.

But Sam Larson's words echoed through her head. *He's not what he appears to be. He's dangerous.*

She had to find out what he meant.

Her body ached to have Dante closer, for his hands to touch her, but her mind screamed for her to guard herself.

To protect her heart.

Mustering every ounce of restraint she possessed, she slowly ended the kiss, pushing him away from her.

"Dante...we have to talk..." She was trembling all over, her legs weak, her self-preservation instinct nearly crumbling.

God help her, she wanted to be back in his arms.

But the killer had brought her into this, and she couldn't run. She had to help stop him before he struck again.

She couldn't live with another death on her conscience.

Dante stared at Marlena, his breath heaving. Dammit, he wanted her.

Wanted to tear her clothes off, lay her down on the floor, spread her legs, and bury himself inside her.

But that would be a mistake.

One time with Marlena wouldn't be enough. And having her more than once would create an addiction.

His hands physically ached as he forced them to his sides. "I'm sorry. You're right. We should talk. Where's the trophy the killer left this time?"

Marlena tucked a strand of hair behind her ear, and retrieved the box from the foyer table. Dante knew there were probably no prints, but he yanked on gloves first, removed the top of the box, and gritted his teeth.

A simple silver bracelet lay inside, crimson splotches of blood dotting the white tissue paper.

Marlena folded her arms around her waist as she stared at it. "It's bloody just like the ring."

He lifted his gaze to hers. "Do you know who it belonged to?"

She shook her head, her face ashen. "Do you?"

"I'm afraid not. But the MO was the same, the girl's carotid artery was severed. He's escalating though. He also carved an S into her chest with a jagged knife before he burned her. And he left her in the woods near my house."

"My God." Marlena sank onto the couch, one shaky hand gripping the sofa arm. "This is personal. He's taunting both of us."

Which made him even more certain that demons were involved, that these deaths were connected to their past.

That the sadistic monster wanted to punish him for refusing to kill Marlena.

So how did Daumer fit into the scenario? What kind of demon was he? He claimed he heard voices in his head—was be possessed by the devil?

Frustration knotted Dante's gut. So far, he'd followed police procedure: used CSI, the ME, organized a manhunt. But none of them had led them to Daumer.

Without an ID, he couldn't even question the second victim's family or search her house or belongings. But when the ME identified her, he'd search for a connection between her and Jordie. Victimology might lead him to the killer.

He considered driving back to the crime scene, but CSI would process it, and the ME had taken custody of the body.

Another glance at Marlena, and he knew he wasn't going anywhere tonight. He had to guard her house.

He'd just have to keep his distance. No more kissing or touching.

If he did, next time he might not be able to stop.

Marlena cleared her throat. "Did you see where the intruder ran? Did he have a car waiting somewhere?"

Dante tensed. He'd wanted to protect Marlena, so he'd kept the truth from her. Now, he might have to tell her to protect her.

~

"No car. He jumped off the ridge into the river."

Marlena gasped. "He couldn't survive a fall like that. Not with the height of the ridge and the frigid water temperature."

Dante's jaw tightened. "Marlena, it's possible he did survive."

"What?" She licked her dry, parched lips. "How?"

The urge to reach for his hands ripped through her, but she remembered the sheriff's warning and wanted answers. "Dante?"

He hissed out a breath, adopting his brooding look, a sign he was shutting down and erecting walls to prevent a personal connection between them. "Do you remember what happened years ago in that forest? What you told the police?"

Déjà vu catapulted Marlena back in time. To the monsters who'd stolen her mother's and sister's lives and who'd haunted her since.

She had to swallow twice to find her voice. "How could I forget?" she said in a choked whisper. "No one believed me. And as I grew up, I figured they were right. That I had imagined those men being monsters."

The silence stretched between them, fraught with tension. The implications filtering through the haze of fear enveloped her.

He scrubbed a hand over the dark stubble on his chin. "They were real," he finally muttered.

At first denial seized her. "No..."

"Yes," he said with more conviction. "They were...are supernatural creatures. Demons."

She gaped at him in shock for several heartbeats. Real? Demons? Monsters just as she'd thought she'd seen...

"Then you saw them back then, too?"

A darkness settled in his eyes that sent a tremor of terror though her.

"Yes. I saw them. I've...seen others since."

Her body trembled violently, and she stood and began to pace, rubbing her hands up and down her arms. Sheriff Larson's words echoed in her head again—he'd seen things, things that couldn't be explained. More deaths after her family's murder.

The anger she'd felt at Dante years ago churned into a

fiery pit in her belly. "If that's true, why didn't you come forward and tell them back then? Why didn't you stand up for me when everyone thought I was crazy?"

He spoke through clenched teeth. "I was trying to protect you, dammit."

She vaulted toward him, clutched his arms, and shook him. "Protect me by denying they existed?"

"Yes." He gripped her arms, stilling them, calming her, when she wanted to pound her fists on his chest.

"Don't you understand?" he growled. "Exposing them as demons, calling attention to them, would only have made them come after you. I couldn't let that happen."

"But the authorities could have hunted them down and destroyed them.

A muscle ticked in his jaw. "They would have killed anyone who came after them. You don't know what you're dealing with, Marlena. These demons are powerful. I was relieved when you and your grandmother moved out of town."

"But the sheriff...Larson, he suspected something."

"You talked with Larson?"

She nodded slowly. "He said that he'd seen and heard things over the years and warned me to be careful." *And to watch out for you.* "But he got so upset, he started wheezing, and his wife ordered me to leave."

Dante's eyes widened. "His wife?"

"Yes. She acted as if I'd brought danger to the town."

A curse rolled from his tongue. "Marlena, Sam Larson's wife is dead. She died fifteen years ago."

Marlena gaped at him. "No...that's impossible. I just saw her..."

"That wasn't Mrs. Larson," Dante said.

"Then who was it?" Marlena whispered.

Dante's big shoulder lifted into a shrug. "I don't know. Maybe a demon who has the power to shift into someone else's form."

Her legs buckled, and he caught her, then guided her back to the sofa. She dropped her head into her hands, dizzy. She didn't, couldn't believe any of this.

She inhaled slowly to calm herself. The minutes ticked by. "How do you know so much about this?" she finally asked. "About demons and the supernatural?"

Tension stretched between them while she waited on a response, his throat working as he swallowed. Marlena clenched her hands, unnerved by his silence.

He's not what he appears to be, Sheriff Larson had said.

Fear crawled through Marlena, the deep-seated fear of her childhood. "You're not one of them, are you?"

Sweat beaded on the back of Dante's neck. Fuck. He'd admitted that demons existed to protect her, but he couldn't confess the rest. If he did, he'd scare her away from him, and then who would keep her safe?

Besides, he didn't know if he could stand for her to look at him as if he was a monster...

A bitter chuckle rumbled from his chest as he fabricated the lie. "Of course not, Marlena. The sight of those monsters plagued me, so I researched demons and the supernatural. I...decided to make it my calling to protect the town." At least that was a partial truth.

Marlena breathed in relief and clutched his hand, sending heat through him. "You think Gerald Daumer is one of them?"

"I don't know," he said gruffly. "It's possible." He pulled her to him, so close that he felt her heart racing, felt the blood boiling through his veins and the heat radiating between them. "Either way, you're in danger."

When she looked up at him again, he saw the wheels turning in her head. Saw her fighting for that strong independence she carried like a shield.

"Do you think this killer is after me?" Marlena whispered. "That he's the same one who killed my family?"

# Chapter Fifteen

Dante stroked Marlena's back, his breath brushing her hair as he crushed her to him. "I don't know yet. But I won't let him get you, Marlena."

Again, his words hammered reality home, and she clutched him. Twenty years ago, she'd felt safe in his arms. It had been the only place she'd felt safe.

She held on to him now, needing his comfort as she had then.

And terrified that she needed it.

The only thing that scared her more than the monsters was the thought of caring about someone again, loving that person—and having him ripped from her.

But she couldn't succumb to her need. Not with all this talk of demons and Daumer still on the loose.

"Are you all right, Marlena?" Dante asked.

"Yes." She slowly separated herself from him. "I need some time. All these years I've wondered, thought I was crazy, and now to find out what I saw was real. That you knew and didn't tell me."

The scars on Dante's hands reddened as he fisted his hands by his sides. If he'd kept the truth about the demons from her, maybe he'd kept other secrets.

Suddenly she wanted to bury herself in her work.

Concentrate on science and research. Things she could explain through concrete data.

"You've had a rough night." Dante stood, too, his body rigid, his expression closed. "Go to bed and get some rest. I'll be down here if you need me."

Fear squeezed her chest. She needed him now. But she didn't trust him. And she didn't want to need him or to think about the things he'd told her.

She wanted to forget her talk with the sheriff, his suggestion that Dante was dangerous.

That her own instincts warned her to stay away from him while her body and her heart screamed to take him to her bed.

His thumb stroked her cheek and sent a tingle through her, and her body hummed with arousal. His gaze met hers again, and something hot, bold, primal passed between them, a moment of longing and desperate need.

But she didn't want to get hurt again. "You can go home, Dante. Go to work, whatever. I'll be fine."

"Protecting you and catching this guy is my job," he said stiffly. "I'm not leaving."

So protecting her wasn't personal. His declaration shouldn't hurt but it did. It was a reminder to her that she was getting too close and had to safeguard herself.

So she turned and rushed up the steps to the safety of her bedroom.

But even then the house, her mother's voice, her sister's cries taunted her.

And she felt empty inside.

～

Dante stayed on guard all night. Hearing Marlena move around upstairs, knowing she was cozy in her bed alone, listening to the shower water kick on and imagining her naked and wet was pure torture.

But he had been tortured before—a different kind of pain entirely—and survived. And he would survive now.

So would Marlena.

But this demon killer would not.

Finally the early morning sunlight peeked through the window, tiny slices of light bleeding through the dark gray clouds hanging heavy in the sky. He brewed a pot of coffee, stewing over the case to distract himself from thinking about Marlena naked in the shower.

When she finally appeared, she was dressed in a black pantsuit that hid her curves, and her hair was pulled back in a low knot at the nape of her neck. A bitter chuckle collected in his throat. That prim hairdo and the suit couldn't possibly alleviate the ache in his groin.

"What's on your agenda today?" he asked as she poured herself some coffee.

"I'm meeting with patients at the clinic."

He crossed his arms to keep from touching her. "I'm going to check with the ME and see if we have an ID on the second body, then forensics. Maybe they'll turn up a lead."

She blew on the steaming cup, then lifted her gaze to his. "I thought you said this killer was like the monsters who killed my family."

He hesitated. "I said he might be one of them. If we find a connection between the victims, it could lead us to him."

"You're right. Studying the victimology would indicate who he might target next," Marlena said.

He nodded. "When you're ready, I'll drive you to the hospital."

"That's not necessary." Marlena jutted up her chin. "I can drive myself. I'll need my car to get to the lab."

He gripped his coffee cup, debating. "I don't want you to be alone, not now the killer has been in your home."

"Dante," Marlena said as she sipped her coffee. "You can't stay with me and do your job. And I can't let this killer prevent me from doing my work."

Damn stubborn woman. "You can't work if you're dead either."

She sucked in a sharp breath. "I've been fighting the monsters and my fear all my life. If this has anything to do with my family's murder or me, I can't run." Her mouth tightened. "I *won't*."

Pain shimmered in her eyes, but determination set in, too, and his admiration for her rose, as well as his hunger for her.

He itched to touch her, tear down that hair and kiss her, destroy any barriers between them. But first he had to find this killer. "Just be careful, Marlena. And call me if you sense any trouble."

"Of course, Sheriff."

His gut pinched.

He didn't have time to analyze her stubborn independence. It was better they forgot about the kiss. Concentrated on work.

She reached for her keys, and he caught her arm. "I mean it, Marlena. If Daumer or anyone suspicious approaches you, don't confront them on your own. Call me."

Marlena looked reluctant to agree, but did so, then grabbed her purse, and he walked her to the car.

Anxiety knotted his shoulders as he climbed into his SUV and followed her to the hospital.

The sooner he found this killer, the sooner he could put distance between him and Marlena. Maybe she'd leave town again. That would be the only way to keep her safe after the fallout.

He couldn't let her find out what he was, or allow his dark side to surface in front of her.

⟜

After making certain Marlena arrived at the hospital safely, Dante ran by his house for a quick shower. He dragged on a shirt and jeans, but a pounding on the front door made him pause. Shit. No one ever visited his private sanctuary.

Suspicious, he moved quietly to the door and checked the peephole. Two big, broad-shouldered men about his size stood on the stoop, looking menacing. Both had dark hair, one with a short cut like a feebie, the other with longer hair, a squarer jaw, and wearing shades.

Except for the scent of their demon blood, they seemed human.

And dangerous.

He opened the door cautiously, braced for attack. Their scent was strong, definitely otherworldly.

He narrowed his eyes. "Who the hell are you?"

The guy with the short hair cleared his throat. "Vincent Valtrez, FBI." With a scarred hand, he gestured to the other man. "This is my brother, Quinton Valtrez, with Homeland Security."

Dante frowned. What did they want with him?

"We have to talk." Vincent shoved a newspaper in front of Dante, and Dante zeroed in on the article about Jordie McEnroe's murder. "We heard there was a second murder last night. Both women were torched."

Dante gritted his teeth. This was all the fuck he needed, damn feebies and Homeland Security breathing down his neck. "You came to take over my case?"

The two men exchanged questioning looks, then Vincent spoke in a commanding voice, as if he was accustomed to giving orders and having everyone drop at his feet to obey. "Not to take over, but we want to know what's going on."

Vincent pushed past Dante, then paused by the floor-to-ceiling stone fireplace. Quinton's boots pounded the floor as he joined him, the two of them a formidable team. They looked as if they expected him to bolt—or attack any second.

Dante crossed his arms. He refused to let them intimidate him. "I don't need help from the Feds or Homeland," he snapped. "I have the investigation under control."

Vincent narrowed his dark eyes. "You have a suspect?"

Hell, more than one. But he didn't intend to reveal anything to these men. "Yes."

Quinton removed his shades, and for a second, Dante felt some kind of strange connection, as if he'd met this man before.

"Who is the suspect?" Quinton asked.

"A psych patient who escaped from the mental hospital nearby."

"Is he one of Dr. Bender's patients?" Vincent asked.

Dante frowned. "How do you know Dr. Bender?"

"She alerted me when some vials of blood from one of her studies were stolen. And the news mentioned her name in connection with the crimes. What do they have to do with her?"

"The killer left his trophies on her doorstep."

"Why?"

"That's what we're trying to figure out."

Quinton's deep-set eyes probed his as if he was dissecting him.

Dante gave him a glacial look. "Why are you looking at me like that?"

Another strange, disconcerting look between the brothers, but this time Quinton spoke, his tone hushed, almost hypnotic. "You don't have any idea who we are, do you?"

Dante stiffened. "I know you're part demon." There, he'd tossed the cards on the table. See if they'd come to attack.

If so, he'd set them on fire with his hands.

Vincent's mouth flattened. "And so are you."

Dante maintained a cool expression. "All right, now we've established that. What do you two really want?"

A tense silence ensued, fraught with distrust. Finally Vincent cleared his throat. "We have reason to believe you're our brother."

# Chapter Sixteen

Marlena finished counseling her morning patients, but she couldn't shake her worry over Prudence Puckett's behavior the day before. She'd tried phoning her but Prudence hadn't answered. She hoped the woman didn't do something rash. She certainly understood her anger and resentment, and she needed therapy badly.

Even more disturbing, often abused individuals grew up to be abusers themselves.

For a brief moment, she contemplated the possibility that Prudence, not Gerald, might have torched Jordie and this other woman. That her resentment of men might have transferred to other women men found more attractive, women men chose over her.

The profile fit. Prudence had been burned by her mother to make her less appealing to men—what if Prudence had snapped and done the same to these women?

But the majority of serial killers were men. And hadn't Dante mentioned that the killer bit the women's necks first, causing them to bleed out?

So why torch the women? That seemed like overkill...

Dante suspected the killer was a monster like the creatures she'd seen years ago in the woods. She still couldn't quite wrap her mind around that.

Pressing a finger to her temple to massage away the headache forming, she glanced at the clock. Time to leave for the lab.

She typed up her notes, saved them, then switched off her computer and headed out of her office. Ruthie Mae Stanton approached her, her complexion slightly pale against her short brown hair.

"Are you all right, Ruthie?" Marlena asked.

Ruthie Mae sank into the chair behind the nurses' station, "Yes, just tired."

"It's only been four months. It takes time to get your energy back after open-heart surgery, Ruthie. You shouldn't push yourself."

"It's not just that I'm tired." Ruthie tugged at her heart-shaped ruby necklace.

Marlena frowned. "Then what's wrong?"

"I've been having weird dreams," she admitted in a distant voice. "Bad ones, filled with violence."

Marlena placed a hand on Ruthie's shoulder. "Do you want to talk about them?"

Ruthie Mae dismissed her anxiety with a shrug. "I guess these murders just have me on edge, but I've dreamed there will be more murders. Sometimes I even see shadows of monsters in the corners at night."

Marlena frowned. "That's understandable considering what's been happening. Sometimes patients experience strange dreams as a result of the anesthesia and painkillers given after surgery."

Ruthie nodded, her mouth pinched. For a moment, she looked as if she wanted to say more, but she stood and brushed at her uniform. "Forget I said anything. I'm sure that's it. My husband always says I worry too much."

Marlena frowned as Ruthie went back to work, then rushed outside and drove to the lab. The temperature had dropped to the forties, the storm clouds hovering as if a permanent grayness had been cast over the sky.

Dr. Sneed approached her as soon as she entered, tapping his pen on a chart. "Come and look at this, Dr. Bender. I think I've found something."

Marlena's pulse kicked up, and she followed him into his lab. He gestured to a printout from the lab. "Take a look."

Marlena studied the notations. "There's an extra chromosome, and other genetic abnormalities."

"Yes. I checked the subject's file and this sample came from Gerald Daumer." He glanced up at her over his thin wire-rims. "This mutated gene might prove that your theory is correct. That his condition is biological and chemically related."

Hope bubbled in Marlena's chest. If they discovered other similar genes and isolated specific abnormal genetic properties, maybe they could alter them, thereby altering the violent behavior as well.

~

Dante clenched his jaw as he stared at the Valtrez men. "I don't have family. Never have. Never will." He jerked a thumb toward the door. "So get the hell out."

Quinton's eyes turned to lasers, piercing and defiant. "Yes, you do. I have premonitions." Quinton removed a newspaper article from inside his jacket.

Dammit, a story Jebb Bates had written.

"When I held this photo, I had a vision of you as a child," Quinton continued. "I saw us together when our mother left us with the Monks. We're fraternal twins."

"Your last name is Zertlav," Vincent said. "Zertlav is Valtrez spelled backward."

Dante's ears buzzed. "What kind of game are you playing? I never knew any Monks."

Yet even as he protested, déjà vu struck Dante. Something about another boy as a child.... He'd been small, scared, as he'd looked up at two mysterious men wearing long dark cloaks. Later they'd locked him in a tiny, dark concrete room.

Was that a monastery?

"The Monks separated us to keep us safe from our father," Quinton continued.

Dante's gaze locked with Quinton's. The man's eyes were just like his. Dark brown, bleak, filled with horrors. Cold, as if he could kill without blinking an eye.

And other resemblances—the wide jaws. High cheekbones. A hint of devil in the voice.

Still, he didn't dare trust them. This could be some kind of trap.

He had no family. He was alone, belonged nowhere, belonged to nobody but himself. And he didn't want it any other way.

"Bullshit," Dante said. "My family was killed long ago."

Quinton frowned. "You were raised by demons. They probably lied to you about your family."

"I didn't believe we were related in the beginning when Vincent came to me," Quinton said in that deep hypnotic voice again. "But blood tests proved Vincent and I are related. Marlena Bender conducted the tests."

Then she'd studied their blood. "Marlena knows you're demons?"

Quinton's sarcastic laugh boomed through the room. "Not exactly."

Vincent dragged an amulet from inside his shirt, and Quinton did the same. "Our mother was good. She gave us these for protection. My bloodstone stands for courage and Quinton's clear quartz stone symbolizes his clairvoyance. She left you an amulet as well."

"I don't have an angel amulet," Dante growled, although another distant memory niggled at the back of his mind. Had he owned one at one time? Had Father Gio taken it from him?

Vincent shifted, his frown deepening with suspicion, then he crossed the room and grabbed Dante by the collar. "We know you're a firestarter. Did you kill those two women and set them on fire?"

Dante ripped Vincent's hands from his collar and shoved him away. "No."

Quinton started forward, but Dante threw up a hand in warning, his fingers burning with the itch to attack. "And for your information, the first woman bled out from bite wounds. The torching was only a cover to hide the real cause of death."

Surprise registered on both men's faces. "Someone drained her blood?" Vincent asked.

"Bastard left a Satanic S symbol at the kill," Dante growled. "Now, why in the hell are you two really here?"

Vincent muttered a string of expletives.

Quinton scrubbed a hand through his hair. "We already told you."

Dante scoffed, then went to the bar and poured himself a scotch. He'd learned the hard way not to trust anyone or let down his guard.

"I don't play games, and I have a demon to find. So either spit out your real agenda or get the fuck out."

"This Torcher serial killer in Mysteria may be related to other crimes we've investigated." Vincent cleared his throat. "Crimes orchestrated by our father, Zion. He's the new leader of the underworld."

Dante downed the scotch in one quick shot, then wiped his mouth with the back of his hand. Something he'd heard when he'd first gone to live with Father Gio nagged at his subconscious.

A time when he'd heard Father Gio talking to the elements, ranting that Dante was meant for bigger things. That he had powers that he hadn't yet come into. That one day when he embraced his destiny, they would bow down to him.

But then he'd defied them.

And now they viewed him as one of the fallen ones. As a weak link unworthy of their respect because he'd failed their tests and hadn't killed Marlena.

Dante frowned. The possibility that the Valtrez men spoke the truth yanked at another memory trying to claw its way from the buried spot in his soul.

He'd been a little guy, three or four maybe, when Father Gio had taken him in. He'd heard rumblings about Zion, about his sons' being all-powerful, future leaders of the underworld.

Then Father Gio had separated him. Exiled him to live with the worst of the demons. They'd put him through hell. Tortured him. Taught him to hunt and maim his prey.

Forced him to live in near isolation and the dark until he was returned for the initiation.

"Zion wants us by his side," Vincent stated. "He'll do

anything he can to turn you, go to any lengths to bring out your dark side and convince you to embrace it as he did."

"He's already made attempts on both of us," Quinton said. "But he failed, so now we believe he's targeted you. One of his soldiers may be in Mysteria now in disguise."

Vincent folded his arms as if in challenge. "If you don't believe us, get tested. Marlena Bender has our blood. See if we're blood-related."

Back to Marlena. He didn't like the fact that these men knew her, that they'd shown up in the midst of a demon attack. That their story was too damn sinister to believe.

That part of him sensed it might be true.

~❧~

Marlena met with Dr. Sneed and Dr. Raysen for a consultation over the results of Gerald's bloodwork. A knock sounded on the glass partition, and she glanced up to see Dante on the other side.

The troubled expression in his eyes sent alarm through her, and she waved him in, then introduced him to both doctors.

"We hope you find this killer soon," Dr. Sneed said.

"Yes," Edmund said. "Then the people in town can sleep again."

Dante tensed. "I'm doing everything I can."

The doctors excused themselves to go back to work and Marlena turned to Dante.

"What's wrong?" Marlena asked. "Has there been another murder?"

A vein throbbed in his neck, drawing her attention to his scar again, but he shook his head. "No. I'm still waiting on the ME to identify the second victim. You haven't heard anything from Daumer?"

"Not a word." She rolled her shoulders, aching from studying her notes.

"I need you to run a blood test for me."

Marlena frowned. "Whose blood is it?"

"Mine."

She dug one hand into the pocket of her lab coat, confused. "What?"

He sank into a chair, rolled up his shirtsleeve, and propped his arm on the patient armrest. "I had two visitors today. Vincent and Quinton Valtrez. They said you took their blood samples."

"Yes," she said cautiously. "Why are you interested in them?" Both men had volunteered their samples, but their blood had revealed abnormalities.

Vincent had even admitted to having violent tendencies, but claimed he channeled them into his police work.

An odd, almost pained look crossed his face, but anger simmered beneath the surface. "They paid me a visit claiming to be my brothers."

His declaration shocked her. "I thought you said your family was dead."

"They are." He scrubbed a scarred hand over his head, spiking his black hair. "At least I was told they were."

"What makes them think you're related?"

"One of them, Quinton, claims that he has psychic abilities, that we're fraternal twins, and that he *saw* us together as children, that our mother abandoned us."

Marlena's head spun with questions. Questions she was afraid to ask. If Dante was related to these men, would his blood also have abnormalities? If they had supernatural powers, did he? "You don't remember either one of them?"

"No." Her eyes flickered with pity as she stared at his scarred arm, and he gave her a self-deprecating look. "I know it's ugly. Just take the damn blood and test it, will you."

She clenched her jaw, grabbed her supplies, and wiped an alcohol swab across his arm, searching for a place that wasn't scarred to draw blood.

Dante's scars had never bothered him; they were part of who he was. But the look in Marlena's eyes tore at him. He was evil, ugly, scarred inside and out, and he lived with the knowledge that he used that dark side to track down predators and demons to protect the town.

But having her see him exposed for the monster he was made his lungs squeeze in pain.

A pain he'd never felt before. One he sure as hell didn't want now.

And judging from the odd look on her face when he'd mentioned Quinton's power, she must have discovered something disturbing about the Valtrez brothers' blood.

"Marlena?"

She jerked her eyes away from his puckered flesh and gave a quick nod. "Yes?"

Her emotions evaporated into a cool professional mask, and she jabbed the needle into his arm. Her hands felt warm, tender, to his skin, and he gritted his teeth at the irony of having a woman who wanted to cure evil taking his blood. Her gaze locked with his, heat flowing between them along with unspoken desires, and for the first time in his life, he wished he wasn't a demon.

A bitter laugh threatened to escape. Hell, maybe she would find some kind of genetic way to cure the darkness inside him and save him.

"There." She removed the needle, pressed a cotton ball to his arm, and tagged and stored the sample. "I'll run it ASAP."

He gritted his teeth as she applied a Band-Aid, then he rolled down his sleeves, buttoned the cuffs, and stood.

"I have stuff to do. Call me if you hear from Daumer or if there are any problems."

She nodded, and he strode out the door wondering just what she'd find in his blood sample. If she figured out who he was, what he was, maybe she'd run from him to protect herself.

He hoped to hell she did. Each time she touched him, his hunger for her mounted.

Determined to get some answers, he had to find Father Gio. Confront him about the past and find out what he knew about Zion.

More storms threatened as he drove to the mountain entrance to the underground tunnels.

For the next two hours he combed the underground searching for Father Gio, at home in the tunnels and the darkness. But his thoughts were in turmoil. He wanted Marlena, but he couldn't have her.

He didn't want brothers, but he might have two. Either that or they'd been sent to destroy him.

And Father Gio and Zion might both be behind their visit and the killer.

Ten minutes later, he paused beneath a jagged overhang and listened to a zombie and a vamp conversing.

"Father Gio is back. I've heard the elements are planning a coup."

"He's holed up in the north quadrant," the zombie said. "Word is that he's going to torture that sheriff for his defection years ago."

"Why now?" the vamp asked.

"He has his orders."

A smile curved Dante's mouth. The north quadrant. He knew exactly where Father Gio was hiding.

It was time his old master gave him some fucking answers.

# Chapter Seventeen

Noises and voices reverberated through the tunnels as Dante strode through the labyrinth of corridors toward Father Gio's haven. The Master had chosen a cave buried deep within the mountain, both for its intense darkness and for its isolation from the others.

Stone pillars supported the front indention with sharp angles jutting outward like spikes, and images of vultures had been carved in the dusty gray concrete. He rapped the gargoyle knocker, causing a resounding lion's roar to thunder through the tunnel.

Shuffling inside alerted him that one of Gio's minions was coming to answer. The heavy stone door screeched open, and a Scorpion demon stood on the other side, assessing him.

Dante adopted a calm expression, not wanting to raise the demon's suspicions. "I need to see Father Gio."

One claw reached up to motion him in. "I'll tell him you're here."

Dante set his jaw to control his burgeoning temper as he paced to the fire beside Gio's throne, where he sat like the Master of Darkness that Dante had always known him to be. In spite of his defection, heat from the flames felt like heaven to his skin, and he drew strength from its warmth and vibrant glow.

But he had to fight its intoxicating draw.

"So you dare to return?" Gio said.

"I didn't come to stay," Dante said, knowing he'd never join Father Gio's side. Not after what he'd done to Marlena's family. "I'm here for answers."

Father Gio's scaly thick skin crackled as he smiled. "Answers to what?"

"How I came to live with you. About what happened to my family and the recent demon attack."

Father Gio ran his fingers through his long white mane. "Your family is dead."

So who was lying? He had no reason to believe either the Valtrez men or Father Gio.

The primal urge to throw fire nearly overcame him, but he quelled it. "Two men visited me, claiming to be my blood brothers. They're demonborn just as I am."

Father Gio simply stared at him, his silver eyes sparkling with menace, as if he was weighing his answer. Finally he sighed. "I see. So they finally found you."

Dante swallowed back rage. "So it's true? They're my brothers?"

Father Gio shrugged as if his lies and secrets made no difference. "Yes. The oldest, Vincent, killed your father years ago. I wanted to protect you from them. He might have killed you, too."

"Vincent claims that my father killed my mother," Dante said, the pain of betrayal stabbing him. "That she was an Angel of Light, of good."

"Your mother had no place with your father. She almost ruined him," Father Gio said harshly. "I couldn't allow you to suffer the same fate or be sidetracked from your destiny. I knew one day Zion would need you. You had to be prepared."

Heat speared Dante's fingers, sparked by his rage. Father Gio was admitting what he'd done. "Why didn't you tell me? Why keep me away from my brothers?"

"Because you had a path to follow," Gio said. "Your destiny is to use your powers for the underworld. I tried to teach you that. And we all believed that one or both of your brothers were the weak links." His long, disappointed sigh echoed in the stench-filled air. "But then you failed, you betrayed us, weren't as strong as any of us thought."

Because he hadn't been able to kill a little girl.

Was that what his father had wanted him to do? Had he been born from that kind of demented evil?

If so, maybe his mother had been right to send him away.

"My destiny is to do as I damn well please." Dante raised his clenched fist, ready to battle.

Father Gio threw up a warning hand, his eyes filled with wrath. "I wouldn't start a war with me."

Dante's gaze fell to the topaz angel amulet against Gio's neck, and fury sizzled through his blood. With one hand, he jerked the amulet off the old man he'd once considered his father and held it in his palm.

Instantly the topaz stone burst to life, an overwhelming heat radiating from the stone as it shot off crystalline red and yellow sparks. Dante felt stronger, empowered, as if he had finally regained something he'd lost long ago.

"You stole this because it gives me power and strength and protects me." He threw a fireball, but Father Gio caught it in his hand with a snarl and tossed it back. It exploded at Dante's feet, heat searing the soles of his boots.

"You don't want to battle with me," Father Gio roared. "I have an army of demons, Dante, many who don't give a damn if they raise Zion's ire by vanquishing you. If you start this war, you'll lose."

Dante gritted his teeth. Father Gio was right. He could defeat a single demon, even two or three, but not Father Gio's army.

And not Zion.

*Together our powers are magnified*, Vincent and Quinton Valtrez had said. He might need them to defeat Father Gio and Zion.

But he wasn't ready to trust them yet. And he'd wait to find out the results of the blood test before he truly believed they were related.

"Are you behind the two bloodletting murders in town?" Dante asked.

Father Gio barked a long hideous laugh. "Bloodletting is not my style. But this new demon, he is quite entertaining."

Dante barely resisted the impulse to attack.

"Get out now," Father Gio growled. "I don't intend to help you defy your father. He is our leader and will rule the world. And I will help him."

Dante cursed. Not if he destroyed this demon and Zion first.

～

Marlena left Dante's blood with the tech at the lab to run the tests, then headed back to her office. She was still contemplating the fact that he might be related to the Valtrez men.

Another storm was rolling in, and she flipped on the radio to listen to while she worked.

"This is Jebb Bates coming to you with some sad news. Sam Larson, former sheriff of Mysteria, is dead. The coroner stated that it looked as if he suffered a massive heart attack, but there will be an autopsy to confirm the results.

"Sheriff Larson served as our sheriff for over fifteen years..."

Marlena flipped off the radio, her chest constricting. She had just spoken with Sam Larson. And she'd upset him.

Guilt washed over her.

Oh, God...had she caused his heart attack?

<hr/>

After his confrontation with Father Gio, Dante stopped by the morgue to confer with the ME.

Dr. Underwood limped toward him, claimed his desk chair, swept aside a stack of files, then spread open the one he'd been carrying and examined it.

"What do you have on victim number two?" Dante asked.

The doctor consulted the papers with a deep frown. "Her name is Brenda Mulligan. We identified her from her medical records. She had a pin in her hip from a car accident. She worked at BloodCore."

Dante gripped the arms of the chair to keep from reacting. If she worked at BloodCore, Marlena must have known her.

Dante straightened. "Did she bleed out like Jordie?"

"Absolutely. He carved an S into her chest, then bit into her carotid artery." He shifted the papers to reveal several photos he'd taken of the bite marks. "Obviously she was killed someplace else and carried to the property near your house."

"Did the blood in the cave match Brenda's?"

The ME nodded.

"Did you find any other blood?"

"I'm afraid not."

This killer was definitely clever.

"Anything else you can tell me?" Dante asked.

"Just that this is one sick, sadistic son of a bitch." Dr. Underwood rubbed at his leg as if it was aching, then pushed up the sleeves to his lab coat and folded his arms. "I haven't seen anything like it in years, not since Larson was sheriff."

Dante started to speak, but Underwood cut him off. "By the way, Larson is dead. EMT said it presented like a heart attack, but he's on my table now for an autopsy."

Dante's mind raced. "Larson is dead?"

Underwood nodded. "The timing seems odd to me," he said. "Perhaps you should call in the Feds. The people of Mysteria won't sleep again until this maniac is caught. And any more deaths are on your head."

Anger raced through Dante. The damn ME didn't have to tell him that. But this killer, this series of murders, was far more disturbing than the humans in Mysteria thought.

Knowing the truth would only create widespread panic. Better they believe one of their own, a human in town, was killing women than learn that demons roamed the underground.

Demons more ruthless and vile and committed to spreading evil than anyone could ever imagine.

＿＿＿＿＞＿＿＿＿

Zion gestured for the Seer to relay her report.

"Vincent and Quinton found Dante," she said with a wave of her black hand. "They have spoken."

"And?"

"Having your minion burn his victims worked perfectly and raised distrust between the men."

"Dante rejected his brothers?"

"Yes. He wants no partnership with them." The Seer hesitated. "He makes his own laws and ways."

"Good. We must destroy their bond," Zion said. "As long as he carries the seed of evil within him, he can be turned."

He simply had to play Dante right. Keep his son from mating with the woman. Turn her against him.

But he'd choose the timing.

The rumbling of footsteps and voices reverberated in the cave, then the first team of soldiers filed in. The demon he'd appointed to the new chair as the Death Angel led the group, and they gathered around the fire.

"The Hunters Moon is upon us. We must prepare our soldiers for war. I've enlisted the elements to dole out their worst." He gestured toward Hypnos. "Your job will be to plant paranoia in the minds of the humans so they turn on each other in anger and fury."

He gestured to the demon on his right. "You will rob people of dreams. Without dreams, the humans can't work out their frustrations, and their tempers and anger will rise." A smile curved his demonic mouth as he gestured to the werecreatures he'd chosen to serve him. "You will begin the pack wars. Kill the leader of the opposing packs so they blame one another, then they'll destroy each other."

The Soul Collectors bowed before him. "Master, we are prepared."

Hypnos bowed his head in supplication. "And this plan begins when?"

"The night of the Hunters Moon. The dead will rise and haunt the humans. And hopefully, my son Dante will join me. Then the anarchy and the end of humanity will begin."

# Chapter Eighteen

Marlena phoned Dante. She had to talk to him about Sam Larson. "Dante, it's Marlena."

"You sound upset. What's wrong?"

Tears choked her throat. "I just heard that Sheriff Larson is dead."

A tense moment passed. "I know. I talked to the ME and he's going to perform an autopsy."

"It's my fault, isn't it?" Marlena whispered. "My fault he's dead because I upset him asking questions."

"You don't know that, Marlena."

"Don't I?" she asked angrily.

"No," he said. "He was a sick man."

She swiped at her eyes. "But you told me it was dangerous to ask questions, and my being there upset him."

"Stop blaming yourself, Marlena," Dante said. "This is bigger than you."

"What do you mean?"

"I can't talk about it right now."

"Why? Did you find Gerald Daumer?"

"No. But the ME identified the second body."

His gruff tone made her tense. "Who was it?"

"A woman named Brenda Mulligan. The ME said that she worked at BloodCore."

Marlena sank into her desk chair with a groan. "Brenda? Are you sure?"

"Yes. Dr. Underwood verified her ID from her medical and dental records."

Marlena leaned her head into her hands. Why was all this happening? First Jordie, now Brenda.

So sad. So unfair. So tragic. She was in the prime of her life, and to have it snuffed out so cruelly...

"Do you know if Miss Mulligan has any family?" Dante asked.

Marlena struggled to think through the grief and shock eating at her. "No, she was an only child. Her parents died in a car crash a few years ago."

"I'm going to her apartment to check it out," Dante said. "Maybe I'll find a lead. Marlena, did Brenda have a boyfriend or lover?"

"No, she only moved here a few months ago. She was fresh out of college, attended UT-Chattanooga. She told me that her boyfriend left her at the altar, so she was reluctant to date again."

"How about other close friends? Someone she might hang out with socially?"

"No one that I know of. She kept to herself. I think she liked to read, and once she mentioned that she kept a journal."

"Okay, if you think of anything else, let me know. Wait at work, and I'll come by and follow you home."

"That's not necessary, Dante. If something happens, I'll call you. Just focus your energy on finding out who killed Brenda and Jordie."

A heartbeat lapsed before he agreed. "Just be careful. And if you think someone is following you or if, when you arrive home, anything looks suspicious, don't go inside this time. Call me."

"I will." Marlena sighed wearily. It had been so long since anyone had worried about her that his concern touched her.

But she had to protect herself from him.

Still, his dark intensity drew her. And he had saved her life.

But she couldn't allow herself to get too deeply involved with him. The pain of loving her family and losing them had been too much.

Her work was her life.

She snapped her phone closed, then walked down the hall toward Dr. Raysen's and Dr. Sneed's lab to break the news about Brenda's death.

Edmund's already pale skin turned chalky white. "My God, who would want to hurt Brenda? She was one of the sweetest girls in the world."

"That is terrible." Dr. Sneed's face grew pinched. "When the sheriff finds this killer, I hope we can draw samples of his blood and test it. I'd like to examine his serotonin and dopamine levels."

Marlena frowned at his impersonal reaction, although the genius doctor had only been working at BloodCore a month, and hadn't known Brenda very well. Science was his life.

Edmund removed his glasses and wiped his face with his hand. "Does the sheriff have any clues?"

"He's still looking for Gerald Daumer."

Dr. Sneed pulled a hand down his chin. "Daumer's blood did have abnormalities. Let's look at it again and compare it to that of other serial killers on file."

"Good idea." Marlena pressed her fingers to her temple, trying to soothe away the tension. "Maybe tomorrow. I'm beat right now."

Exhaustion and guilt weighed on her. She hadn't slept well the night before, not with Dante downstairs, so she headed home. She wanted to mourn Brenda alone. And think about Sam Larson's death and Dante's comment that this situation was bigger than her.

Storm clouds thickened, thunder rumbling, the moon barely discernible in the black sky as she walked outside, jumped into her car, and drove from the parking lot. Rain began to sprinkle as she wound up the mountain, fog making visibility limited. She amped up the defroster and heater, glancing over her shoulder for headlights, but the road was deserted, the endless sea of trees groaning from the weight of the wind.

An eerie sensation flooded her nerve endings, and once again, she imagined she saw eyes watching her from the forest as she parked in her drive. The house appeared to be just as she'd left it. Doors and windows closed. A sole light burning in the kitchen.

Wrapping her coat around her shoulders, she grabbed her umbrella, then rushed up the front steps to her house, unlocked the door, and fell inside with a sigh. Despite her fatigue, adrenaline pumped through her, and she had to take deep breaths to calm herself.

But suddenly a noise jarred her. A creak from upstairs. A rocking sound as if someone's foot was tapping repeatedly.

Then a low, keening cry like a baby's.

She clamped her teeth over her lower lip and dropped the umbrella. Gerald? Prudence?

She tugged her cell phone from her purse, grabbed the fire poker, and tiptoed toward the stairs. Slowly, she inched upward. A quick check showed that the bedrooms were clear.

The attic again? Gerald? Had he come back for help?

Dust motes floated in the haze of the stairwell, a dank odor seeping from the corners, but she forged ahead, then eased open the door, prepared to run if necessary. She tried the light switch, but the light was out, so she picked her way up the stairwell until she reached the clearing at the top. A tiny sliver of moonlight wove through the tree-tops and spilled through the narrow window, just enough to illuminate a figure in the room.

A man huddled in the corner with his knees pulled to his chest. He wrapped his arms around his legs and was rocking himself back and forth.

Gerald Daumer.

When he looked up at her, his eyes gleamed an odd shade of burnt orange, and the raspy gurgle that erupted from his throat sounded inhuman and terrifying.

⌒

Dante met a CSI team at the Mulligan woman's apartment. The manager of the complex let him inside with his master key, and Dante scanned the front room, mentally logging the details.

A combination kitchen and den. A green floral sofa, pine end tables, a mismatched chair, a small wooden table with dried flowers in a vase in the center. A painting of a farmhouse on the wall. A bookshelf overloaded with paperback novels, psychology books, and travel magazines. A small desk in the corner with a laptop on it.

He pulled on gloves, then strode through the den to the bedroom on the left, once again cataloging the contents and looking for anything out of place. Bed made neatly with a dark green comforter. Yellow and green towels hanging haphazardly in the small bath. Hairdryer, curling iron, makeup case—all the things he'd expect to find in a woman's apartment.

He checked the drawers, the medicine cabinet, the closet. Women's clothes, lab tech jackets, sensible shoes, and toiletries.

No sign that a man had lived here or stayed over.

He returned to the den and checked her phone log. The lab. A few unknowns. Nothing that created suspicion. He located a small address book on the counter and flipped through it. The number for the local dry cleaner's, police, fire department, pizza delivery place, BloodCore, the psychiatric hospital where Marlena worked, and a few numbers whose area code indicated they were from Chattanooga. Probably college friends or acquaintances.

Hoping to find something helpful on her computer, he booted it up, then checked her email log, but it had been erased. Suspicious.

He searched to see if she belonged to any online groups, chat rooms, or single clubs but found nothing. No Facebook or MySpace page either.

Odd. Had the killer erased any evidence of her social networking life to protect himself?

Other than living in the same town, was Brenda connected to Jordie in any way?

Maybe the CSI tech team could recover the deleted files and they'd find a link, maybe a club or singles group where the killer might have met the victims.

Remembering that Marlena said Brenda kept a journal, he rummaged through the desk drawers in search of it, but found nothing except a few bills and brochures on local tourists sights. He shut down the computer, then checked the kitchen drawers and the end tables and felt between the sofa cushions.

A journal was private—where would a woman keep it? Her bedroom?

Pulse racing, he hurried into the bedroom and checked the bedside table. A Bible had been tucked inside the drawer, but no journal. Hoping the killer hadn't found it, he walked over to the closet, searched through the pockets of her coats, felt along the top shelf, then looked inside the shoeboxes on her floor.

Eyes narrowed, he turned and peered across the room, and suddenly moved to the bed. He felt beneath the pillows, then lifted the mattress and skimmed his hand between it and the box springs. His hand brushed across a rectangular leather-bound book.

Maybe her journal would finally give him a lead.

～

Marlena took a step back, bracing herself to run and call for help.

"So cold, so cold, so cold," Gerald whispered. "Make the voices be quiet. Make them be quiet."

Marlena released a pent-up breath, but kept her distance. She had to remember that Gerald might be a killer, or he could just be a frightened mentally ill patient who needed her help.

"Gerald," she said softly. "It's Dr. Bender. What are you doing here?"

His crying continued as if he hadn't heard her, and he started beating at his temple just as he had in her office.

"Gerald," she said again. "Can you hear me?"

Slowly, his cries softened, then he looked up at her with swollen, bloodshot eyes. His skin was ruddy and chapped as if he'd been out in the elements too long. His teeth were chattering, his hair damp and matted, and beard stubble grazed his face. The scent of sweat, body odor, and smoke wafted off of him.

Fear mingled with an adrenaline rush and the need to help him. He was her patient. She wanted to help him, convince him to turn himself in for questioning before he got hurt.

"Gerald, tell me why you're here," she said, lowering her voice. "I thought you were going to stay at the hospital for treatment."

"No, no hospital," he cried. "They do awful things to me there. They lock me up and tie me down. Then he can get to me."

"Who can get to you, Gerald?"

"The devil. He's after me. He tells me to do bad things and if I don't, he'll kill me and send me to hell where he'll torture me for eternity."

She touched his arm. "Let me get you a blanket and something hot to drink. Would you like that?"

"Don't leave me." His eyes darted around nervously. "He's here now. He's watching."

"Who's watching?"

"Zion. He's *here*. He keeps whispering in my head. He wants me to kill for him."

"Whom does he want you to kill?"

He pressed his hands over his ears, slapping at them. "Stop it, make him leave me alone!"

"Gerald, tell me what happened. Did you kill Jordie?"

"Blood. Blood. Blood. So much blood everywhere," he screeched. "He likes to bite his victims, sink his teeth in deep, and watch the blood spurt out. It's everywhere."

"Did you see the person who killed Jordie?"

"*He* killed them," Gerald cried. "He told me how it felt. How the blood tasted so succulent and delicious that he was dizzy." He suddenly lurched up, the childlike voice disappearing as a roar of rage burst from him. "He wants me to kill the rest of them. He says you can't save them, but you have to."

Marlena backed up, gripping the fire poker tighter. "Save who?"

"You," he shouted. "And I have to obey him." Then he lunged toward her, his teeth bared, his eyes gleaming, wild and delusional.

# Chapter Nineteen

———

Marlena screamed and swung the fire poker to fend him off.

"Gerald, stop, don't do this. I can help you. Let's sit down and talk."

"No, he says I have to kill you! Finish what he started. Finish what he started." He ground his hands against his ears. "The devil says do it!"

She jabbed the poker into his stomach, and he doubled over with a wail. Her heart racing, she turned and ran down the steps, but he charged her from behind, and they both tumbled downward. Her shoulder hit the steps, her knees scraped the wood, and he slammed his fist against her head.

Stars swam in front of her eyes, and she screamed as he yanked her hair. "He's going to get you, Marlena. He'll kill you if I don't."

"Stop it, Gerald!" Marlena kicked and fought, one foot connecting with his knee. He rolled her to her back on the landing, and she clawed his face.

He howled as blood trickled down his cheek, then lifted one hand to wipe at it, his lips curling back over his teeth in a sinister look at the sight of the crimson stain. The momentary reprieve allowed her to escape. Heaving for breath, she stumbled up and raced down the steps.

A second later, footsteps pounded behind her. She grabbed her purse and ran outside, fumbling with her keys. Gerald was on her tail, reaching for her, when she jumped into the car, started the engine, and fled down the mountain.

With a trembling hand, she dug her cell phone from her purse and punched in Dante's number.

"Dante, Gerald Daumer was just at my house." Her breath hitched. "He tried to kill me."

Dante's deep voice boomed over the line. "Where are you now?"

"In my car."

"I'll call Hobbs and order a search team out to your property. Meet me at my house." He gave her the address. "I'm on my way."

Marlena checked her rearview mirror, grateful not to see a car following her. In fact, she hadn't seen one in her driveway. Gerald must have been on foot. Had he been hiding out in the woods behind her house?

Where would he go now? Would he murder some other poor unsuspecting female because he'd failed to kill her?

The rain picked up, pelting the windshield, the wind jarring the windows. She veered onto the side road leading up the mountain to Dante's, the night sounds of the woods growing more eerie, the property so isolated that for a second she questioned her sanity in coming to his house.

Thick woods and dense trees clouded the house, which had been built underground, as if the stone structure were literally carved from the side of the mountain. The only windows she could detect were skylights, and the big, gnarled branches of the giant trees towering overhead gave the exterior an ominous and sinister feel.

Suddenly a wall of blinding rain fell in front of her, and she hit a pothole. She braked, but the car skidded and fish-tailed toward a hulking oak tree. She tried to steer into the skid, but rocks spewed, the rain thickened, and her tires squealed as she struggled to maintain control.

Through the foggy haze, the silhouette of a man in a black cape appeared in front of her like a ghostly image that had materialized from nowhere. But he wasn't a man—not exactly.

His features were grotesque and distorted. A halo of red surrounded him in a hazy glow, his cape billowing out like wings. Sharp fanglike claws protruded from his fingers, and his skin glowed a fiery red.

Terrified, she clenched the steering wheel and swerved to avoid hitting the creature. An animal's howl rent the air, then the creature leaned forward and blew a puff of fire at her.

Marlena screamed. The rain should have extinguished the flames, but the fireball rolled toward her as if untouched by the rain. She swerved to avoid it, and the car skimmed a row of trees, bounced over the gravel driveway, and skated toward another copse of oaks. She tried to brace herself as the vehicle spun out of control and slammed into a thicket.

The impact flung her neck back, the air bag exploded and slammed into her chest. She screamed as the creature leered at her through the window, then her head spun, stars swam before her eyes, and darkness swept her into its abyss.

～

Dante's jaw ached from grinding his teeth as he sped up the drive to his house. He spotted Marlena's car jammed into a tree, and panic assaulted him.

Cursing, he threw the SUV into Park, jumped out, raced to her, and yanked open the car door. Her face was pale, her head slumped forward against the air bag, and blood dotted her lip.

His chest clenched as he felt for a pulse. "Marlena?"

Relief surged through him as he heard her shallow breathing and felt her pulse beat beneath his fingers. He removed his pocketknife, slashed the air bag, then gently stroked her back. "Marlena?"

She groaned, and he gently eased her head back against the seat to examine her. Fortunately, the bleeding was minimal, just a trickle where she must have bitten her lip. "Marlena, can you hear me?"

Slowly she opened her eyes and looked up at him. Her pupils were dilated, and she looked dazed and confused.

"Marlena?" He cradled her face between his hands. "I'm here. I'll call for help."

She clutched his arm in a panicked grip. "No, please don't leave me..."

"I won't," he said gruffly. "Tell me what happened. Where are you hurt? Did you hit your head?"

He tried to tilt her chin to examine her more closely, but she pushed his hands away. "No. I'm all right."

"What happened?" he asked. "Did Daumer follow you?"

She shook her head. "No, but he said the devil, Zion, was in his head, that he wanted him to kill me." Her voice cracked. "And then in the driveway, through the rain, I saw...I think I saw him."

Alarm ripped through his gut. "Exactly what did you see?"

Marlena's eyes darted toward the woods. "He had

blood-red lips and claws and he...he shot fire from his hands."

Holy hell. She'd just described Zion.

Had he appeared in front of Marlena?

*Zion will do anything to get to you,* the Valtrez brothers had said.

Was he going after Marlena to punish him?

❧

Marlena replayed the images of the monster in her head. She had seen a monster, hadn't she? Some kind of creature with glowing eyes and fire shooting from his paws...

"Let's go inside," Dante said in a gruff voice.

She pushed at the steering wheel to get out, but Dante slid his arm behind her back, scooped her up in his arms, and carried her to his house.

Marlena tugged at his arms to let her down. "I'm not helpless. I can walk."

"Just relax," he said between clenched teeth. "I still think I should call an ambulance and have you examined."

"I'm a doctor," Marlena said. "I'm fine, Dante. I was just spooked."

But he didn't release her. Instead he strode to the door, unlocked it, and carried her inside. Marlena's head was aching, her muscles stiff and sore from the impact of the air bag. He carried her to the sofa and gently placed her on it, but his determined look pinned her down. "Move your arms."

She rolled her eyes, but bent them to prove she wasn't hurt.

"Now your legs."

She sighed in disgust then tried to stand, but swayed, and he cursed.

"I can walk, I'm just shaken," she admitted as she sank back against the seat with a shudder.

He placed an afghan over her, his jaw tight, his eyes glittering with anger.

Without another word, he turned away from her, strode outside, and returned a minute later with an armload of firewood.

She took in her surroundings, aware the walls and bookcase were bare and void of personal items. The sense that they were isolated once again hit her. Sam Larson had warned her to be careful around Dante. And he'd admitted that he dealt with demons.

Was he dangerous to her?

No, he wouldn't hurt her physically. But emotionally...

The wood began to crackle and pop, the scent of burning timber filling the air, the heat emanating from the blaze warming her. The rest of the house was dark, the only light the sliver of moonlight trying to weave its way through the thick storm clouds in the skylight.

But Dante's sullen silence sent an icy chill through her.

She clutched the afghan to her chest. "Dante?"

He stiffened, his shoulders squaring as he angled his head to stare at her. Her insides quivered at the intensity in his eyes, her heart thundering as she waited on his response.

Instead of answering, he walked to the bar in the corner of the den, poured a glass of red wine for her and a scotch for himself, then handed her the glass.

"How did you know I like red wine?"

The corner of his mouth tilted in an almost-smile but

quickly fell back into a tight grimace. "I noticed at your place. Drink it."

Her hands trembled slightly as she accepted the glass, then she took a sip of the Merlot, grateful for something to soothe her nerves.

He sipped his scotch, then stood in front of the fire again, his shoulders rigid.

"Dante, talk to me." Marlena pushed the afghan away, then walked over to him and forced him to look at her. "Tell me what's happening. First two women are murdered, then the old sheriff dies shortly after I ask him about the past."

Rage darkened his eyes, but another emotion flashed there as well. Fear.

And pain.

Pain she didn't understand.

"Dammit, Marlena." His voice sounded tortured as he set his drink on the mantel; then he yanked her into his arms and crushed her in his embrace.

Dante inhaled Marlena's erotic feminine scent, savoring the sweetness seeping from her. He didn't deserve to touch Marlena, much less hold her.

He was born evil. And just as Father Gio had taught him, evil would never die.

In spite of all the innocents he might have saved, that side of him thrived, tempting and alluring.

The evil flowed through his blood and soul, dark and hot, hungry to be fed.

Yet Marlena buried herself against him as if he was

her savior, and he was helpless to resist her. She felt soft and warm and so damn feminine and sexy that his body stirred to life. His hands burned to touch her, his mouth watering for a taste of her flesh, his cock throbbing and begging to find a home between her thighs.

His baser instincts shoved his conscience aside, and he dropped a kiss into her hair. Desperate to be closer, he trailed his hands over her shoulders, down to her hips, and cradled her between his legs. She shivered against him, and he swept one hand up, lifted her chin, and looked into her eyes.

He'd protected her as a child.

He wanted to do the same now. But he wanted so much more...

Things he couldn't have. Like the taste of her on his lips. The feel of her bare skin against his fingertips. Her body quivering as he swept his tongue and hands over her naked flesh.

Dammit. He wanted Marlena in his bed begging him to fill her.

# Chapter Twenty

Marlena's lips parted, her gaze flicked to his mouth, and her hand swept up his chest. Raw need overwhelmed him, and he lowered his head and fused his mouth with hers. For a brief second she stiffened, and his gut clenched. She didn't want him. She knew what he was, that he was a monster.

Then she moaned his name and moved against him, and hunger surged through him. He deepened the kiss, teased her lips apart with his tongue, delved inside her mouth to taste her sweetness and independence. Arousal swelled inside his body, arousal so painful that his head swam, obliterating any thought except the fierce need to take her.

To make her his.

He raked his fingers along her cheek, then her jaw, and tilted her face so he could lick the soft skin of her neck, nibble at the sensitive zone behind her ear. Her breath hitched as she moved seductively against him. Her thigh brushed his, and white-hot pleasure shot through him, heightening his lust. He traced his tongue along her neck, then lower, his fingers literally itching to tear off her clothes.

Passionate, desperate, he rasped her name. She lifted her chin and her foggy gaze met his. Her eyes were clouded with hunger, need, yet a sliver of fear lingered. His hands stilled as an image of the terror in her eyes the day her family was brutally murdered replayed through his head.

His demon family had put that terror there.

He knew who had killed her family, and he hadn't stopped them. Hadn't turned them in or seen that they were punished.

As if to remind him of his place in the world—that he belonged nowhere—the sound of a wolf's lonely cry rent the air. The lone sound stirred others, and the screech of a pack in hunt mode echoed through the hills.

A pack of werewolves. Not the BlackPaws. He recognized their call. This was a predatory pack, one that had come to Mysteria to war with the BlackPaws.

There were others out there, too, the demons who'd entered Earth, passing by the Twilight Guards and threatening humanity on all Hallows' Eve.

Marlena was searching for a cure for violent behavior, for evil, for a way to eradicate the monsters like him.

But that was impossible. Evil would always survive.

And with the new leader of the underworld, the demon world was mounting in force. Zion had unleashed hundreds of demons into the universe to prey, and more violence and trouble would come.

Dammit. Even if he wanted to kill the beast within himself, to cure the darkness, he needed that monster's strength and drive to protect the town from others like him.

～

Marlena's heart was pounding, the scent of Dante's masculine body swirling through her like an aphrodisiac. His lips had paved a blazing trail of fiery sensations down her neck, stirring desires and hungers that needed sating, that made her skin tingle and her insides hum with pleasure.

But he suddenly pulled back, and a barrage of emotions warred in his eyes. The intensity sent a shudder through her.

For a moment, he looked dangerous.

Jaw clenched, he released her abruptly, then spun around and stepped outside on the porch as if he needed to put some physical space between them.

Had she done something wrong? Why had he stopped?

Shaking with unspent desire and anger, she followed him outside. The wind swirled through her, icy cold and frigid.

She wasn't asking for a relationship, didn't want to care for someone else and then lose him. She just needed comfort tonight. That was all she'd allow herself. "Why did you stop, Dante?"

He leaned against the porch rail, his hands cradling the banister. "Because you don't know what you're doing."

She bit her lip, irritated at his condescending tone. "Yes, I do. I'm not a child anymore."

He spun around, his deep brown eyes skating over her with a look that bordered on predatory. "Believe me, I know that."

She stepped forward to reach for him, but he threw up a warning hand. "Go inside, Marlena," he said gruffly. "You're in danger, and I have to do my job and find this serial killer."

"That doesn't mean we can't be together tonight."

"Trust me, Marlena. Sex with me won't solve your problems. It will only complicate them."

Hurt rippled through her. She wanted to be back in his arms. She'd wanted to feel him against her for years. He was the only one who understood her past, her pain, who knew what had driven her to search for a medical way to eliminate violence.

A noise outside startled her, and she scanned the darkness beyond, suddenly feeling naked, vulnerable and exposed, as if an endless sea of eyes was peering through the woods, monster's eyes watching them.

"I know sex won't solve all our problems or help us find Gerald Daumer." She placed her hand on his shoulder, stroked the tension from his knotted muscle. "But I want you anyway, Dante. I want you to help me forget about the demons tonight."

How could he forget about the demons when he was one of them?

He couldn't. But he could give Marlena that gift.

Emotions clogged his throat as he yanked her against him. He shouldn't be here with her now. Shouldn't get this close.

Caring for her, wanting her was a forbidden passion.

But his body hummed with raw need, and he couldn't stop himself from holding her or wanting her.

Dammit, she could have died tonight.

First Daumer had attacked her, and now a demon had shown himself to her at his house. A firestarter, an upper-level demon.

And this one might be his own damn father.

He tightened his hold on her, inhaling the sweet

scent of her body, desperate to calm the rage fueling his bloodstream. Marlena wasn't safe with him.

But would she be safe without him?

The image of the Satanic S shot through his mind, then the image of Marlena's mother and sister's sadistic murder. The idea that the murderer had left her trophies from his kills, that he might have found Marlena dead like the other girls, ate at his gut.

She clutched his back and tilted her face toward him, and a fierce hunger spiked his heart rate. Knowing she might have died tonight made every bone in his body ache. Stirred every primal desire he'd ever possessed.

"Dante?"

"Shh." He didn't want to talk about the demon now. He couldn't.

He just wanted to hold her and let her warmth rid him of this relentless cold. Wanted to feel her soft body against his hard one. Let her tenderness remind him that he was part human, even if his own soul was lost.

Resistance fled, the intense need to be closer to her overwhelming him, and he cupped her face in his hands, tilted her chin up, lowered his head, and fused his mouth with hers.

~

Ruthie Mae Stanton had wanted to tell Marlena everything. But she was too ashamed.

Ashamed, but not enough to change. No, she wasn't ready for that. She had always been a prude, a good girl, had only slept with one man, the boy she'd married years ago. And she'd only had sex in the missionary position with her husband, Gene.

Gene the deadhead, she thought with a bitter laugh.

He was boring and fat now, and bald, and after his nightly six-pack of PBR, the asshole couldn't get it up. Not that he had much in that department anyway. He was about the size of a cocktail wiener.

Judge Brannigan's stately image flashed into her head. Now *there* was a man.

Strong, big, and powerful, both in his job and in the bedroom.

He'd taught her so many things between the sheets, had taken mundane sex and turned each touch into a titillating journey of exploration and endless pleasure.

She finished her shift at the hospital, then hurried home and changed into a slinky red dress, one she'd bought off the Internet in a shopping frenzy. It hugged her curvaceous figure and had a split up the side to midthigh. Unfortunately, she couldn't show off her ample cleavage because of that nasty scar from her bypass surgery, but she had killer legs, even in her forties.

The judge didn't seem to mind her scar or her age.

She dabbed on perfume and powder, then hopped into the car and raced through traffic, battling the horrific weather. She parked at the hotel. The judge was waiting in the hotel room, dressed in his judge's robe as if holding court, his steamy look raking over her from head to toe. He slammed his gavel on the wooden desk, then waved his hand as if to order her to fall to her knees.

"You're late," he said harshly.

A sliver of fear shot through her, yet excitement heated her blood. "I'll make it up to you," she whispered.

His wicked laugh boomeranged off the walls, then he tossed down a shot of whiskey and grabbed the thick rope on the table. "Oh, you'll pay," he said, then reached for her dress, ripped it off, and shoved her to the floor. "Tonight I'm going to punish you. You're going to suffer for all your sins."

"Yes, Master." Her nipples hardened as she bowed to him. But for a split second, she contemplated being the dominator, making him suffer. Following through on the orders from the evil voice inside her head.

Except that she would kill the women who'd stolen the men from her. She would strap them down, carve an S into their chests, watch the blood trickle down their bodies and drip to the floor in a beautiful crimson river.

# Chapter Twenty-one

Hunger spiraled through Dante as his lips closed over Marlena's. She moaned his name, and raw lust and need inflamed him.

He wanted to strip her clothes off and feel her naked against his greedy fingers, to feel her body opening and welcoming his thick cock between her moist thighs.

A wicked smile curved his mouth, and he cupped her face in his hands. For a moment he allowed himself to indulge in forbidden fantasies—he could hear her panting his name as he brought her to the brink, then teased her until she begged him to make her come.

She wet her lips, but her gaze remained locked to his. Dammit. For the first time in his life, a deep-seated fear crowded his throat.

Not fear for himself but fear of losing her to the demons.

She was warmth to his cold, life to his dead, empty soul.

So he lowered his mouth to hers, claiming her as he'd craved to from the very moment he'd met her.

She moaned and leaned into his chest, her body trembling against him.

A fierce hunger overtook him, his body twitching with

arousal to the point of pain. Firelight flickered over her beautiful face, and he slid a hand over her breast, then ripped open her blouse and sucked a plump pink nipple into his mouth.

Still, even as her goodness soothed the need in his body, the call of evil beckoned beneath the surface. He wanted to throw her down, take her fast and furious, force her to pleasure him, to serve his every need, tie her to him forever.

It was wrong, and he knew it. Wrong to take a human, wrong to seduce her when she was vulnerable. Wrong because she wasn't part of his world and never would be.

Wrong because he had secrets he didn't want her to discover.

~

Need rippled through Marlena, her body tingling with it, her nipples hardening. Dante's touch ignited a fire in her belly, the flames of desire burning so hotly that her knees nearly buckled.

He was the sexiest, strongest man she'd ever met. And something about him, maybe the mysterious danger underlying his eyes, his tone, even his control, made her crave his touch.

She didn't want to die without at least being with him one time.

Muscles bunched in his chest as he pressed her against him and nipped at her lips, teasing her mouth. With a low moan, he plunged his tongue inside, while his hands raked over her and tore at her clothes. Seconds later, they dropped to the braided rug by the fire, and he trailed kisses along her jaw and neck, then lower, to her breast.

Marlena whispered his name as the erotic sensations pummeled her.

He kneed her legs apart as he suckled her, and wanton needs possessed her as if she'd lost control over her conscious mind.

Dante's touch felt electric, addictive, comforting, erotic, mind-numbing, as if nothing mattered but their bodies mating and becoming one.

He traced a finger over her bare stomach, dipping his fingers into the wet folds of her body, and she bucked upward, needing more, craving his length inside her.

"Marlena," he said in a hoarse voice, "give yourself to me."

A blinding ache filled her, and she parted her legs, unable to deny him. "Yes," she whispered.

His gaze met hers as he rose above her and shoved her tangled hair from her eyes. Smiling wickedly, he stripped off his clothes.

Her stomach clenched. His big body, illuminated by the firelight, looked like that of a male god. She'd never seen anyone so powerful and strong, so dark and fierce, so terrifying and sexy.

His shoulders were broad, with corded muscles that rippled down his stomach, his thick hard sex pushing between her thighs.

Yet scars marred his arms and torso. Scars that made her wonder who had hurt him.

Scars that made her want to kiss away any pain he had ever suffered.

Rising to her knees, she pulled him toward her and she did kiss them. One by one. As her lips soothed his flesh, his low growl echoed in the room, rumbling with hunger and need.

Instinct drove her to slide her fingers over his powerful length. His gruff groan of pleasure gave her the courage to stroke him from the base of his cock to the head where moisture beaded on the surface.

He shoved her hand away, cupped her hips, and thrust inside her, filling her, stretching her until she wound her legs around him, closed her eyes, and relinquished control completely. Pain and pleasure ripped through her with mind-numbing intensity.

He cradled her face with his hands and kissed her again, then nibbled at her earlobe gently. "Look at me, Marlena."

Her eyes flew open, and her gaze latched with his, the passion flaming in his expression sending her over the edge.

Her orgasm exploded in a blinding sea of white light and brilliant colors. She cried out, clutching his back with her fingers, urging him to move faster. He undulated his hips, then thrust inside her again, harder, so deep she thought she would die, and he came inside her with a raw, guttural sound that echoed off the mountain.

His body was burning hot, pinpricks of fire leaping through her nerve endings everywhere he'd touched her. Another strange feeling swept over her, fear erupting. It felt as if her body no longer belonged to her, as if it belonged to him and would forever.

~

Dante's body ached with need, a fiery burning sensation more intense and vibrant than he'd ever experienced flooding him. Sex normally revived him, but this was different—it was almost as if his heat had melted into her, her goodness had revived his humanity, as if their bodies and souls had collided.

The scent of her skin suffused him, sending a wild ache through him that needed to be quenched again and again and again.

Some primal beast inside him railed at the thought of her being with another man after him.

She pressed a kiss to his chest, and tenderness for her pummeled him. He rolled them sideways, then turned to face her. But regret about his lies fueled his blood as he looked into her trusting eyes.

Still, his dark desires ran hot, and he traced his finger over her breast, then down to where their bodies were still joined.

Pain and guilt streaked through him, nearly robbing him of breath as his past played through his mind. The days of captivity, the brutal punishments, the beatings, the hunts. His fellow demons attacking Marlena's family, her horrified face, her screams of terror...

If she knew the truth, she'd run from him in horror.

She angled herself so they were nose to nose, so close that the scent of her made him hard again. "I hate that I'm afraid," she admitted softly. "I wasn't like that as a kid. Before that awful day when my mother and sister were killed, I used to be fearless."

His throat tightened, the lies and betrayal burning his throat like acid.

She smiled softly, reached for his hand, and threaded her fingers in his. "I wish you could have known me then. I used to fly on my bike down the hill. I used to dive off the ridge into the river. And I loved lightning storms. Once I even climbed that old tower in town when a storm was brewing." Her voice hitched. "Now, I hate storms."

Dante squeezed her hand, an image of a playful young Marlena nagging at him. She had been young and daring and innocent.

But his demon family had stolen her innocence that day.

Suddenly her smile faded and she lowered her gaze and stared at their joined hands. "It was my fault my family was killed."

She lifted her gaze and the anguish in her eyes clawed at him.

He had to clear his throat before he could speak. "That's not true, Marlena, and you know it."

"Yes it is." Tears glittered on her lashes. "My sister hated the woods. She was afraid there were monsters there. But I insisted on going camping. I begged and pleaded and called her a sissy for being afraid."

He tilted her chin up with the pad of his thumb. "Marlena, you were only a child. That's what kids do."

"But I didn't believe her," she said in a broken voice. "I always thought I was invincible, that I had to show off. My mother gave in to me, but she couldn't find a babysitter so Carrie had to go with us." The tears she'd been trying to hold at bay streamed down her cheeks. "If I hadn't begged, if I hadn't called my sister a chicken and pleaded with Mama, we would have been home that day, not in the woods."

"Marlena," he said gruffly. "It wasn't your fault. Those monsters came out of nowhere and attacked you."

"But if we hadn't been in those woods," she said, choking on a sob, "my mother and sister would still be alive."

The words he needed to say to comfort her failed him.

Telling her the truth now would only hurt her more and
make her see him for the monster he'd been back then.

The monster that still lived within him. The one he
constantly had to battle to keep that side of him at bay.

Damn. He'd kill himself and any demon who tried to
hurt her.

~~~~~~~~~~

Marlena curled against Dante and wiped her eyes. She'd
never felt so close to anyone in her life.

The thought terrified her.

Yet pure pleasure from their lovemaking still rippled
through her. Confessing her guilt somehow eased her
conscience.

"Dante?"

He thumbed her hair from her cheek. "What?"

"What happened to you after that day? Where did
you go?"

He stiffened, that cold, shuttered look crossing his face.
"It's not important."

"Yes, it is. You just disappeared. Over the years, I wondered where you were. What you were doing. About your
family."

He completely shut down, then threw his legs over the
side of the bed.

"Please don't go." She tugged at his arm, coaxing him
back to her. "I just want to know more about you and how
you got those scars."

He gritted his teeth. "That's the last damn thing you
want, Marlena."

"No, I really want to know."

"Drop it. You know all you need to know about me."

"That's true, I guess," she whispered. "I know you saved me, and you've been protecting me since this killer surfaced. I have faith in you, Dante. You're going to find this killer and put him away."

Dante clenched his jaw but cradled her in his embrace, then lapsed into a silence that tore at her. The walls he was erecting stood between them like mountains she feared she could never cross.

She knew the killer was still out there, that there were other monsters. And poor Brenda was dead now at the hands of the madman...

But lying in Dante's arms enabled her to forget them for a moment, to forget the pain and grief, the guilt, to allow herself to feel pleasure.

So she closed her eyes and fell asleep, praying that at least for tonight, the nightmares wouldn't return.

But Dante's refusal to discuss his family worried her. Something bad had happened to him in the past, something that had left him scarred and bruised, unable to trust.

Something he didn't want to share.

He obviously had his own monsters and nightmares to deal with.

Another thought niggled at her. If Vincent and Quinton had supernatural powers, did Dante? Was that how he'd been able to run so fast that day? How he'd been able to escape the demons?

⁓

Zion roared his displeasure as he stared into the fire where the Seer had used her magic to give him a vision of his son Dante in bed with the woman.

Dammit. Dante was weak like the others.

If Vincent hadn't killed him when he was a mortal on Earth years ago, he would have raised his sons in his image and now they would be a team, as it should have been.

"She does not know what he is," the Seer said. "Or that he was sent to kill her the day her family was destroyed."

A slow smile curved Zion's demonic mouth. "Then she must find out. But the timing is important. I will use it to destroy their bond."

"It may be too late." The Seer's eyes turned a molten lava color, her sharp intake of breath sending alarm through Zion.

"What do you see?" he growled. "Did she conceive a child from his seed tonight?"

The Seer bowed and nodded. "The magical child is within her."

A thunderous roar ripped from Zion. "Not for long. When the female realizes she's carrying a demon child, the spawn of the Dark Lord who belonged to the demon family who stole her own family's life, she will do away with it. After all, this woman's goal is to destroy evil."

And if she didn't rid herself of the child, he would do it for her.

~

The woman had to die tonight.

He smiled and zipped his pants, the exhilaration of sex still rippling through him as his gaze homed in on her naked flesh.

Fucking her senseless had been the last thing on his mind when he'd seen her. Instead he'd hungered for the sweet taste of her blood and imagined watching her body light up in flames.

Time to get the party started now. Time to let the world know that he had power.

He grabbed her by the ankles, huffing out a breath as her limp body jerked in an attempt to rouse herself and fight.

With a bitter laugh, he dragged her across the charred and parched land, the jagged rocks and crumbled pebbles scraping her naked skin.

Skin that would soon scent the air with its acrid odor, an odor he craved as he craved the fire.

He settled her into the heart of Devil's Canyon next to the lone tree with its gnarled, bare branches and scaly trunk, a fitting place to leave her.

"Please let me go." She stirred and kicked at him, but her feeble attempts were childlike and pitiful, sweet music to his ears.

He yanked her arms behind her and tied them to the tree, then spread her legs and tied them to stakes in the ground, posing her for all the world to see what a whore she was.

"Why are you doing this?" she whispered.

He barked out a bitter laugh. "You have to die."

"No," she cried. "Please don't do this…"

He hissed. "You used your fleshy body to entice me. That's a sin."

"But you liked it!" She struggled against the bindings, kicking and pawing at the dirt like a dog. Obviously her demonic powers hadn't kicked in yet. He was in time.

The bad blood hadn't yet overcome her, not as it had him.

He raised the knife, jabbed it to her chest and smiled as

her scream of terror pierced the air. With one quick flick, he carved the Satanic S in her chest, his body stirring with bloodlust as her blood began to flow and drip down her flesh.

The red, sticky life force drained from her and soaked the ground as the life faded from her. A smile curled his lips over his teeth as he removed a small can of lighter fluid and doused her and the tree. Methodically, he removed a pack of matches from his pocket, struck one, then lit a branch.

Grimly, he watched the frail limbs burst into flames, mesmerized by the beautiful orange and yellow colors as they blended together. Heat radiated through his fingertips, the thrill of being alive made more potent by the fire.

Flames erupted, shooting upward and spreading, engulfing the tree, the wood crackling and popping in a small explosion. The smell of burning skin filled his nostrils, drugging him with pleasure as her skin began to sizzle.

The fleshy white turned a reddish brown in seconds, her hair swirling as it ignited. Smoke curled upward in a sea of gray, floating toward the heavens, boasting of its victory. He reached out and pressed his finger into the flames, watching in fascination, savoring the euphoria engulfing him.

Below, the underworld rejoiced and chanted his name.

He held his hands up in victory.

# Chapter Twenty-two

Dante left Marlena sleeping, grabbed his phone, and punched in his deputy's number. "Did you find Daumer?"

"No," Hobbs said. "I called in a couple of deputies from the county and they've been combing the woods but so far nothing."

"Keep looking. And let me know if you find him."

Dante disconnected the call, then sat in the chair beside Marlena and watched her sleep, his body coiled like a viper's. When she'd asked about his family and his past, he'd wondered briefly if she suspected what he was. If his blood tests had given him away.

But she wouldn't have slept with him if she'd known the truth.

Her description of the creature she'd seen in front of her car still disturbed him. If it had been Zion, he was closing in on him. Had found out where he lived.

He scraped his hair back from his forehead. Dammit. He might need help, might have to contact the Valtrez brothers.

No. not yet. He didn't trust them.

He was powerful in his own right. Had never needed anyone before.

But Zion was the leader of the underworld. He

possessed powers beyond the imaginable, and had a multitude of soldiers to enforce his commands and wreak destruction.

His cell phone vibrated, and he checked the number and saw it was the crime lab, so he connected the call.

"Sheriff, this is CSI Evans in forensics. Sorry to report this, but that computer showed nothing."

Another dead end. "Thanks. I appreciate the follow-up."

A noise outside startled him, and he closed his phone, yanked on his jeans, strode to the den, and checked the door. But everything seemed secure.

Outside, the howl of an otherworldly creature echoed off the mountain, the earth trembled, and rocks tumbled down the ridge like a small avalanche.

Senses alert, he stepped outside, making sure to lock the door, although there was no way a locked door would keep demons at bay. The scent of smoke and demonic blood filled the air, swirling around him in a sensual rush.

He glanced to the left to the top of the ridge and watched the dark clouds hovering over the mountain in an ominous gray as if waiting to unleash a mountain of rain. The earth rumbled, the echo of the underworld chanting that danger was on its way.

Footsteps sounded near the creek, and he strode down from the porch and followed the path into the woods. His body honed for attack, heat seeped through his fingertips, his baser instincts bursting to life.

The scent of the demon faded, drifting away in the raucous wind, although the hollow sound of the demon's laughter boomed from below.

And when he looked into the clear crystal water, his cold demonic reflection stared back.

His eyes were glowing a bright hot orange, a dark aura surrounding him as if the devil had surfaced from deep within his core to remind him that he was not human. That he shouldn't have touched Marlena.

But the memory of her lithe body beneath him, of the passionate, glazed look in her eyes when he'd touched her, taunted him. The beautiful sound of her soft moans and cries of ecstasy filled him with the need to take her again.

The screams of her sister and mother from years ago followed, resurrecting the guilt he'd never overcome.

An image of Zion tearing Marlena's heart out ripped at his gut, and the animal in him howled his rage to the heavens.

He would stop this killer and Zion, even if he had to die to do so.

A sliver of morning light seeped through the dark clouds and flowed through the ceiling skylight in the bedroom. Memories of making love with Dante returned, warming Marlena and sending a fresh stab of need and desire through her.

Hungry for him again, she rolled over and felt for Dante, but the bed was empty. For a moment, her heart ached as if she knew he'd deserted her just as everyone else in her life had.

Then panic and fear clawed at her. What if something had happened to him?

She threw off the covers, grabbed his shirt, and pulled it on, hastily fastening the buttons. Her pulse racing, she hurried into the den in search of him.

Relief spilled through her when she spotted him sitting

at the kitchen table, a cup of coffee in front of him as he studied some kind of book.

She touched his shoulder, frowning as he tensed. Obviously this was going to be an awkward morning after. "Don't you ever sleep?"

"Rarely," he said matter-of-factly.

She waited for him to look at her, but he remained focused on whatever he was reading. Irritated he was shutting her out after they'd been so intimate, she moved to the counter, rummaged through the cabinet, and found a mug, then poured herself a cup of coffee.

Contemplating the best way to approach the topic of the night before, she blew on the steaming brew. His jaw was set firmly, his gaze focused on the book, his posture rigid and standoffish.

"Dante, what's going on? Why won't you look at me?"

His hand rolled into a fist on the table. "We have a killer to catch," he said in a gruff voice. "I need to focus."

She tapped her fingernails on the table. "You don't want to talk about last night?"

A muscle ticked in his jaw. "No." For the first time since she'd entered the room, he looked up at her. His eyes were dark and unreadable, the passionate haze from the night before gone completely.

Obviously their lovemaking had meant nothing to him.

Fine. She was an adult. She could have casual sex. It wasn't as if she was in love with him. But they couldn't repeat the act or she might lose herself emotionally.

Turning her thoughts back to the case, she warmed her hands on the coffee mug. "Did they find Gerald last night?"

His face twisted. "I'm afraid not."

She gestured toward the book on the table. "What are you reading?"

He pushed back his chair, his jaw tight. "Brenda Mulligan's journal. You need to take a look at this."

She lowered herself into the chair facing him, then sipped her coffee.

He flipped back a couple of pages, then began to read. "I think it was a mistake to trust him, to join the project, but I believed in him. But since the experiment, he's behaved strangely."

Marlena scooted forward to look at the page. "What experiment?"

"She doesn't go into detail. But there might be something here."

He flipped to another entry. "I've been having headaches and experiencing memory lapses. Yesterday I woke up and was in the park. I have no idea what happened to me that night, but I had dirt on my clothes and blood on my hands. My medication must be causing blackouts. Still, I'm worried. We're both different since the transfusions."

Marlena curled her fingers around the coffee mug. "Transfusions? Does she mention who administered these transfusions?"

"Not that I've found yet." He flipped to another page. "She says here that he was going into rages, that she was afraid of him. She mentions her own aggressive tendencies mushrooming. That she was gaining strength and literally tore the door off the hinges in a fit of rage. She was also having violent thoughts."

Marlena's grip on her cup tightened. Gerald had complained of hearing voices and having violent thoughts, and it seemed that Brenda had experienced similar thoughts.

He flipped a few more pages. "Here, she says that she intends to confront him. Make him tell her if the others are acting on the violent impulses. And..."

"And what?" Marlena asked.

"If they're exhibiting signs of supernatural powers."

Coffee sloshed over the rim of Marlena's mug, and she grabbed a napkin to mop it up.

Dante stared at her, his jaw clenched. "This entry was made the day before she died."

Dante's fingers stilled on the pages of the journal, "The project you were working on—it has to do with aggressive and violent tendencies?"

She nodded. "Several of the vials were blood samples from prisoners and violent offenders. There were a few from people claiming to have gifts. A woman with telekinesis. A man who claims he has prophetic dreams."

He stewed over the possibilities. "What would happen if that blood was injected into another person?"

Marlena shrugged. "I don't know. That wasn't the purpose of our research."

Dante considered her answer. With Daumer, he'd sensed both demonic blood and human blood. The same with that woman he'd met at the Dungeon, Prudence Puckett. What if some negative genetic marker in the blood had been transferred to the recipient?

"About the missing blood—do you think one of your coworkers or employees might have taken it?"

Marlena shook her head. "No. I talked with each one of them, and the FBI questioned and polygraphed everyone at the lab."

An odd look flickered in Marlena's eyes. "Blood from the Valtrez men was in two of the missing vials. They both claimed they have supernatural powers."

His hands tightened into fists.

"I asked you once if you did, Dante. Do you?"

The temptation to spill the truth seized him, but the lie floated out easily. "No." He suddenly stood. She was asking too many questions, getting too close. "Let's go. That security consultant finally called and is going to meet us at your house."

He had to focus now. And being around Marlena made that impossible.

He'd assign Hobbs to watch her.

If Zion wanted to hurt her because of him, then it was better if she was nowhere near him.

Marlena rushed to dress. A dozen questions pummeled her as Dante followed her to her house. She'd studied human behavior, and although Dante had looked her straight in the eye, she sensed he was lying.

The notations in Brenda's journal disturbed her as well. If her death was connected to the experiment she referred to, what kind of experiment was it and who had conducted it? Did it pertain to the blood stolen from BloodCore?

And if so, how did that connect to Gerald Daumer?

He hadn't mentioned taking part in any kind of experiment when they'd talked.

Flipping on the radio to distract herself, she listened to the weather report. "Meteorologists around Tennessee are warning that a blizzard is on its way. Reports of odd swings in the weather are coming in across the States. The

Southeast has reported sudden flooding, tornadoes are ripping across Kansas, a hurricane has been spotted off the coast of Florida, and the western drought has caused major brush fires, which are spreading out of control."

Marlena flipped off the sound, hoping the flooding didn't extend to Mysteria. The town had enough problems. She parked at her house, and Dante met the security consultant at the door while she showered and changed.

The next hour passed in a tense silence as they waited for the security consultant to finish installing the alarm system. The technician showed Marlena how to activate and deactivate it.

Dante's cell phone buzzed, and he checked the number, then connected the call with a frown. "I'll be right there."

He snapped his phone closed, and her stomach clenched at the grim expression on his face.

"There was another murder?" Marlena asked.

"Yes. A woman torched at Devil's Canyon."

Marlena sighed, the gruesome image playing through her head. "Do you know the victim's identity?"

"Not yet."

Marlena ran to the front door and stepped outside to search the porch. Dante was right behind her. "He didn't leave me a trophy this time."

Dante leaned one hand against the rail. "There were cops all over your place last night, and we're here now. We could have spooked him away."

"I wish he'd just show himself," Marlena whispered.

"But that would ruin the fun for him," Dante said. "He likes the game, likes toying with us, watching us chase after him."

"That's three women so far." Marlena's heart ached. "And only a day apart. That means he's escalating."

Dante wanted to comfort Marlena. But she was right.

He had to find this demon before he hurt Marlena. No more babysitting her himself.

And no more sex.

"I have to go," Dante said. "But stay here. I'm sending a deputy to escort you to work."

"I don't need an escort," Marlena argued.

"Listen, Marlena, this is not up for debate. He may be waiting until you're alone to strike."

Fear flickered in her eyes, and he hated himself for putting it there. But she had to realize the danger.

"Set the alarm. I'll phone for a deputy on my way."

She reluctantly agreed, and he rushed to his SUV. He phoned for a deputy as he drove out to Devil's Canyon, and the officer said he would be at Marlena's within minutes.

The snowfall intensified, gathering on the boughs and branches, collecting on the mountain ridges and peaks. There were miles and miles of mountains for Daumer and demons to hide among.

He pulled his jacket around him as he parked and climbed out, rocks skidding down the canyon as he descended the hill. Years ago, a prison had stood on this land, but a fire had erupted and the entire prison had gone up in smoke. All the prisoners, guards, and staff had died, trapped in the blaze. The scent of their disgruntled spirits wafted through the canyon, the sounds of their screams echoing in the silence.

Deputy Hobbs was already on the scene, a crime unit

searching for evidence and snapping photographs. The scent of smoke and charred flesh mingled with death and the sulfuric odor of the spirits.

He studied the tree where the killer had left the woman, her torched body, the bite marks on her neck, the Satanic S carved into her chest and another burned into the ground. Considering the weather the night before, the rain could have extinguished the fire, meaning the killer must have stuck around and watched to make sure the woman was sufficiently torched.

The sick son of a bitch. He was truly evil. If not a demon by birth, a demon at heart.

But why torch the women when they were already dead?

By now, the killer had to know the ME had discovered that the women had bled out first.

Jebb Bates, the pesky reporter who'd splattered news of Jordie's and Brenda's deaths appeared, jogging down the hill.

Deputy Hobbs cursed. "I'll ward him off."

Dante's cell phone buzzed, and he checked the number. Marlena. Shit, he hoped she was okay.

He punched the connect button. "Marlena?"

"Dante, I just got to the lab. The killer left the box for me here."

His chest tightened. "Open it and see if you recognize the trophy."

He heard shuffling, then Marlena gasped. "Oh, my God..."

"What is it?"

"A ruby necklace..." Tears laced her voice. "It belongs

to Ruthie Mae Stanton, one of the nurses at the psych hospital."

Dante frowned. "I'll tell the ME and bring Stanton in for questioning.

"I want to be there when you talk to him," Marlena said.

"Why?"

"Because Ruthie Mae was my friend."

Her voice cracked, and he gave in. "The deputy will pick you up."

He didn't wait for her to argue. He hung up and stared at the Satanic S. This damn killer had to be working for Zion.

And he had to stop him.

Emotions welled in Marlena's chest. Ruthie Mae was dead. Killed in the same brutal way as Jordie and Brenda.

Ruthie Mae, who was kind and loving and a dedicated nurse.

If evil was here in Mysteria, if those monsters did exist as she'd thought as a child, all the more reason for her to continue her work.

Dante might be able to stop this one.

But her work could be used to stop more, to create a cure, to eradicate violent offenders and save more lives.

She had to finish in honor of her sister and mother.

But Gene Stanton was going to need her when he heard the news about his wife.

She removed her lab coat and went to the front door of the lab to meet the deputy. They arrived at the sheriff's office before Dante and Gene, and when they entered, Gene looked rumpled and irritated, then more confused when he saw her.

"What's going on, Marlena? The sheriff dragged me in here and he won't even tell me the reason."

"Let's go sit down," Dante said, then ushered him into a small room that Marlena realized was used for interrogations.

Gene rolled his beefy hands into fists on the table. "What's going on, Sheriff?"

"Where were you last night, Mr. Stanton?"

"I pulled a swing shift at the warehouse. Why?"

Dante rapped his knuckles on the table. "Can anyone verify that?"

Anger flashed in the man's blue-gray eyes. "My boss and two other workers. Now what the hell is going on?"

Dante glanced at Marlena, and she decided to take the lead. "Gene, I'm so sorry to tell you this, b—but Ruthie Mae was killed last night."

Gene vaulted up, rocking on his work boots, his face turning a pasty white. "What? No...No..."

"I'm so sorry," Marlena said softly.

"Sit down," Dante said. "I need to ask you some more questions."

Marlena glared at him. "Gene, please..."

He collapsed with a heavy breath, then leaned his elbows on the wooden table, tunneling his fingers into his thick white hair. "God, no...what happened?"

"She was murdered," Dante said quietly.

A hiss escaped the man's mouth, then he lifted his face and shock widened his eyes. "What? You don't mean like those other women?"

"I'm sorry, but yes," Dante said.

"No!" He pounded the table, fat tears streaking his pocked face. "Not my Ruthie Mae. Not like that."

Marlena placed her arm across his shoulders to soothe him and he broke down and cried like a baby.

Dante stood, left the room, and stayed gone for half an hour. Finally he returned with a bottle of water for Gene and propped one hip on the table.

"Who did this?" Gene stammered. "Why haven't you caught him yet, Sheriff? Why? What have you been doing?"

Dante's shoulders tensed, and Marlena patted Gene. "The sheriff has been exploring every lead, Gene. I promise you that."

"Then why is this maniac still out there?"

"Because he's smart and cunning," Dante said, seething. "That's why I need your help."

Gene sank back in the chair and scrubbed a fist over his face with a grief-stricken sigh. "All right. What do you want to know?"

Dante crossed his arms. "How long have you two been married?"

"Fifteen years." His voice broke. "Just had an anniversary last month."

"Were the two of you happy?" Dante asked.

Anger flashed in his expression again. "We had our good times and our moments. But . . . yeah, we were mostly happy."

Marlena heard the warble in his voice as a sign there had been trouble. "Is there anything in particular that you remember? Had Ruthie mentioned someone or something bothering her?"

"No." He parted his legs, braced his elbows on his knees, and propped his head in his hands as if struggling to get through the session.

"She mentioned to me that she'd been feeling odd since her surgery," Marlena said. "Did she talk to you about it, or had her behavior changed in any way?"

Ruthie Mae's husband frowned and cut his eyes toward her. "Lately she had a short temper," he admitted. "Wasn't like Ruthie Mae, but she became more demanding and..."

"And what?" Dante asked.

Gene chewed the inside of his cheek. "Horny," he said. "Ruthie Mae used to not like sex that much, but lately she wanted it all the time. I thought that was odd for a heart patient. I figured she'd be scared after surgery."

Marlena glanced at Dante but he gave no reaction.

"Do you think she might have been seeing someone else?" Dante asked.

The big man shrugged, his look anguished. "Maybe. She was late a few times, and when I called the hospital, they said she wasn't working."

"So she lied to you?" Dante asked.

He nodded. "I confronted her a couple of times, but she blew up." His voice cracked. "I've never seen her act like that. She even came at me with her fists."

Marlena gaped at him. "Ruthie Mae physically attacked you?"

"Yeah, I swear she never was like that before." He turned to Dante. "And before you ask, I never hit her. My mama raised me never to hurt a woman." Emotions clogged his voice, and he dropped his head into his hands. "God help me, I loved Ruthie Mae. She didn't deserve to die like this."

"No, she didn't," Marlena agreed. It was obvious that Gene loved Ruthie Mae; he would never have hurt her.

"We will find out who killed her," Marlena said.

"I hope to hell you do." Gene glared at Dante. "If you'd found the son of a bitch before now, Ruthie Mae would still be alive." Cursing, he stomped out the door.

Marlena understood his frustration and felt helpless. But he didn't have to blame Dante.

Three women were dead now and the killer was still out there. No telling when he would strike again.

$\sim$

Dante watched Stanton leave with a grimace. He didn't blame the man for being angry. If his wife had been murdered, he'd be furious, too.

Wife? Sweat exploded on his skin. He'd never considered marriage...

Shaking off the thought, he tried to focus on the case. He had been investigating, but he had to work harder. He had allowed his concern for Marlena to distract him.

No more.

He'd have Hobbs watch Marlena and he'd work around the clock. He might not have trusted Hobbs in the beginning, but so far, he'd held up his end as deputy.

It was time for him to go underground with the demons.

# Chapter Twenty-three

It had been two days since Marlena had seen Dante. She understood his need to focus on the investigation, but she missed him.

And she hated that he'd assigned his deputy to guard her. Not that Hobbs wasn't nice, and he'd made certain she arrived at work and home safely, but he wasn't Dante.

Brenda's journal and Gene Stanton's comments about his wife disturbed her. Their surgeries, transfusions, an experiment, the missing blood vials...Could they all be connected?

On a hunch, she phoned Jordie McEnroe's mother. "Mrs. McEnroe, this is Dr. Bender at BloodCore."

"Yes, what can I do for you?" Mrs. McEnroe said in a tired voice.

"Did Jordie undergo any kind of medical treatment lately, a surgery of some kind?"

"As a matter of fact, she ruptured her appendix a few months ago and had an appendectomy."

Marlena's fingers tightened around the phone. "Did she receive a transfusion?"

Mrs. McEnroe's heavy sigh echoed with anguish. "Yes, she did. It was really scary, but she survived." The older woman sniffled. "We were so relieved...But now she's gone, and in such a horrible, violent way..."

Marlena's lungs constricted. "I know, I'm so sorry. She was a sweet girl."

"Yes, she was. I just wish that sheriff would find the maniac who killed her," Mrs. McEnroe said angrily. "I'm afraid to leave my house. And business at the diner is terrible. Everyone in town is panicked, looking at their neighbors like they might be a killer."

"I'm sure the sheriff is doing everything he can."

"Well, it's not enough," Mrs. McEnroe said bitterly.

Marlena bit her lip. Dante was taking a lot of flack from townspeople about this killer. Something had to break soon.

The tech she'd left Dante's blood with knocked on her glass window and she gestured him in.

He must have the results of Dante's bloodwork. Now she'd know if he was related to the Valtrez brothers.

~⟶

Dante had been searching the tunnels for the past two days, listening to the barrage of talk about Zion. He was the all-powerful leader. The demons had to obey his commands. The anarchy was coming.

And dammit, he hadn't found Daumer or any connection to him.

He studied the photos of all the murder victims on the wall of the conference room again. Daumer's shrine of horrors was there as well, along with every detail he'd uncovered so far about each of the victims, including their family histories, friends, job choices, and physical descriptions.

So far, the only connection he'd found was that Jordie and Ruthie Mae both had undergone surgery. But they had had different doctors, so that had been a dead end.

He'd also sent Daumer's photo to the Feds and had one of their specialists compile a group of photographs suggesting what Daumer might look like wearing different disguises. The press had run with it, printing the photos across the States and posting them on every TV news broadcast available.

So far, several calls had come in, but none had panned out.

The town was in a panic. Everywhere he went, locals glared at him with hatred, as if he'd failed them.

Where the hell was Daumer? Had he moved on to another city to choose his next target? Or was he hiding out, biding his time, planning a surprise attack?

Planning something even bigger...

He glanced at the other board, where he'd posted a list of the victims and the blood types he'd requested from the ME. He'd also asked him to evaluate them for any abnormalities and checked tox screens but none of them had been drugged.

He glanced over the notes from the interviews of the employees at BloodCore but nothing stood out. Dr. Sneed and Dr. Raysen had impeccable reputations and references. Both had been written up in medical journals and were respected in their fields. Neither had motive to steal blood from their own lab.

His phone buzzed, and he checked the number. Marlena.

Shit, he'd avoided her for days. But he missed her like the devil.

And what if she'd received another trophy?

Bracing himself to remain professional, he punched connect. "Sheriff speaking."

"Dante, it's Marlena. I have the results of your blood tests."

His chest tightened. "And?"

She hesitated. "The tests were positive. You and the Valtrez men are brothers."

So they hadn't been lying about that.

Another call beeped in. "Thanks for the information. Have you heard from Daumer or received any more gifts?"

"No. Dante—"

"Another call is coming through, Marlena. I have to go." He connected the other call, cutting Marlena off. It was better, he reminded himself. She was safer away from him.

"Sheriff speaking."

"Sheriff, this is Jebb Bates."

Shit. What did the asshole want?

"I know you're avoiding me, but you need to make some kind of statement to the public. The town is anxious to know what you're doing to find the Torcher."

"I can't divulge the details of the investigation without compromising the case," Dante snapped. And compromising his secrets.

"I know you're hiding something," Bates said snidely. "And I also know that Marlena Bender went to see Sheriff Larson about her family's murder shortly before he died."

"How do you know she went to see him?"

"I have my sources."

The damn weasel. "You were following her?"

A hesitant pause. "I think she's connected to this killer, that her family's murder was, too. In fact, she may have caused Larson's heart attack. That is, *if* it was a heart attack."

Dante saw red. "Leave Dr. Bender out of this."

"She's already involved," Bates said. "And I intend to find out exactly how."

"I'm warning you, Bates, stay away from Marlena. She's an innocent in all this."

"But you're not." Bates dropped his voice and adopted an ominous tone. "I know you're not who you say you are, Sheriff, and I plan to expose the truth to the people of this town."

Dante slammed the phone down, cutting him off. But Bates was ruthless and sneaky and wouldn't give up. What would he do if somehow the bastard found out the truth?

The next few days dragged by. Marlena had thrown herself into her work, but there was still no change in the case. On the positive side, there had been no more murders.

But Gerald was still missing. If he was the killer, why had he stopped?

She wondered if he might be hurt. Or if he had committed suicide.

Dante had orchestrated a massive search for Gerald, spreading the word nationwide in case he had left town.

Dammit, Dante was still avoiding her. When she'd phoned with the results of his bloodwork, he'd been curt, almost rude, as if he didn't want to talk to her.

They never should have made love. Had he been afraid she'd get clingy?

Well, she'd gotten the message loud and clear.

Damn the man. She wasn't a clingy woman. Yet she

had dreamed about him at night and craved his touch so badly it was driving her crazy.

But she'd *never* tell him so.

She noted the abnormalities in the genetic markers, as detected by the microarray system. The biosensor unit had detected unknown organisms.

She wished she had more information on the men. In her interviews with Quinton and Vincent, both men had professed to have supernatural abilities. Vincent had a telekinetic power. Quinton said he could read minds and had premonitions.

When she'd ask Dante if he had a power, he'd denied it.

Edmund poked his head in. "How's it going, Marlena?"

Not ready to share what she'd learned about the Valtrez men, she shrugged. "The research is slow."

"I noticed that deputy following you to work and home. Has Gerald broken into your house again?"

"No. I guess the security system scared him off."

"Good." Edmund's eye twitched. "I hope he's gone for good and the town will be safe again."

"I've been thinking more and more about the missing blood vials and wondering what would happen if the blood was transfused into someone else," Marlena said. "The sheriff found Brenda's journal. She talked as if someone was conducting experiments with blood, and she said that she'd been a part of the experiment."

"What kind of experiment?" Edmund asked.

"She didn't elaborate, but she said that she felt different since she'd had the transfusion. And that *he* had changed. He was having blackouts and thoughts of murder."

He shifted, rocking on the sides of his Italian loafers.

"Did she mention who gave her the blood or where this so-called experiment took place?"

Marlena shook her head. "No. Did she discuss it with you?"

"No." Edmund cocked his head sideways. "I wish she had. I'd like to know the nature of the experiment, and who was in charge of it. If someone is crossing the line and the experiment is illegal, they need to be reported."

He excused himself, then left to go to lunch. She dove into her work for another forty minutes. Suddenly the scent of smoke filled the air, and she glanced up at the glass partition and saw flames creeping along the floor and walls of the connected room.

She jumped off the stool and hurried to the door, but it was jammed. She yanked on the knob and turned it, but it still wouldn't budge. Finally, she raised her foot and kicked at it, but with no result.

Her heart pounding, she ran to the opposite side of the room, to the exit. But when she pressed a hand to the wood, it felt hot.

The fire alarm sounded, screeching madly, and down the hall, footsteps pounded as employees raced to escape.

She grabbed the phone to call for help, but there was no dial tone. The line was dead.

Panic stabbed her as smoke curled beneath the door, seeping into the room. She covered her mouth with her hand to stifle a cough, trying to formulate a plan. Flames inched higher along the walls, crawling toward the cabinet of chemical supplies. Dear God. She had to hurry. If that cabinet exploded . . .

She had to make a run for it.

Grabbing a towel and covering her mouth with it to

keep from inhaling smoke, she kicked the door again, with all her force, and it finally gave. Once in the next room, she pivoted, scanning the room for a way out, but a thick wall of smoke nearly obliterated the doorway at the far side of the room.

Heat scalded her as she raced across the room and vaulted through the burning doorway. Flames engulfed the structure, roaring all around her.

Dear God help her. She was trapped!

Another cabinet filled with supplies exploded behind her. She screamed as the impact threw her to the floor, and heat scorched her face as the flames danced around her. A wall crashed and ceiling titles pitched downward. Smoke thickened, choking her, and she covered her head with her hands.

Debris pelted the back of her skull, and the room spun into darkness.

Hunched on the ground in the woods outside BloodCore, Gerald Daumer rocked himself back and forth, tugging his tattered coat around him. He'd been hiding out for days, living in one cold, ratty cave and then another like some damn wild animal. Horrible creatures lived in those caves.

Evil beings that ate humans and devoured their souls.

He'd escaped one of them, although the monster had taken a chunk out of his leg. The wound was yellow and full of pus and hurt so bad he could barely walk.

He couldn't go back to those caves.

But he couldn't turn himself in. His picture was all over the news. Everyone was looking for him.

Because he'd tried to hurt Marlena.

The voices screamed at him again. They were getting worse. Horrible, vile sounds that made him want to die. "Do it," the voice shouted in his ear. "Kill her. Finish her off."

"Shut up!" he screeched. He banged his fists on the rocks by the river until blood dripped down his arms. "Leave me alone."

"You coward. You're evil. Show Satan that you love him."

He covered his ears with his bloody hands, screeching to drown out the voice. The evil, twisted images of the dead girls played through his head, taunting him, the bloody scenes driving him insane.

He had to stop it. Put an end to the madness.

Even if he had to die.

Rising from his haunches, he slithered through the woods, sneaking between bushes and trees until he made his way to the service entrance to the lab.

"Kill her," the voice commanded. "Then you can have eternal life."

"No," he muttered. "I know who you are and I'm going to tell her so she can stop you."

He crawled into the building, hiding in the shadows of the storage room, waiting until footsteps died before he crept into the dark hallway to find the stairs. Marlena had promised to save him.

She had to, before the devil completely swallowed him.

# Chapter Twenty-four

The call about the fire at BloodCore sent Dante running to his SUV. He'd been working day and night on the investigation, had been combing the underground tunnels listening to the demons talk, hoping to find Daumer. A couple of times he'd even detected his scent in the caves, had sensed that he'd just missed him, that he might be closing in.

But then he'd escaped.

Dammit, Marlena was supposed to be safe at the lab. And a fire...

The SUV ate the miles, tires skidding on black ice from the recent ice storm. He shouted for cars to move over, blaring his horn to get drivers to let him pass, then finally turned onto the road leading to BloodCore.

The minute the lab appeared in view, he spotted the smoke curling in the sky. Flames were shooting from the top of the building. The sound of metal and wood crackling mingled with panicked voices and cries as employees poured from the building onto the snow-packed ground.

Frantically he searched the sea of faces for Marlena as he jumped from the SUV and rushed through the crowd.

"How did the fire get started?" someone asked.

"Did you hear that explosion?" a young man said.

"Oh, God, oh, God, I thought I wasn't going to get out."

Dante grabbed a lab tech's arm. "Where's Dr. Bender?"

"I don't know," the young girl screeched.

Dante released her, then pushed through a half-dozen more people, asking each one, but no one had seen her.

An older woman with red hair finally approached him with terror-stricken eyes. "You were asking about Dr. Bender. Her office is down the hall where the fire started."

His chest tightened. Marlena might be trapped inside.

Rage fueled his blood, and he sprinted to the front door, inching sideways as another employee stumbled out. Behind him, the fire engine roared up and screeched to a stop. Another police car and an ambulance wailed to a stop, lights flashing, and rescue workers jumped into action.

"Everyone get back, clear the area!" one of the fire-fighters yelled.

Dante ignored them and headed inside the building, yelling Marlena's name as he scanned the smoky entrance. The front office was ablaze, smoke clogged the hallway, and ceiling bits caved in with a loud crash.

Dragging a handkerchief from his pocket, he crammed it over his mouth and plunged into the smoke-filled hall-way. Normally he would have been mesmerized by the flames, sucked in by the heat and the intensity and power of the fire.

But all he cared about was that Marlena was inside.

That she might be dead. Killed by his first love, the fire.

For one brief moment, he suddenly hated it. Wished he had the power to extinguish the flames, not give life to them.

But he didn't.

Flames licked his jacket, teased his face, and scalded his hands and legs as he forged on. The thick smoke nearly blinded him as he dashed up the stairs, and he blinked to clear his vision.

"Marlena!"

Glass shattered as a window exploded, and he kicked aside burning rubble and wove through a maze of debris. "Marlena!"

Finally he spotted her lying on the floor in the hallway, face-down, the flames licking at her. His pulse pounded, and he jogged over to her, dropped to the floor, and checked her pulse. Seconds ticked by. "Come on, Marlena, you can't die…"

Finally he felt her chest rise, and her pulse kicked in.

It was faint, but she was alive.

The wall behind him collapsed, splinters of burning wood flying. He snuffed out the sparks on his sleeve, then scooped Marlena into his arms, shielding her with his body as he raced back through the burning building. Another wall crashed, blocking his exit.

He cursed, searching for an escape route. Then he spotted an opening and wove his way back to the stairs. Desperate to get her out, he jogged down the steps, dodging crackling wood and ceiling tiles flailing down.

Marlena moaned in his arms, her breathing labored as he carried her outside. Chaos reined, the lawn crowded with frightened and shaken employees.

"Dante…"

"Shh, I've got you," he murmured.

Paramedics were tending to an older woman, and he hurried toward the ambulance. "Dr. Bender needs medical attention," he yelled.

One of the medics glanced up, then nodded and retrieved a stretcher from inside the ambulance. Dante carried her to the stretcher and eased her down onto it.

A strangled sound made him jerk his head up, and he glanced sideways and noticed Prudence Puckett standing at the edge of the crowd. She was hunched in her coat, her hair draped down to hide her scar, but the cold way she was staring at him and Marlena made him pause.

Marlena stirred as the medic shoved an oxygen mask over her face, and Dante jerked his attention back to her.

"How did the fire start, Marlena?" Dante asked.

She pushed at the mask with a cough. "I don't know."

Rage shot through him as he looked back at the blaze. He'd bet his life it was arson, that the killer had intentionally set the building on fire and was somewhere close by, taking perverse joy in the havoc.

Out of the corner of his eye, a woman's image caught Dante's attention. He jerked his head sideways. Prudence Puckett.

A sinister smile curled her lips, then she ducked her head and dashed through the crowd away from the burning lab.

Dante squeezed Marlena's arm. "I'll be right back."

Instincts alert, he jogged after her. Why was Prudence running away? And what was she doing outside Blood-Core?

The crowd had thickened as the news reporters arrived, cameras rolling. Damn, Jebb Bates was right in the thick of things, interviewing employees, asking questions, probably planting suspicion.

Dante darted through the spectators, but Prudence disappeared into one of the side alleys between two other buildings housing other medical offices. The acrid scent of smoke clogged the air as he chased her through a row of parked cars.

She broke into a full run, but his speed kicked in, and a second later, he snagged her arm.

"Let me go," she said in a shrill tone.

Dante tightened his grip. "What are you doing here, Prudence?"

She tried to jerk away, but he forced her to look at him. "I asked you a question. What were you doing at the lab? Did you set that fire?"

"Of course not. I came to talk to Dr. Bender." She yanked her arm free. "But when I arrived at the lab, it was already on fire, so I didn't go inside."

He narrowed his eyes. "Then why were you running away?"

She stared at the smoke curling into the sky with an odd, faraway expression. "I don't like fire," she said, then touched her cheek self-consciously.

"What about Dr. Bender? Do you have a grudge against her?"

A bitter laugh escaped her. "Don't be ridiculous; I've been seeing her for therapy." Prudence rubbed at her wrist as if he'd hurt her.

Dante studied her for another moment, sensing she was holding back information. "Do you know any of the other doctors here?"

She folded her arms. "Dr. Sneed," she said icily. "I'm having plastic surgery, and he was giving me therapy to increase my immunity against rejection of skin grafts."

She touched her cheek again with a shaky hand, her fingers lingering over the puckered flesh as if the memory was raw, fresh.

"What kind of therapy?"

She pressed her lips together as if she didn't intend to answer him.

"Come on, Prudence, tell me, what kind of therapy? Was it some new technique, maybe experimental?"

"He gave me injections to boost my immune system," she said defensively. "Now let me go. I don't have to discuss my medical condition with you. It's private." With a snort of disgust, she turned and ran from him as fast as she could, the snow swirling around her as she disappeared.

Questions ticked in his head as he watched her go. He still didn't trust her. She'd been at the scene of the fire, had been watching in the crowd.

How exactly had she been burned? Could she be a pyromaniac?

Adrenaline pumping, he strode back to the lab. One of the firemen met him at the edge of the lawn, tugging at his hat. "Are you the sheriff?"

Dante nodded.

The firefighter crooked a thumb toward the building. "We found a man's body inside. Poor guy didn't make it."

Dammit. Dante followed him to a second ambulance, scanning the crowd, but a sea of faces swam in front of him and no one stood out.

Gritting his teeth, he pulled back the sheet to view the body. Bruises and burns marred the man's face and hands, and his clothes were torn and ragged. His face had suffered minor burns, but not enough to disfigure him.

"His name is Gerald Daumer," Dante said tightly. "The

police have been looking for him." He shifted on the balls of his feet. "I want an autopsy performed on this man, and the fire investigator and CSI team to look for evidence of arson."

"Why do you think arson?" the firefighter asked.

"Because Daumer's wanted by the police for questioning in the murders of the three women in town."

"You mean he's the Torcher?" the fireman muttered.

Dante grimaced. Jebb Bates had dubbed the man with that name. "That's what I'm trying to figure out."

But if he was the serial killer, how had he ended up dead?

～

He smiled as he watched the chaos on the lawn beside the lab, the frightened lab employees, the rescue workers, the horrified expressions of the spectators, the tears from the terrified and injured.

Valtrez looked stumped as he conferred with the fire chief, and one of the deputies canvassed the crowd asking questions, trying to sort out what had happened.

Firemen dragged hoses and dumped water on the burning building, desperately trying to extinguish the flames. The beautiful flames that spurted into the sky, shooting off brilliant colors; red, yellow, orange, even a faint purple streak from the chemicals stored in the lab.

Smoke thickened the stormy sky, mingling with fresh snow and painting a haze that reminded him of the gray areas in the underworld, the planes where life ceased to exist but hell had not yet claimed ownership of the spirit.

His smile quickly faded as Dante hurried to his car and followed the ambulance. He'd chased after the scarred woman and questioned her. What had she told him? About the evil blood that now ran through her veins? That she was turning evil?

That Marlena Bender wanted to help her?

Foolish. Marlena couldn't stop it from happening, couldn't keep the scarface from embracing the darkness within her. Couldn't stop the evil.

The blood was too powerful.

Dammit.

He'd wanted Marlena for himself.

But not now she'd slept with the demon.

Now he wanted her dead.

# Chapter Twenty-five

Marlena slipped in and out of consciousness in the ambulance, the nightmare of the past few hours reminding her that life could be snuffed out in a split second.

But Dante had saved her again.

Why did she feel such a powerful connection to him?

Now they'd made love, she felt it even more strongly.

With one touch, he'd ignited a raging, burning need and desire inside her. Even exhausted and frightened and angry that he'd avoided her for days, she wanted him beside her.

Yet he didn't want her.

Sleep pulled at her, silly dreams of marriage and babies and a life with him teasing her. But the fact that someone might want her dead and that demons actually existed intruded.

The ambulance jerked to a stop, the back door swung open, then the paramedics lowered the stretcher and rolled her into the emergency room.

"Her name is Dr. Marlena Bender. She was caught in the fire at BloodCore. Her vitals are good," one of the medics told the nurse and doctor who met them. "Check her for smoke inhalation."

Sirens wailed around her, the voices of doctors and

nurses echoing through the noise. Wheels squeaked, and she closed her eyes, slightly nauseated, as they pushed her through the double doors to the emergency room.

A warm hand closed over hers, and she opened her eyes and gazed up at the physician with blurry eyes. "Dr. Bender, I'm Dr. Able."

She nodded, although images of faceless demons suddenly surfaced. Terrible, hideous faces of creatures attacking her.

And this man was one of them. He had shifty eyes, jagged teeth, misshapen ears...

She blinked, but then his face morphed into that of a normal man.

Heaven help her. She must have inhaled more smoke than she'd thought—she was delusional.

"Don't worry." The doctor patted her arm. "We'll take good care of you."

She nodded sluggishly, although a tingle of nerves rippled up her spine as they rushed her into the exam cubicle. The doctor examined her, then stepped aside, and a nurse treated her cuts and abrasions and drew a blood sample. An IV came next to hydrate her, and she dozed off while the saline dripped into her system. When she opened her eyes the next time, the doctor stood over her, one hand in his lab jacket, the other on her arm.

"Are you feeling better, Dr. Bender?"

She licked her dry lips. She was so thirsty. "Yes. I just want to go home."

"I think that can be arranged." An odd look settled in his eyes. "By the way, we ran your bloodwork."

Something about his tone alarmed her. "What did you find?"

"Did you know that you're pregnant, Dr. Bender?"

Marlena's stomach clenched.

A low sound echoed from the doorway, and she looked up. Dante stood in the doorway, a savage look in his eyes.

Had he heard the doctor's report?

Shock momentarily robbed Dante of speech.

With demons, he'd never had to use birth control. Had never worried about having offspring.

But with Marlena . . . his hunger for her had blinded him to anything but the fierce need to live in the moment. To indulge in the passion he felt for her.

Myriad emotions played across her face, and her hand automatically fell to her stomach. Silence stretched between them, filled with memories of the erotic night they'd shared, filled with questions, with tension.

If Marlena knew the truth about him, would she want this child?

*His* child?

Emotions he'd never expected to feel welled in his chest and nearly choked him.

The thought of Marlena carrying a Dark Lord both thrilled and frightened him. For a moment, he allowed himself to imagine what their child would look like. A beautiful, spunky little girl with silky blond hair and green eyes. A son with dark hair and brown eyes. A little boy torn between a world of good and a world of evil.

A Dark Lord who had to live with the evil gnawing at him constantly.

But he would also carry Marlena's blood. Marlena who was an angel compared to him.

Marlena who wanted to use genetic therapy to eradicate violence.

*Zion will use anyone you care about to get to you.*

Would Zion use his own grandchild?

A possessive streak ripped through him, and he had the urge to sweep Marlena and his unborn child away to someplace safe. Someplace Zion could never find them.

The doctor cleared his throat and pivoted as if he'd just realized that Dante stood in the doorway. The craggy old man smiled again, then patted Marlena's arm. "I'll get the papers ready to release you. That is, unless you think you need to stay here tonight and rest."

Marlena propped herself on her elbows. "No, I want to go home."

"All right, but take it easy for the next few hours." The doctor excused himself and disappeared down the hall.

Dante stood, immobile. For the first time in his life, he considered the possibility that he might have a life with goodness in it. A future with Marlena and a child.

But doubts quickly crept in. There were too many demons out there who might come after him. Demons, and Father Gio, and Zion.

Marlena tugged self-consciously at the hospital gown.

He crossed his arms to keep from pressing his hand over her belly where his unborn baby lay. "You're sure going home is a good idea?"

"It's fine," she said sharply.

He gritted his teeth. "What about the baby?"

Confusion and worry knitted her brows. "Dante, I really don't want to talk about this right now."

His temper flared. She obviously didn't like the idea of having his child. "Why not?"

"It's just a surprise." She closed her eyes and massaged her temple. "I need time to process the fact that I'm going to have a baby."

"*We're* going to have a child," he said in a tone that brooked no argument. But concern for her and the baby overrode the foreign emotions pummeling him.

"Please," she whispered. "I can't deal with it now."

He studied her for a long moment, remembered the ordeal she'd just been through. "All right. But we *will* talk, Marlena. You can't run from me forever."

A hiss escaped her, then she opened her eyes and looked at him defiantly. "Why does it matter to you, Dante? You made it clear that one night of sex meant nothing to you. I heard the message loud and clear when you pawned me off on your deputy."

He cleared his throat, determined she know he was serious. "That was before."

A bitter laugh escaped her. "Don't think for a minute that you're going to hold this child over me. I'm an independent woman. I earn a good salary, and *if* I choose to have this child, I can and will take care of it by myself."

Rage obliterated any rational thoughts, and he stepped closer, the darkness inside him fueling his words. "You won't do anything to hurt this child, Marlena," he growled. "And as long as I live and breathe, neither will anyone else."

~

Dante's threatening tone sent a shiver up Marlena's spine.

She had no idea why she'd baited him by even suggesting she might terminate the pregnancy. She was a doctor, sworn to heal and save lives. There was no way she'd consider hurting her own child.

But she'd been in shock over the news herself, and she did have some pride.

Fortunately, the doctor saved her from a response by returning with release forms. She hesitated for a second, wondering if she should stay overnight—not because she physically needed medical attention, but because if she did go home, she strongly suspected that Dante would not leave her alone or with his deputy tonight.

Dante stepped aside and looked out the window as the doctor removed her IV, and she signed the release forms.

The doctor handed her a bag holding her clothes. "Be sure to make an appointment with your OBGYN."

Marlena rolled her eyes. "Of course. I know what to do, Doctor."

He nodded and patted her shoulder again. "I'll get the nurse to bring a wheelchair."

"I'm perfectly capable of walking," Marlena said, then stood, one hand reaching for the gurney as a dizzy spell assaulted her.

"You're taking the damn chair." Dante rushed to her and took her arm, steadying her. Yet his heady scent and strong arms made her want to hold on to him.

He urged her to sit down, his movements gentle, almost tender, and emotions welled in her chest. She hated showing any weakness.

The doctor stood watching them, his brows raised, a smile in his eyes. "It is policy, Dr. Bender."

Marlena glared at them both, hating to be ordered around by men. Dammit, she could take care of herself.

But she had a child to think of now, so she accepted the fact that she'd have to accept hospital policy.

"I need to get dressed," she said. "Please turn around, Dante."

A sarcastic laugh escaped him. "You're kidding, right?"

"No," she said between clenched teeth.

"Marlena..." He lifted a strand of hair and rubbed it between his fingers with a devilish grin. "I've already seen every beautiful inch of you. I've touched it and tasted it and I will again."

A blush stained her cheeks. "That was before," she said repeating his very words. "We were caught up in the moment." She clutched the sheet to her chest, suddenly feeling vulnerable.

"You're damn right we were." His sultry gaze raked over her with an intensity that made her nipples harden as if he'd touched her naked flesh.

As if he was reliving the moment as well, he growled an obscenity, then pivoted, his arms folded. "All right. Get dressed."

"You're insufferable," she whispered. He had the audacity to laugh, and she shook her head in agitation.

Hastily, she shed the gown and pulled on her clothes, wincing as her muscles stiffened, and she inhaled the smoky odor lingering on her clothing.

Seconds later, a knock sounded, then the nurse appeared in the doorway pushing a wheelchair. Dante stepped forward and took her arm, and she humbled herself enough to allow him to steady her into the chair.

While the nurse wheeled her to the elevator, Dante retrieved the car. By the time she reached the front door, he was parked in front. He jumped out and helped her into his SUV. A tense silence settled between them as he drove her back to her house. A storm raged outside, the clouds dark and rumbling, a funnel cloud swirling behind them.

"Damn, it looks bad," Dante said as he dodged a falling branch. "Do you really think it was wise to leave the hospital?" Dante finally asked.

She shot him a deadly look, frowning as she glanced ahead at the swirling wind and rain. "I'm a doctor, Dante. Don't insult my intelligence by questioning me."

A muscle ticked in his jaw, but he kept his comment to himself. The ride stretched out painfully slow, the weather escalating, the funnel cloud chasing them all the way along the mountain until they reached her house. Afraid he was going to do something ridiculous like try to carry her inside, she opened the door and climbed out before he could make it to the passenger side of the car.

But he quickly circled the front, slid his arm around her waist, and helped her slog through the snow-packed ground and blinding rain to her porch. Shivering with the cold and roar of the storm, she huddled inside her coat while he took the key from her shaky hand and unlocked the door.

She punched in the security code while he flipped on a lamp in the den and searched the house. When he returned, he stopped and stared at her. "Do you want to go to bed?"

Exhaustion clawed at her, but she was too anxious to sleep. "Not yet. I might make some tea."

"I'll make it and build a fire. Just sit down."

"I'm perfectly capable of making tea," she said.

"For God's sake, Marlena, stop being so damn stubborn. It's just a cup of fucking tea."

She moved to the kitchen, but he took her hands and

coaxed her into a chair, then filled the teakettle with water and dropped a tea bag into a mug.

She hugged her arms around herself. "Dante, you don't need to baby me. I'm fine."

"You're pregnant," he said gruffly. "And you almost died in that fire."

"But I didn't," she said softly. "And I can take care of myself now."

"The hell you can," he snarled. "Someone tried to kill you tonight."

She jerked her head up. "What? You think someone intentionally set that fire?"

He gave a clipped nod. "The arson investigator is searching for evidence. And yes, I think it was arson. Someone who wanted to hurt you."

The teakettle whistled, and he poured water into the mug, then handed the cup to her.

Too tired to argue, she cradled the mug to warm her hands, then carried the tea to the den and curled up on the sofa.

Dante rushed outside, brought in firewood, and built a fire. For a long moment, he studied the flames, as if they held the answers to all their problems.

She sipped her tea, trying to ignore the echo of the doctor's words telling her that she was pregnant and the flutter of arousal stirred by being in the same room with Dante.

When he turned back to her, though, the flutter turned to a nervous spasm. "What aren't you telling me?" she asked.

He cleared his throat, then leaned against the mantel. "Gerald Daumer was at the lab."

She swallowed, tea sloshing over the rim of her cup as her hands trembled. "You saw him?"

"Yes." His mouth tightened, and he took the cup from her and clasped her hands in his, then blew on her fingertips to alleviate the sting from the hot tea. "He was dead, Marlena. He died in the fire."

Marlena clenched his hands. She'd never lost a patient before. "My God. You think Gerald set the fire?"

"It's possible that he started the fire, then got trapped inside. An autopsy should tell us more. Maybe forensics will find evidence of an accelerant on Daumer's hands or body."

"Poor Gerald," she said in a whisper. "He came to me for help and I failed him."

Dante cursed. "Marlena, he tried to kill you. And he may be responsible for three other women's deaths. And there could have been a lot more tonight."

A sudden clap of thunder shook the walls. The windowpanes rattled and a shrill whistling sound screamed through the house.

Marlena glanced at the window and gasped.

It was a tornado.

＿＿＿＿＞

Prudence Puckett touched the hideous, pocked purple and red skin on her cheek, painful memories wracking her. Pain from the lesson her mother had wanted to teach her—that she shouldn't use her flesh to entice men, that she had to control her sinful, lustful ways.

Still, as she entered the Dungeon, the spot she'd found by following Dante one night, her body yearned for the touch of a man's hands, for his fingers and tongue doing wicked things to her flesh. For the pain and pleasure of his cock inside her and the orgasm that would come.

But the men didn't look at her now. Not with lust or want.

They saw her disfigurement and turned away in revulsion.

She hated them for not wanting her. For choosing the pretty girls instead.

She wanted Dante Valtrez.

But he had the hots for Marlena Bender. The selfish bitch wanted all the men for herself.

Dante Valtrez had seen her at the lab. He thought she'd tried to kill Marlena.

Hell, she should have. The fucking bitch wanted her to stay ugly.

But she was strong now. The transfusions had given her power and brought out her will to fight.

A tall, dark-haired man approached her, a predatory gleam in his eyes as he slid down on the barstool beside her. Judge Brannigan. What was he doing in a bar filled with demons?

He'd come from one of the back rooms, and the scent of sex permeated his skin.

He slipped his hand into hers and gestured for her to follow him. Excitement warred with fear as he led her through the dark tunnels, then into a dimly lit room. The chains on the wall sent alarm though her, yet titillating sensations rippled through her as well.

"In here, I am the judge and jury," he said as he jerked her arms up and snapped the metal clamps around them. "I am everything to you."

She smiled as he fastened the chains around her wrists, exhilarated by the lust in his eyes.

"Yes, Master. I'll do whatever you say."

The demons met and chanted, circling Marlena Bender's house. They had their orders. The woman was carrying the demonborn's child. A child who would be the grand-child of the leader of the underworld.

A child who could destroy Zion if his sons didn't do it first.

A child who had to die so Zion's plans would be ful-filled and the anarchy could begin.

Storm reared back and blew a puff of air toward the Bender woman's house and the entire structure rocked with the force. The ground trembled and shook, the earth cracking and tearing apart. An avalanche began to rumble from the ridge above and rocks cracked and began to roll down the mountain in a maddening crash.

Clouds exploded in fury and tore at the roof of the house, sending shingles flying. Trees splintered and broke, raining down in a thunderous roar. One slammed into the roof of the house.

Inside, the woman's screams echoed over the noise, screams that were music to his ears.

Yes. It was beautiful to hear her scream. Screams of fear first.

And then she had to die.

# Chapter Twenty-six

Marlena screamed as the house shook and vibrated and windowpanes exploded, sending glass spraying the den. A thunderous roar reverberated through the structure, and tree limbs scraped the house. The lights flickered off, then on, then off again, pitching the room into total blackness.

Dante cursed and dove over Marlena to protect her as a branch shot through the broken window like an arrow heading for her heart.

"What's happening?" Marlena cried.

"I don't know," Dante growled, although he had a strong suspicion the elements had attacked. Damn Storm and Father Gio and the whole fucking bunch.

"Come on." He grabbed her arm and pulled her toward the hallway, jerked open the basement door, then coaxed her down the steps. Darkness bathed the interior, and he reached for a light, but when he flipped the switch, the power was off.

"Careful," he said gruffly. The wooden boards creaked, and the roar of the wind and storm shook the walls, wood splintering. The boom of a tree being ripped up by its roots echoed above, the sound of the tree crashing following.

"My God," Marlena whispered. "It sounds as if my house is coming down…"

He wanted to tell her to forget the damn house, but this was Marlena's childhood home, the one place where her memories of her mother and sister remained intact. Fury rose inside him to think that she might lose that, too.

And all because of him.

Another tree splitting rent the air as they made it to the bottom of the steps, and he felt his way along the rail, then urged her beneath the staircase against the cement wall.

"I can't believe this is happening," Marlena whispered. "This isn't tornado season."

No, just the season for demon attacks.

She sat down and wrapped her arms around her knees while the wind wailed, more trees thundered down, and the walls and ceiling collapsed above them. The sound of the china cabinet crashing followed, glass and china shattering.

Marlena trembled, and he curved his arm around her and pulled her up against him, cradling her close while the storm ripped apart her house. She buried her head against his chest, and he stroked her hair and back, trying to soothe her as the storm raged for hours, the constant sounds of wood splintering and collapsing forcing them to remain huddled together to stay safe.

Fury mounted with each second that passed. Father Gio was behind this.

It seemed like days that they sat in the darkness, clutching each other, his rage escalating with every passing second.

Dammit, the demons could attack him.

But the beast inside him wanted revenge for their attacking Marlena.

But finally, slowly, the winds began to die down. The

tornado passed. A deathly quiet fell over the house, an ominous silence suggesting that the demons were outside watching, waiting for them to emerge.

Or to see if they had died.

Marlena lifted her head from his chest, but he couldn't quite release her. Not yet.

"Do you think it's over?" she whispered.

A low growl escaped him. "The storm? Maybe, for now."

"But?"

"But the danger isn't. That was the elements, and they've only just begun."

She turned those innocent eyes toward him. "What do you mean?"

Dare he tell her the truth? Would she go running?

But how could he not tell her—she had to know the depth of the danger she faced.

"The elements were sent by the demons," he said. "They'll most likely attack again." He stroked her cheek with the pad of his thumb. "I'm going to take you to my place, where you'll be safe for the night." He'd built it in the side of the mountain as a fortress against Father Gio and his team.

He wanted her there now, tucked away, so nothing could hurt her or his child.

She shoved fingers through her hair as she stood. "I'll have to clean upstairs."

He doubted there was much left to clean. "Marlena," he said gruffly as they made their way to the stairs. "I'm sorry."

"It's not your fault," she said softly.

If she only knew the truth...

They silently climbed the steps, and when he pushed open the door, the destruction was worse than he'd imagined. Marlena gasped, a soft cry escaping her as she spotted the pictures thrown from the walls, the scattered, dilapidated furniture, the overturned china cabinet, the shattered dishes, the broken windows, and the tree that had broken through the roof. He clutched her hand and helped her step over broken glass, wooden beams, and ceiling plaster that had fallen. Rainwater stood inches deep.

"I can't believe this," she said in a hoarse whisper. "First the lab catches fire. And the same night my house is torn apart."

He gritted his teeth. It was way too damn coincidental. "At least you're alive." He gestured to the door. "Come on," he said. "Tomorrow you can call a crew to start cleanup and repairs."

Her features were strained, her expression pained, but her silent acceptance of his hand at her back as he ushered her through the debris indicated the depth of her shock.

He grabbed his keys from his pocket, the jangling sound echoing in the ominous quiet as he eased open the front door and looked out. Immediately, he sensed demons surrounding the house.

For a brief second, one of them materialized at the edge of the forest, then a second pair of eyes and a silhouette moved beside him.

Vincent and Quinton?

The images disappeared as quickly as they'd appeared, as if they had literally faded into the night.

Was it really them? Had they lied when they'd come to see him? Were they working for Zion now?

Or had those been shapeshifters, wanting him to think that his brothers were against him?

⋙

Tears blurred Marlena's eyes as she turned to assess the damage again. She spotted the photograph of her, her mother, and her sister on the floor and jerked away from Dante's hand, climbed over the overturned broken lamp and splinters of ceiling, and retrieved it from the floor.

Dust and other debris covered the back of the frame, and she wiped it off with her hand, then flipped it over. The glass was broken, but the picture was still intact. She traced a finger over her mother's and sister's faces, then hugged the picture to her chest. She couldn't leave it here. She had to take it with her.

When she glanced up, Dante stood in the doorway watching her with a troubled expression. "On the way to my place, I'll call someone to come out and cover the roof in case it rains or snows again."

She swallowed, barely able to make her voice work. "Thanks."

Her chest clenched as she took one last look at her demolished house. But as they rushed down the broken porch steps and ran toward his SUV, another torrent of wind swept through, nearly knocking them down.

From the shadows of the forest, she saw the silhouette of a creature, its eyes glowing, its fangs flashing. Suddenly it roared toward them with a hideous sound. Another creature vaulted from the thicket of trees to the left, then another, the inhuman sounds they made sending terror streaking through her.

Dante jerked open the SUV's door and shoved her inside,

then turned and flung out his hands. Marlena watched in shock as a stream of fire oozed from his fingers and spewed in violent rays of light toward the creatures.

One of the creatures roared an attack sound, wings sprouted from his sides, and he flew into the sky, squawking as he dipped toward them with a spiked beak.

Marlena screamed, and Dante flung another fireball at the soaring beast. The fire caught the creature's wings, and a hideous howl split the night, then the creature turned and flapped madly in the direction of the river.

Dante jumped into the SUV, started the engine, and sped down her drive, sending gravel and muddy snow spraying behind them as he maneuvered the curve on two wheels.

"Fasten your seat belt." He spun the vehicle around, gears grinding as he veered onto the road that led toward his house.

Marlena's hands were shaking but she complied. But shock was still rolling through. Real demons had attacked them, and Dante had fought them off with his bare hands.

Hands that had shot fire.

The furious gusts of wind escalated, tossing the SUV across the road; tree limbs smacked the windshield and leaves and branches flew through the air. Normally the winter was beautiful, but the bitter winds and foggy conditions now seemed steeped with eeriness and a cold that made her ache deep in her bones.

Dante struggled to keep the SUV on the mountain road, but the wind knocked the Jeep toward the guardrail. He cursed, gears grinding as he braked and tried to keep them from going over the embankment.

"My God, this can't be real," Marlena cried.

Dante jerked his head toward her, but another railing wind swept them toward the cliff. Tires squealed and screeched, and he shouted another obscenity, throwing out an arm to shield her as the car lurched forward.

They barely managed to miss going over the ridge, but somehow he righted the SUV just in time and sped onto the winding drive to his house.

Cursing, he checked over his shoulder. A sea of vampire bats swarmed behind them, hovering above the vehicle like winged devils closing in, ready to strike. They dove toward the car, attacking the glass, and he veered sideways to fend them off.

Dante shoved Marlena's head down with his hand. "Stay down," he shouted.

She ducked and covered her head with her hands just as the window on her side cracked and one of the bats started to attack. Dante flung out his hands, and the bat burst into flames. More converged, attacking the car, pecking at the metal and glass, their violent screeches echoing over the roar of the wind.

He spun up his drive, swinging the car left and right to try to shake off the bats, then careened to a stop in front of his house.

Her heart was pounding as he turned to her. "I'm going to fend them off. Run to the house, unlock it, and go inside."

She gripped his hands, terrified. There were dozens of them—they could rip him to shreds. "No, Dante, they'll kill you."

The screeching grew louder, more ominous as the vampires attacked, and he cupped her face in his hands. "I'll be fine. Just do as I said. You have to protect the baby."

She gulped back a sob, horrified at the thought of Dante dying to protect her. But the creatures were vicious, the car rocking with the force of their assault, and the front windshield shattered. He threw his coat over her head.

"Run!" he shouted, and flung open her door.

She jumped out and raced toward the house. He vaulted from the driver's side and ran behind her, flinging fireball after fireball at the creatures as he rushed her to safety. Her hands shook as she unlocked the door and a bat dove toward her, but Dante appeared, caught the bird with his hand, and snapped its neck.

She stumbled inside, trembling and crying, her body reeling with shock.

A second later, Dante rushed inside and slammed the door shut, then leaned against it, chest heaving. Outside, the wind roared, the bats flailed and screamed, and reality crashed down on her just as her house had earlier.

Her pulse racing, she turned to him, her body quivering with fear. "You... what are you?"

His expression turned tortured, but he gripped her arms and hurled her toward the den, then insisted she sit down. A reddish tint gleamed in his eyes, sending another pang of fear through her.

"Dante, what happened?" she asked. "You said those were demons, but you fought them off."

"Are you all right?"

She frowned, but nodded, and he dropped to his knees and placed a hand over her stomach. "What about the baby?"

"We're fine," she whispered. "Now tell me what the hell is going on. That fire... it came from your hands?"

He hissed a labored breath, then paced across the room.

Outside, the noises railed, the earth shook, and another storm broke loose.

Dante lit a fire in the fireplace, then stood with his back to her and stared into the flames for so long that she thought he wasn't going to answer.

Her chest hurt from the ache inside. He had lied to her. "Dante, please talk to me."

Finally he cleared his throat. When he turned to her, the glow had dimmed, replaced by a darkness filled with hostility and pain.

"Yes, those were demons," he said. "And they're after me because I have a gift," he said. "I'm a firestarter. I can throw fire with my hands."

A flash of her past resurfaced, and she remembered fireballs being thrown the day her mother had died.

She'd thought the demon had thrown them, but Dante had actually done it—because he was protecting her. Just as he had today.

"So you lied...you have powers," she said, testing him.

He nodded. "Yes, I'm part demon, just as Vincent and Quinton are," he admitted in a haunted voice. "But we're all working on the side of the law."

She had to swallow hard to make her throat work. "If you're part demon, then our child will be, too?"

He closed his eyes as if to gain control. When he opened them, his tortured gaze locked with hers. "Yes."

Nausea flooded her throat, and she had to lean over to catch her breath. "Will he be...like those creatures who attacked us?"

Dante shook his head, but worry tightened his features. "No. Those were vampires in bat form."

Her pulse raced. "You mean vampires really exist?"

"I'm afraid so. And those were after blood."

She clenched her hands, shook her head in denial. "What about our child? What will he be?"

"I don't know." Dante cleared his throat. "He or she will look human, will have your human blood, the blood of my mother, who was an Angel of Light, good. But he will have my blood as well." He hesitated. "He may have a gift, a power of some kind."

Her chest squeezed at the gruff fear in his voice. But he was part demon, had lied to her.

Nausea and exhaustion weighed her down, and she stood. "This is too much. I ... need to lie down."

He studied her for a long moment, then nodded, the cold acceptance in his eyes disturbing her even more. Sam Larson's warning reverberated in her head, adding to her fear. And then the images of the monsters who'd taken her family's lives.

Needing time, and distance, she rushed away from him, desperate to be alone and process everything that had happened.

She didn't know what she was going to do. How she would raise a child who wasn't completely human.

And she would never trust Dante again.

～

He hung Pru from the tree, the moon silhouetting her naked body.

She had had to die. She was a sinner, her dark side emerging. It would only have been a matter of time before the evil urges possessed her just as they had him.

He bit into her neck, felt the warm, sticky lifeblood wash down his throat, then watched the blood drip down her body. He had to purge her of the bad blood just as he had the others.

Smiling, he touched a branch of the tree, a tree that had been shrouded by other, larger ones keeping it dry. He doused the limb with lighter fluid, then lit it with a match. The limb took a moment to ignite, but finally it caught and sparks of fire shot onto the branch and caught. The limb crackled and popped, and flames slowly began to creep up the limbs and light up the sky.

Despite the snow falling, the flames grew bolder, licking at her bare feet, the heat beginning to char skin. Soon it would be ablaze, melting off bone and turning that sinful flesh to ashes.

Two more to go and his list would be finished.

Two more, and then the demon baby.

# Chapter Twenty-seven

Dante stared into the darkness as the hours ticked by while Marlena slept. He'd lost her tonight.

Lost her with his lies and secrets—and the fact that he was a demon.

It shouldn't bother him, but dammit, it did. He hated the pain and fear he'd put in her eyes. Hated what he was.

What his kind could do to her.

His cell phone jangled, and he saw it was Hobbs, so he punched the connect button.

"Sheriff, it's Hobbs. We have another body."

Dammit. "Was she torched like the others?"

"I'm afraid so." Hobbs cleared his throat. "And I think we have an ID. Prudence Puckett."

His jaw tightened. Holy hell, he'd seen her at the Dungeon and then at BloodCore. He'd even suspected her of torching the lab.

But now she was dead.

Shit.

"Where are you?"

Hobbs gave him the location, and Dante scrubbed a hand over the back of his neck. "Call a CSI unit. I'll be right there."

"They're on their way."

Dante disconnected, knowing he had to get his head back in the case. But Marlena stumbled from his bedroom, throwing him off with her tousled hair and sleepy eyes.

But she didn't make a move to come near him, kept herself planted by the door. "I heard your phone. What's going on?"

"It looks like Daumer wasn't the killer after all."

Marlena paled. "There's been another murder?"

Dante nodded. "Hobbs IDed the body as Prudence Puckett."

Shock strained her features. "My God, she was just at the clinic."

"I know," he said. "I saw her running from the fire, chased her down, and questioned her."

Her eyes turned wary. "You thought Prudence might have set the fire?"

He gave a noncommittal shrug. "She was acting suspicious."

"She was one of my patients, too." Marlena sank onto the sofa. "Somehow...this all seems connected to me."

"It's not you," he said gruffly. "It's about me."

Her eyes widened, remnants of fatigue and the shock of the night blurring her eyes.

She hated him now.

Part of him knew that was best. Best that he let her go.

But demons might come after his child to get to him. And his child was going to need him and so was she, even if Marlena didn't think she did.

Her cell phone buzzed, and she checked the number, then answered. "Yes, Dr. Raysen."

Dante went into the bathroom to splash cold water

on his face, then returned and reached for his jacket. He needed to get going.

Marlena ended the call, then turned to him.

"We need to go by the lab. Dr. Raysen went in to clean his office and found a flash drive belonging to Dr. Sneed. He sounds upset and thinks it's important."

"Are you up to going?" Dante asked.

She stiffened her spine and retrieved her coat. "Of course."

Dante clenched his jaw at Marlena's stubborn determination. Dammit, she needed to be in bed resting, not chasing down clues.

But he didn't have time to argue.

"Tell me about his flash drive and why Raysen is upset," Dante said.

"There's a list of subjects from one of his experiments, and all of the murder victims' names are on it."

This might be the break they needed. "Then we definitely need to take a look at it and talk to Dr. Sneed. Is he at the lab now?"

"No. Edmund said he tried to contact Dr. Sneed but couldn't reach him."

"Let's go look at that flash drive." Dante gestured to the door, and they hurried outside. The snow had thickened, the wind swirling the white flakes in a blinding haze. He started the engine, turned on the wipers and defroster, and chugged toward BloodCore.

Dr. Raysen met them when they arrived, his glasses askew, his fingers twitching at his chin. "Here's the flash drive," he said, then led them toward his office. Debris and smoky ashes still littered the building, but his office was in its north side, and barring some water damage, had suffered very little.

"Here, look at my computer." Dr. Raysen slid his chair aside and gestured for Marlena to sit down beside him. She claimed the chair, and Dante studied the screen over her shoulder.

Marlena clicked on icon after icon, both of them skimming for details. Spreadsheets of the results of various blood tests filled one of Sneed's files, another listed data from other sources that might affect his research, a third information from Germany on similar studies with lab rats that pointed to definite genetic predispositions to violence and mental disease leading to aberrant behavior. One study specifically involved the study of serial killers.

"This is what you want us to see?" Dante growled in frustration.

"Just look," Raysen said.

Marlena noticed a file coded with numbers and clicked on it, then exhaled in relief when the data they'd been looking for appeared on the screen.

Six names:

Jordie McEnroe.
Brenda Mulligan.
Ruthie Mae Stanton.
Gerald Daumer.
Prudence Puckett.
Judge Beau Brannigan.

"Judge Brannigan?" Dante said in surprise.

"I thought it was odd, too," Edmund said. "What does it mean?"

"It looks as if Sneed altered these subjects' genetic makeup, some through blood transfusions and others through injections." Marlena narrowed her eyes, skimming his notes. "And here, it looks as if he kept notes of changes in their behavior."

"The subjects exhibited more violent tendencies after the treatment," Dante said.

"That and other psychological problems." Marlena scrolled down the page. "Jordie was becoming paranoid. Brenda manic-depressive and suicidal. Ruthie Mae became addicted to sex and craved domination. Gerald thought he was possessed by the devil and admitted to hearing voices telling him to kill. And Prudence hated beautiful women and the men who ditched her for them. She talked of making them suffer the way she had to suffer. And Judge Brannigan, addicted to S&M."

"If he's sadistic, Brannigan could be the killer," Edmund suggested. "Or maybe Sneed killed his subjects."

"But why would he kill his own subjects?" Dante asked.

"Perhaps he didn't get the results he intended," Edmund said.

Marlena sighed. "If his experiment was illegal, he might have been afraid that if the truth got out, his reputation would be ruined."

He was creating bloodborn demons, Dante thought. "So his subject list became his hit list?"

Marlena clutched the edge of the desk. "Oh, my God. Look." She pointed to a separate file and opened it. Silence stretched between them as they read the notations.

"Look at the date," Marlena said. "Sneed first tried the experiment on himself, then the others."

"And look at this date. Three months ago, he noted changes in himself. Symptoms he was experiencing mimicked the others." Marlena skimmed further. "He had fantasies about committing murder, about craving the feel of someone dying at his hands. And he was obsessed with blood."

"Then he realized his subjects were starting to exhibit the same tendencies and that they would only escalate so he decided to kill them himself," Dante concluded.

But why would Sneed keep these notes on file where someone could find them?

"Jesus. The man thinks he's some kind of savior," Dr. Raysen said in a grave voice.

"He's no savior," Dante muttered with a snarl. "He's a monster."

~

Zion stood over his minions, listening to their reports. The elements had wreaked havoc the night before. And more was on its way. As soon as he had Dante by his side, the true anarchy could begin.

The tidal wave, the tsunami, the deaths . . .

Then the demons could rule the world.

Yet Marlena Bender had survived the tornado.

All because of his son.

He gestured toward the Seer. Time was running out. The anarchy must begin, with or without his sons. And if they chose not to follow him, they would have to be destroyed. "You planted the images of Vincent and Quinton for Dante to see?"

"Yes." The Seer smiled, her teeth gleaming against the darkness. "Two shapeshifters appeared outside the Bender woman's house. It should plant doubt in Dante's mind."

Good. And he had appeared in front of the woman twice now. First at his son's house when he caused the Bender whore to crash. The second, at the hospital when she'd been brought in after the fire and he'd momentarily morphed into the doctor's body.

She would remember his eyes when he finally orchestrated his plan and she saw him again. She would realize that she carried Satan's child.

And that his son's people had taken her family's lives.

Laughter boomed from his chest, echoing through the cave of black rock. Then she would turn on his son and break the bond that could save his soul.

And Dante would realize that trying to fight his demon side was useless.

# Chapter Twenty-eight

Dante hated leaving Marlena for a moment, but she would be safer with Raysen than with him. He met the security guard on the first floor by the front door. "Be sure to call me if Sneed shows up. I need to question him concerning the recent murders in town." He paused. "And be careful. He could be dangerous."

The security guard frowned but agreed, then Dante hurried to his car, climbed in, and headed toward town. While he drove, he phoned Hobbs and explained his suspicions. "I'm on my way to the judge's house. Make sure forensics doesn't miss anything at the crime scene."

"Look, get off my back. I've done everything you've asked so far," Hobbs said.

"Just keep doing your job," Dante snapped, then abruptly ended the call.

The blizzard forced him to slow down as he steered through town to the courthouse, the wind screeching. He tugged his jacket around him as he raced up the steps to the building, then went straight to the receptionist's desk to ask about Brannigan.

"I'm sorry, Sheriff, but he's not in today. He called this morning and asked for his schedule to be cleared."

"I need his home address."

She gave him a wary look. "I can call him for you."

"No," he said, not wanting to tip off the judge. "I'll do that on my way."

A bald-faced lie, but he didn't want to share his suspicions with her. And if Brannigan wasn't a killer, he might be the Torcher's next victim.

Every second counted.

"All right." She scribbled the judge's address and phone number on a sticky note and handed it to him.

Evening was setting in, the storm intensifying and making visibility difficult, the wind-chill factor nearing zero as he approached the estate on the outskirts of town.

The stately Tudor house was set on a five-acre estate on the outskirts of Mysteria. Dante cut the lights and parked beneath a cluster of trees in the drive, pulling his gun and bracing himself as he inched up the drive to the front stoop.

He quickly conducted a visual sweep of the property. The place was isolated, miles from another house. A private lair where Brannigan could kill without notice, where no one could hear a woman's screams or pleas for mercy.

He hesitated, debating his approach. He didn't have a warrant, so he decided to just ring the doorbell. One, two, three minutes passed but no one answered.

Warrant or not—hell, these were exigent circumstances. He had to go in anyway.

He glanced through the front window. The house was dark, the heavy drapes drawn in the back, yet the sound of dogs barking ferociously echoed through the walls. He tried the doorbell again and tapped his foot while he waited, but still no answer.

The cold seeped through him, and he heard fragile

limbs breaking with the force of the wind and weight of the snow.

Dante moved quietly around to the backyard, pulled on gloves, then jimmied the back door. Two Dobermans pounced immediately, teeth gnashing, charging at him, threatening attack.

He didn't like to hurt animals, but he wouldn't be their dinner either, so he reached out and pressed one hot finger to each of their necks. Just enough to send a slight burning sensation through them and to make them back off. The dogs whimpered, then ducked their heads and allowed him to pass as they settled into a corner.

He strode through the house, his eyes easily adjusting to the dimly lit rooms with their thick velvet drapes and dark wood paneling. No one was inside. No pictures of family, a wife, or children. No collectibles. A portrait of the judge hung above a stone fireplace behind a huge, polished cherry desk. It was immaculate, with matching desk paraphernalia, and as he would have guessed, there was a safe, securely locked and camouflaged by a portrait of hunters.

A gun cabinet held what appeared to be a collection of shotguns and rifles, and another glass case displayed a collection of coins dating back centuries.

He stalked through the rest of the house and found the man's bedroom. More masculine furniture and drab colors, yet no sign of anything to indicate an obsession or fetish.

He was missing something.

If the judge was a sexual deviant, into kinky stuff and S&M, he would probably have a secret chamber where he

engaged in his twisted sexual activities, one that wouldn't
be visible to any visitor.

Dante checked the bedroom again, searching the closet
to see if there was a private door, but found nothing.

Years ago, many of the houses had been built above the
underground tunnels. If Brannigan's had, he could have
followed the tunnels and discovered the Dungeon.

Determined to find the judge's fantasy room, Dante
returned to the man's office and searched the bookcases
for a key or secret door, but again found nothing. Damn.
Was he wrong?

No... it had to be here.

Dante strode into the kitchen, then checked the walk-in
pantry and discovered a second door in the back of the
closet. He searched the pantry shelves for a key, but didn't
find one. The judge probably kept it with him. Then he
had another idea. Maybe he'd missed it.

He dropped to his knees and felt along the bottom of
the lower shelf.

Adrenaline churned through him as he grabbed the key
and unlocked the door. The stairs were pitch-black, the
scent of smoke, linseed oil, and blood wafting up toward
him. He braced himself in case the judge was downstairs
hiding and slowly inched his way down the staircase.
When he reached the landing, he paused, listening.

Again, the scent of blood and smoke assaulted him,
stronger this time, and he found a low lamp and turned it
on. He had to blink at the sudden light, then saw the bed
in the corner, the ropes and harnesses, the dog collars,
whips, and chains.

The judge's chair, as if he held court here.

The hairs on the back of his neck prickled, and the

sound of pinging made him turn in a wide arc. His lungs tightened at the sight of blood dripping onto the floor.

The judge had been strung up with his own S&M straps, a wooden gavel crammed in his mouth, his naked body charred, the imprint of the Satanic S burning on the bare soles of his bloody feet.

# Chapter Twenty-nine

Dante fisted his hands by his sides. He couldn't touch anything in the judge's private sex chamber. CSI would have to process the scene, and the last thing he wanted was for his prints to be mixed with the killer's. He also wanted them to open that safe—maybe he'd find more information on the experiments inside.

But he studied the Satanic S and knew its significance. The killer was a Satan worshipper. He'd made a deal with the devil.

Whether he was human, one of Sneed's bloodborn demons, Sneed himself, or a true demon was the question.

He had to locate Sneed.

The upstairs door had been locked, meaning whoever had killed the judge had returned upstairs to lock the door and replace the key. But there had been no blood upstairs, no signs of a cleanup, suggesting the killer had escaped through the underground tunnels.

The tunnels where the demons thrived.

Where Zion would find willing soldiers.

He searched the dank room and located the door into the underground. It was unlocked but closed, a partial handprint marring the surface. He knelt and examined it, then sniffed the faint scent of sulfur and charred ashes.

Assuming the judge had kept recordings of his sexual escapades, he glanced around and noted the cameras on the walls, the CDs arranged in a shelf above the computer. They were labeled by date, and he popped one in and grimaced. A woman was tied to the same S&M ropes from which the judge now hung, and the judge raised a whip to strike her.

The woman was Prudence Puckett.

So the judge had fucked her before he'd killed her. What about Jordie, Brenda, and Ruthie Mae?

He removed the CD, stored it in its place, then checked the row again, searching for others. He discovered one for Ruthie Mae but not one for Brenda or one for Jordie. He checked the camera and computer, hoping the murder might have been caught on tape, but they were empty.

Damn.

Leaving the evidence intact for forensics to analyze, he glanced at the judge's torched skeleton once again, then quickly climbed the stairs. He phoned Hobbs, explained his findings, and requested a CSI team.

"Don't let this get out to the press yet," he said. "Not until we find Sneed and have a chance to interrogate him."

Hobbs agreed and Dante slithered through the darkness back to his vehicle.

Time was critical.

He had to find Sneed before he came after Marlena. If he was cleaning up after himself and thought that Marlena was on to him, he'd go after her next.

⤐

Marlena tried to wrap her mind around the fact that Dr. Sneed might be a murderer.

It just didn't fit with what she knew about the man. He had seemed so young, almost naïve in personal relationships, and gentle.

And although he was severely allergic to bees, once she'd seen him use a jar to capture a bee and carry it outside instead of killing it when it could easily have sent him to his death.

Besides, his motives in assisting her research were pure and altruistic, not evil.

Several documents appeared on the display, and she narrowed her eyes, trying to decide where to start. The project Sneed called Project X.

She clicked on the icon to open it and noted a spreadsheet of various blood samples and tests he'd run on the subjects, subjects he'd labeled with numbers, not names. Tests for diseases, various blood disorders, immunities, white blood cell counts, red blood cell counts, genetic markers, and so on.

Markers indicating the propensity toward violence.

Edmund rapped his knuckles on the counter. "At first, I didn't know if I could decipher his code," Edmund said, "but he's not as smart as you thought."

She opened a second file and realized it held another spreadsheet, this one chronicling more detailed behavior and changes in the various subjects. Behavior that the subjects reported had changed since they received the treatments. Behavior and thoughts indicated an escalating pattern of violence, aberrant thoughts, and increased sexual deviancy.

All of which fit their theory about the blood altering the subjects' behavior. "I still don't understand why Dr. Sneed would do this," Marlena said. "He doesn't fit the profile."

"What you knew about him was obviously a lie," Edmund said.

Marlena's gaze met his. "Was it?"

Edmund's eye twitched. "He was a narcissist," Edmund said. "He wanted attention, for everyone to think he was this super-genius kid. And you had your theory, so he decided to steal your research to make a name for himself."

Marlena pinched the bridge of her nose. "I suppose it's possible that he fooled me. But that would mean he's a true sociopath, that he's a charmer who fits in easily, and that wasn't true."

"Why do you continually defend him?" Edmund said with a bitter edge to his voice.

Marlena tensed. "I'm not," she said. "But I just can't believe I was so wrong about him."

"Maybe you had your head in the sand while you were busy with that sheriff."

The animosity lacing Edmund's voice caught Marlena by surprise. "I've been trying to help him find this serial killer," she said. "In case you've forgotten, the murderer sent me trophies from the first victims."

Edmund folded his lean arms, his eye twitching more violently. "Why do you think he chose you?"

Marlena contemplated his question. "To get my attention," she said. "Because he wanted me to know who he was. He wanted to be stopped."

"Or maybe he wanted to impress you?" He moved closer, then reached out and touched her hand. "Maybe he wanted you to finally notice him."

"I always paid attention to Dr. Sneed's work," Marlena said, but an iciness she'd never noticed before lined

Edmund's face. Suddenly an odd feeling nagged at her. She sensed they weren't talking about Sneed now.

And something about Edmund looked different. His eyes...they were almost wild, his pupils dilated...

Dante raced toward Sneed's condo, his anxiety mounting with every passing second. Everyone on the list of subjects in the experiment was dead now.

Sneed would want to cover his tracks and kill anyone who might be able to expose him. He'd sent Marlena presents, souvenirs, from the victims to taunt her because he obviously wanted her to know what he'd done.

That he'd proven violence could be related to genetics, markers carried in a person's blood.

And if he killed Marlena, he could take full credit for the research.

The wind rocked the SUV, and he slowed to avoid a patch of black ice, the blizzard so thick the haze obliterated his view. Tree branches snapped and cracked, the wind hurling them across the road, the roar so loud that it echoed off the mountain ridges. Was it another tornado?

He swerved, barely missed a limb flying at his windshield, then swung the SUV to the right and veered into the parking lot of the condo complex where Sneed lived. The steel and concrete high-rise looked out of place next to the mountain, and most locals viewed it as an eyesore, standing in opposition to the history of the small town and the wild ruggedness of the mountains.

He threw the SUV into Park, pulled his jacket around him, battling the heavy winds and icy patches as he jogged to the entrance. A security guard stood at the front, and he waved his ID, then caught the elevator to the third floor. When the doors whizzed open, he strode to the last unit on the end and punched the bell. Impatience gnawed at him as he waited, but no one answered.

Adrenaline surged through him. He raised his fist and knocked, then pounded on the door. Inside he thought he heard a sound, maybe a clatter? No, a moan...

His pulse clamored, and he jerked his gun from its holster, then picked the lock and eased open the door.

"Sneed, it's the sheriff." He inched into the foyer, quickly scanning the cold room, the lack of furnishings, searching for the young doctor. Scuffmarks marred the tiles, and the scent of blood and death seeped toward him.

Demon blood?

No...

Human.

Easing forward, he spotted the kitchen–living room combination, the sound of the TV echoing through the empty room. He glanced at the patio; the door was closed, the sheer curtains drawn. A bedroom sat to the right, and he stepped onto the plush white carpet, then spotted Sneed slumped in a desk chair in the corner, blood streaming from his neck, dotting the white carpet.

Dante inhaled the scent and fought his bloodlust, then inched forward and spotted the computer screen. The words "I'm sorry" blipped across the screen repeatedly.

A suicide note?

Dante reached out and pressed two fingers to the man's wrist to make sure he was dead, but a low moan, almost indiscernible, sounded, and he felt a pulse. Low but thready.

Sneed was alive.

He lowered his gun and considered calling 911, but if Sneed had killed all those people, he deserved to die. He wanted to hear that confession.

He spun the chair around, then lifted the man's face and forced him to look at him. "Sneed, Sneed..." The man's eyes rolled back in his head, his breathing so low Dante knew he might lose him any minute.

"Sneed, stay with me. Did you kill those people?"

Sneed moaned and his eyes flicked open slightly, but he looked dazed and disoriented. "What?" he said in a hoarse whisper.

"Did you kill those women? Were you conducting blood experiments on them?"

Sneed slowly shook his head and groaned.

Dante gripped his face firmly. "Don't lie to me now. You injected those people with blood, with genetic markers, to see if it changed their behavior, and it did."

"No..."

"Then you realized they were turning violent and you killed them to stop the transition."

"No... not me," Sneed ground out.

Blood was still flowing down the man's neck, his face gray and chalky, sweat beading his skin. He choked, blood spurting from his nose.

Dante gripped him tighter. "Tell me the truth, you coward."

Sneed shook his head, his eyes rolling back again. "Not me... Raysen... obsessed with Marlena..."

Dante's blood ran cold. Raysen was obsessed with Marlena. Raysen had known about her work, had conducted the experiment to impress her, had pretended the flash drive belonged to Sneed to frame him.

Panic and terror seized him.

Marlena had trusted Raysen.

Holy fuck. Raysen had tricked both of them by framing Sneed.

And he had left Marlena with the sick man.

Marlena scraped back her chair and stood. "Edmund, what's wrong? You're scaring me."

Edmund raked his fingers over his chin. "You think you know everything about human behavior, yet you can't see what's in front of your eyes. You believe Sneed was some god but you never noticed me."

"That's not true," Marlena said, his harsh tone making her inch backward. "I've always admired your work, Edmund."

"My work?" He growled. "What about me? I tried to befriend you, but Sneed came along and snowed you. And then that sheriff did, too."

"Dante is just doing his job," Marlena said.

Edmund growled an obscenity. "His job was to screw you?"

Shocked at his boldness, Marlena took another step back. "What? That's none of your business."

Edmund smirked. "You were fooled by Sneed. You have no idea." He poked her in the chest. "I know who Dante Zertlav really is. He's a demon, Marlena, the son of Satan."

"What?" Her heart clenched. "Why are you doing this? Why are you trying to hurt me, Edmund?"

"Because it's true," Edmund shouted. "You slept with a demon and now you're going to have his demonic baby."

"How did you know I was pregnant?" Marlena gasped and inched toward the door. She had to get away from him, had to talk to Dante. Edmund's tone was crazed, his eyes wild—dangerous.

"I told you I know more than you think." He grabbed her wrist, his nails digging into her skin. "Dante is not only a demon, but he grew up with the demons who killed your family. He was sent there that day to kill you."

"No..." Nausea rolled through Marlena and she tried to pull away. But he suddenly jabbed a needle into her arm. "What are you doing, Edmund?"

"I wanted you, Marlena, but you chose the demon over me. Now I have to destroy the demon child."

Her head begin to spin in a drunken rush as reality dawned. Edmund was the Torcher. He had made that flash drive and framed Sneed to trick her. He had killed the women, set the fire, and killed Gerald... "No, Edmund, stop, we're friends, you can't do this..."

"It's too late," he said in an ominous tone. "I made a deal with the leader of the underworld, and you and your child have to die."

Zion extended his hands and waved them across the top of the mountain. He was the all-powerful...

"The future lies in the palm of my hands," he said with a boom of laughter.

He leaned over the ridge, blew his fiery breath across the land and watched as the heat began to melt the thick snow banks and run down the mountain. Soon the river and creeks would swell and flood, overflowing into the streets and rising in the town to destroy homes, and businesses, and lives.

Hypnos was primed and ready to plant paranoia in the minds of the humans, to create panic, fear, and chaos so that they turned upon one another in anger and rage.

Soon the evil would wash away any remnants of the good left behind and nothing his sons could do would stop the anarchy.

# Chapter Thirty

Marlena winced as Edmund dragged her through the delivery exit, pushing her behind a doorway to hide from the security guard until he passed, then down to the basement and into the tunnels below.

She didn't know what kind of drug he'd given her, but it had paralyzed her arms and legs, her throat had grown thick, and when she'd tried to scream, no sound had come out, as if her vocal cords had frozen shut.

She wanted to fight Edmund and run, but she was too weak to do anything but let him lead her through the darkness like a puppet on a string.

Soon the drug would have to wear off, she consoled herself. Then she'd find her chance and escape. She had to in order to save her child.

Edmund was deranged now, completely out of his mind, and he was going to kill her.

"This is where your demon boyfriend grew up," Edmund said as he shoved her deeper into the abyss. The acrid stench of wet rock, a dead animal, urine, and blood swirled around her, nauseating her.

"He was raised by the demons who killed your family. And he was supposed to kill you that day."

Marlena sucked in a sharp breath at his words, then

stumbled over something slimy and almost fell, but Edmund yanked her back up and dragged her forward.

The sound of low, hideous voices, inhuman growls, screams, and sinister laughter echoed through the chambers. What kind of evil creatures were down here?

Aboveground, cars honked, thunder roared, and it sounded as if it had started raining again, a heavy, gushing downpour, as if the skies had opened, dumping a tidal wave of water.

Edmund's fingers dug into her arm, his nails like spikes, his grip painful, almost superhuman as he pushed her through a doorway. Inside, the room was dark, except for two ancient-looking torches lit with fire.

"This is the Dungeon," Edmund growled near her ear. "The bar where your boyfriend comes to find his fuck buddies."

Shock and pain seared Marlena as she spotted the bartender. He had thick, glossy black hair and black eyes, yet his skin was the palest white she'd ever seen, his lips a blood red. As if he sensed their presence, he angled his head and fangs protruded in his mouth.

He was one of the vampires? Had he attacked them the night before?

To the left, she spotted a woman wearing a cat costume—no, Marlena realized in shock. She was part cat...

Her gaze skimmed the rest of the room. This was a gathering place for the demons, a place no one in town knew existed. A place where inhuman creatures met to party while above them people moved through their daily lives, oblivious.

Did they meet here to plan attacks on the humans?

Did Dante really frequent this place? Had he known about these demons and kept quiet? Had he posed as sheriff to protect the town—or to protect his demonic friends?

Another wave of nausea clawed at her stomach, and she staggered against the wall, her legs buckling.

Edmund slid an arm around her waist to hold her up. She tried to lift a hand to push him away, but it wouldn't cooperate and fell limply to her side.

Denial rolled through Marlena. Dante couldn't be evil like the monsters who'd killed her family. Not the man who'd saved her and made love to her. Not the father of her child.

"Enough of this place. Now let's go have our own private party." Edmund dragged her from the room back into the dark tunnel and shoved her down another pitch-black hallway. The air thickened with sweat and the odor of refuse, and odors that now registered as inhuman.

"Your baby will be evil," Edmund said in a brittle tone. "That's why Dante seduced you. His father is the leader of the underworld. Dante planned to give the child to his father as an offering."

Tears filled her eyes, and she tried to scream again, but her voice died in her throat.

Dante had never explained why he'd been in the woods that day years ago. He'd refused to talk about his childhood or family.

And Edmund was right—Dante was a demon. She'd witnessed him use his powers.

God help her . . .

Did he plan to offer their child to the leader of the underworld?

Dante pressed the gas pedal as he punched Marlena's number to warn her about Raysen. Prudence Puckett and the judge had been killed only hours apart, Daumer the night before. And Sneed had almost died as well.

Which meant that Edmund was closing in, finishing off his list.

And he was with Marlena.

Three, four rings, and no answer.

His pulse pounded, and rain fell in heavy sheets. The SUV slid on the wet pavement as he careened up the mountain toward the lab. He shouldn't have left Marlena for a moment.

Another ring and her voicemail picked up. "Marlena, it's Dante, dammit, call me!"

He ground his teeth, steering around a truck puttering along the curve, his gears grinding as he maneuvered the sharp angle and tried to avoid clipping the guardrail. The weather had taken an odd turn, and the blizzard had stopped, the temperature warming. He heard the rush of water and realized the snow was melting quickly. Too quickly. Mixed with the torrential rain, it would cause massive flooding.

Damn. The elements were wreaking havoc again. The mountain runoff would cause heavy flooding from the river and creeks.

He punched Marlena's number again and let the phone ring, his mind spinning. Fuck. What if Raysen had already killed her?

Snow and slush spewed behind his SUV as he spun into the lab. He slammed on the brakes, threw the SUV into Park and jumped out, then jogged up the steps. Yanking his gun from his holster, he held it at the ready as he entered the lab.

But before he could make it inside, his cell phone vibrated on his hip.

He checked the caller ID box, though, and saw it was Drake Mortimer. "Dante here."

"It's Mortimer. You said to call if I saw anything suspicious."

"What is it, Mortimer? I'm in a hurry. I think I know who the killer is, and he has Marlena."

"Damn. That's why I called. A man was in here a minute ago with her. And something definitely was wrong. She looked scared shitless."

"Raysen had Marlena in the Dungeon?"

"Yes. Then he shoved her out the back door into the tunnels."

"Holy fuck." Sweat trickled down his neck. "Thanks, Mortimer. I'm on my way to the tunnels now."

Impatience gnawed at him as he ran back to his SUV, fought his way around traffic, and veered on the mountain road to the closest entrance to the tunnels.

Moving on blind instinct, he wove through the maze of corridors toward the Dungeon, then tried to think of a place underground where Raysen might take Marlena.

Footsteps sounded behind him, crunching on glass, and he spun around but the shadow slithered into an overhang. Damn demons.

To the north lay Father Gio's lair, to the west a unit carved out for the undead, but to the east lay a series of caves more isolated and not yet inhabited. Ignoring the group of demons gathered having an orgy, he jogged toward the northern end, the scent of despair and fear thickening the air as he left the more populated nooks and crannies.

The footsteps sounded again, and he spun around and saw Jebb Bates trailing him. Shit. Then suddenly a pack of demons jumped him.

Bates screamed, his eyes widening in horror. Dante's first instinct was to save the jerk, but the demon pack was too fast. Before he had time to toss a fireball, the demons mauled and mutilated the man and began slurping down his blood.

Son of a bitch. He'd deserved it, but Dante didn't like that a local had fed the demons, even if it was the slimy reporter who would have exposed him if he'd had the chance. And now this demon pack would want more blood.

Up ahead, the scent of smoke drifted toward him. Fear that Raysen had killed Marlena knocked the air from his lungs.

No...he couldn't lose Marlena and his child.

He stiffened and glanced around the dark interior as he approached the entrance to a side cave, his eyes adjusting to the dim light as he searched for the predator.

A vile spirit was here now, Dante could feel him.

The scent of smoke intensified, then a deep moan reverberated from inside, paralyzing him.

Marlena.

Dammit.

She was strapped to a chair in the center of a circle of flaming Satanic S's drawn on the floor in an infinity pattern—the pattern that signified that the devil lived forever.

Rage and fury blackened his heart and heated his blood as she slowly lifted her head. Bruises marred her cheek and her green eyes were filled with pain, sadness, and horror.

And something else—anger, fear, accusations…
betrayal.

"Hello, Dante."

He gripped his hands into fists at the sound of Raysen's
maddening voice.

He'd met him before, but this time he looked different,
almost wolfish, like an animal. His hair seemed to have
thickened, a thick beard grazed his jaw, and claws protruded from his hands—now paws.

But it was the predatory gleam in his eyes, the cold
harsh hunger that sent Dante's blood flowing in a mad
rush. He was going to kill Marlena and his child.

And he looked as if he would enjoy every minute.

Edmund smiled as the truth dawned on Zertlav's face. His
deal with Zion had been pure genius. Now Marlena would
know *he* was superior.

And Zion's son would suffer.

Wielding a knife, he paced behind Marlena. Dante's
demonic scent still lingered on her skin. He'd once loved
the woman and wanted her as his. They could have done
such marvelous work together.

They could have had a brilliant child, one who would
help the world as he'd tried to do with his work.

Before the bad blood had flooded his system.

But she had destroyed that love the moment she'd slept
with Zion's son.

Now he would rip that baby from her gut and then
kill her and Zertlav. Then Zion would honor him and he
would receive his redemption.

Marlena stared at Dante with a mixture of hope and despair. Were the things Edmund told her true? Had his people killed her sister? Had he seduced her to keep her from suspecting the truth? Had he impregnated her to offer their child to his father?

"Let her go," Dante said in a harsh tone. "You're problem is with me, not her."

"She's carrying your demon child," Edmund said. "The child has to die."

A sob welled in Marlena's throat. She didn't know if the child would be evil, but she didn't want him to kill the baby...

"Don't do this, Edmund," Marlena pleaded. "I'll find a way to save you and the others from the project."

"No, it's too late," he said. "They were turning evil. I had to destroy them." He jerked his hand toward Dante.

"You were playing god with people's lives," Dante muttered. "You killed Gerald Daumer and Sneed."

"They were weak," Edmund shouted. "Gerald wanted to tell Marlena everything. And Sneed...he discovered what I was doing and was going to turn me in." His voice grew shrill, his eyes demented. "And how can you judge me?" Edmund growled. "You kill for fun, for sport. Just like your people did when they killed Marlena's mother and sister."

Marlena flinched and looked up at Dante, praying he would deny the accusation. But guilt pierced his dark eyes, and his jaw tightened.

Her heart shattered into pieces. It was true.

How could she have loved a man who was a demon, whose people had killed her family?

Pain knifed through Dante at the anguish in Marlena's eyes.

"I'm sorry, Marlena," he said in a hoarse whisper. "Please, let me explain."

She shook her head, tears streaming down her cheeks. He took a step toward her; he had to make her listen. Had to save her from Edmund.

"I told her everything," Edmund said. "How you used her, seduced her to give Zion a grandchild. How you were sent to kill her that day. How you live with the demons and protect them in town. How your brothers are demons, too. They have already joined your father in worshipping Zion."

"I don't give a damn what they do. But Marlena is not evil, so let her go."

"She has evil growing inside her," Edmund snarled. "Your evil child."

"Just let her go," Dante said again. "I'll join Zion, and do whatever he wants."

"It's too late for that. The child...cannot live." Suddenly Edmund whipped a sharp knife upward, grabbed Marlena by the throat, and slid the blade to her neck.

"I said let her go," Dante growled. "You have me. That's all you need. My father will reward you greatly if you take me to him."

"But he ordered the baby dead first," Edmund said.

No...He hadn't been able to save Marlena's sister, but he had to save her and his child.

The rage in his bleak soul rose to the surface, and he flung his hand, tossing a fireball behind Edmund to get his attention.

Edmund laughed bitterly, then suddenly thrust the knife downward into Marlena's chest. Marlena screamed and slumped forward, blood spurting from her heart.

"No!" Dante lunged forward, but Edmund's laughter seared the walls.

"She'll die with the baby inside her," Edmund said. "I have honored Zion."

Fury drove Dante. He raised both hands and threw another fireball at Edmund. Edmund dodged and lunged through the flames at Dante, stabbing at him with the knife. The blade caught his arm, but Dante ignored the sting and the blood seeping from the wound and focused his energy on his power, pulling it from deep within him.

He flung one hand and sent another sizzling fireball soaring toward Edmund. Edmund ducked, but the flames caught his hair and lit up the darkness. Edmund beat at his head, screaming in terror, but rage spurred Dante on, and he hurled another fireball and another and another.

Edmund howled in pain and jumped back to beat at the flames, but Dante was relentless. He continued his assault until fire totally engulfed Edmund's body, and he collapsed onto the floor in a swirl of flames, screaming in agony as his body disintegrated into ashes.

"Marlena!" Dante's heart was pounding as he raced over to her. She had to survive. He couldn't lose her or his child.

He dropped to his knees and lifted her chin to look into her eyes. "Marlena?"

Her eyes were wide open, staring into space, glassy. Panic clenched his muscles, and he reached up and felt for a pulse, his breath stalling in his chest.

Emotions welled in his throat, the flames dancing

higher and higher around them, clawing at his shoes, at the chair, at her feet. He frantically untied her, grabbed her from the chair, and carried away from the circle of flames.

He had to save her. Had to.

But the knife had punctured her heart, blood soaked her blouse and body, and she wasn't breathing.

He eased her down onto the floor, leaned over, and started CPR, trying desperately to breathe life back into her. One, two, three—he did the chest compressions, praying, begging God to save her.

Over and over he performed the motions, blowing air into her lungs, but she lay limp, stiff, her body turning colder and colder by the second, her skin paler as the blood drained from her body.

Precious minutes passed, dragged by, rolling into half an hour, and slowly reality returned. Aboveground, the floods poured through the streets, but the silence in the cave was ominous and eerie.

He dragged Marlena into his lap and rocked her back and forth in his arms, emotions suffocating him—rage, grief, anguish.

He'd never loved anyone before, never had a connection or needed anyone in his life. But he loved Marlena and his son.

And now they were dead because of him.

# Chapter Thirty-one

⌐

Shock immobilized Dante, a deep-seated rage choking him. There was no reason to kill his unborn child, not unless the child had some kind of power Zion feared.

"Marlena, I'm so sorry," Dante whispered into her hair. "I'm so sorry."

He clutched her to his chest, rocking her back and forth, unable to release her. Pain and sorrow wrenched his gut. He couldn't believe his child was gone, that he would never be born. That he'd failed again.

That he'd lost any chance of having a family of his own, someone who might love him, demon and all.

Moisture trickled down his cheeks and dripped onto her limp body.

Even worse, Marlena had died hating him.

He howled out his pain, grief and emotions overwhelming him, then stroked her hair from her face and swallowed hard so he could speak. "I was sent to kill you, Marlena," he whispered. "I was only thirteen, and it was the initiation for our pack of demons." He rubbed her cheek with the pad of his thumb. Her skin was already cooling, her body so still that he wanted to shake the life back into her.

"They wanted me to kill you. It was part of my initiation, but I couldn't do it," he mumbled. The vicious scene played before him like a camera on rewind. "You were so young, even younger than I was. I'd done bad things before, things they made me do when they tortured me. Things I thought I was supposed to do. It was our way of life. To hunt and to kill."

He dropped his head forward and held her tightly, willing the time back but knowing it was impossible. If only he hadn't been so stubborn, had called for help.

Maybe called his brothers.

Marlena might be alive and he might have stopped Edmund.

Grief overwhelmed him, and he lay down beside her and pulled her into his arms. He'd never let her go.

"That day, I said no to the demons. I saved you and then I left them. I went undercover for months, hiding out. I lived in isolation for years."

He touched her stomach, an intense pain ripping through his gut. Only now he had killed his own child, because he hadn't been able to protect him and his mother.

Rage erupted inside him, overpowering his grief.

He had to avenge their deaths.

Zion was responsible.

He tenderly stroked Marlena's hair, his heart wrenching, then pressed a long, slow kiss to her lips. They lay there for what seemed like hours, him holding her, unwilling to let her go, drinking in her scent, memorizing every inch of her, every moment they'd shared together, every sweet and wonderful thing about her.

Choking back sorrow, he finally released her, then stood. But his grief ebbed and flowed, an entity that would never end, fueling his thirst for vengeance.

He'd fought for his independence, had sworn he never needed anyone. Not the demons who'd raised him, the brothers who claimed they wanted a reconciliation, or Marlena.

The woman who might have loved him.

Until he'd crushed that love with the truth of what he was and what he'd been.

Vengeance was his only friend now. He would get it, then to hell with whatever happened to him.

But he didn't have the power to vanquish Zion alone.

He needed his brothers and their combined powers. He didn't know if he could trust them, but he had to take the chance.

He couldn't leave Marlena here, though. The demons, the vampires, might find her and feed off her, so he picked her up and carried her through the tunnels to his house. Her limp body lay in his arms, her skin growing colder by the minute, until he laid her on his bed.

"I'll be back for you," he whispered, then pressed a kiss to her lips. "I won't let Zion get away with this. I swear to you, I'll make him pay."

And if his brothers had already joined Zion, had had anything to do with Marlena's death, he would kill them and bury them with his father.

Zion laughed as he watched his son Dante mourn over the woman. His grief would soon turn to anger and the need for revenge.

Dante was, after all, his son.

Edmund's spirit drifted from the body and floated in front of him, a series of glowing particles and ectoplasm that shimmered in the stunning darkness of the night.

"I obeyed your commands, Master. Please give me life again," Edmund pleaded.

Zion merely laughed. "You failed to bring me my son."

Edmund's ghostly form shimmered and fluttered. "But I killed his demon child."

"Yes, but you should have continued to make new demons for me instead of killing the bloodborn ones. Defying me in any way is unacceptable." Zion raised his hands and flung them at the ghostly form, then issued his demands.

"You will be sent to the lowest realm of the underworld and live in the fiery pit of hell forever."

"No!" Edmund screamed.

With one flick of his hand, the sentencing was done, and Edmund's spirit disappeared into the underground.

Zion smiled in glee and gathered his minions around him to prepare for his sons. He called upon Father Gio and instructed him to send all the elements out with their weapons.

The war had begun.

━━━━━

Dante stalked through the tunnels, the anger in his dark soul stirring fantasies of death and torture, of destroying his father and watching his body turn to ashes and fade into the ground.

Excitement heated his blood at the thought.

The memory of Marlena's cold body in his arms and an image of what his child would have looked like surfaced, adding to his guilt, yet intensifying his primal need for revenge.

He'd never thought he'd ask his brothers for help. But the time had come to either join with them or fight to the end.

He punched in Vincent's number, his pulse clamoring as he waited on a response. Five rings later and he had to leave a message.

He threw the phone on the seat of the SUV with a vicious curse and drove toward his place. He needed to hunt. To kill. To taste the blood of a demon as he had so many times before.

The dark beast within him hungered for flesh, for blood and death and destruction.

He parked at his house, stared into the dark woods beyond, and knew there were demons in the midst hunting as well. Some hunting the animals, others who would feed from the town if not stopped.

The evil pulled at him, beckoned him to venture into its erotic abyss, to take what he wanted without question. To vent his pain on others as he'd been taught by the demons.

Moving on instinct, he shuffled forward into the deep recesses of the woods. The snow and wind whirled around him, the clouds threatening another downpour. The elements were probably laughing now, enjoying themselves as they wreaked havoc on the land and forest. The sound of the creek rising to the east roared through the night, promising destruction to the town.

He blundered on, the scent of a wild animal driving him, the smell of blood, a demon and the sound of werec-reatures beckoning.

He belonged here in this tangle of lost souls and spirits and evil cravings.

Not in a home with beautiful Marlena or a child. But God help him, he'd wanted that.

His legs buckled, and he sank to the snow-packed ground and howled his fury and anguish. Somewhere close by, he heard laughter echoing off the mountain.

His father's hideous laughter.

No, he didn't belong with Marlena or a child of his own.

But dammit, he wanted them with every ounce of his being.

Only he'd lost them forever.

And his father was celebrating his victory as pain racked him senseless.

But suddenly a noise erupted through the fog of his grief.

He lifted his head and inhaled the scent of a human in the woods. An innocent.

His dark, baser instincts surged to life, the blood roaring in his head. He stalked toward it, the rage eating at his soul spurring him forward. The need to vent, to remember the man he used to be when caring about a human was not part of him, when he didn't feel, when he didn't know this kind of grief and loss, overwhelmed him.

He had to drive away the pain. Remember what he was.

Who he was. What he was meant to be.

What had been drilled and beaten into him for years, that he was a demon, a killer. He needed to draw on those lessons so he could tap into his demonic soul.

That demonic part of him would bolster the strength he needed to kill his father.

He kicked snow and brush aside, waded through the overflowing creek, stalked through the forest. A vulture was feeding on the dead carcass of an animal, then he heard noises—voices—floating to him in the wind.

"It's spooky out here," a young girl said in a shaky voice. "Come on, Jon, let's go back."

"No, it's raining. Let's sneak into the cave and we'll have some privacy."

Stupid teenagers. Any demon in the area could attack them and chomp them to pieces in seconds. Him included.

The girl spotted him, then gasped and jumped behind the boy, clutching him with blood-red fingernails. The boy's eyes widened, but he squared his bony shoulders as if he was ready to fight for his girl. "Sheriff?"

Her innocence reminded him of Marlena as a child and resurrected his humanity. "Get out of there," he shouted. "This area is dangerous."

The young couple scurried away in fear, and he turned and stalked back toward his house. He wouldn't waste time on any of the smaller demons tonight. He wanted Zion.

His message light was blinking when he let himself inside. He grabbed the handset and checked the number.

Vincent.

A minute later, Vincent spoke. "Dante?"

Dante pinched the bridge of his nose and gasped for a breath as he connected the call. "We have to destroy Zion."

"What happened to Marlena? Quinton had a premonition that she died."

He choked back emotions. "He killed her. Zion used Raysen to kill her."

A tense second stretched between them. "Meet me at my house," Vincent said. "I'll call Quinton and tell him to come. Together we can bring Zion down."

Dante's throat thickened as the image of Marlena dying taunted him. "Just give me the address. I'm on my way." If Vincent or Quinton was lying to him, he'd kill them then. But first he needed to know where to find his father.

Vincent gave him GPS coordinates, and Dante hung up and rushed to his SUV. He started the engine, then scrubbed at his eyes as he tore down the mountain. His entire life spread before him in an array of sickening images. His life with the demons, with Father Gio and the elements when he was young. The torture and the brutal exercises they'd forced him to endure. The battles and hunts for innocents to be sacrificed.

The fights with opposing demons to prove his strength.

The day of the initiation. Father Gio ordering him to kill Marlena. Her mother screaming at the demons to let them go.

His first sliver of humanity surfacing when he'd seen the fear and youth and hope in Marlena's eyes.

Being with her had almost made him *feel* human.

His hands gripped the steering wheel in a white-knuckled grip, and sweat beaded his skin as he fought to keep the car on the road. The creek running beside the road was overflowing, flooding the street, and cars were already stranded along the highway. He flipped on the radio and tensed at the news report. "The residents of Mysteria are being asked to evacuate to higher ground. There are reports of two deaths already from flood-related accidents, the subdivision on the east side of town is half under water, and the weatherman has predicted that more floods and tornadoes are on the way. But Mysteria isn't the only town having problems. A hurricane is due in the Gulf, and California has reported an earthquake—"

Dante flipped off the radio, certain Zion was responsible. If he thought Dante would join him in the underworld now, he was wrong.

He would destroy him instead and put an end to his reign of terror.

It wouldn't bring Marlena or his child back, but he'd do it in memory of them.

～～

Marlena was so cold. Cold and alone.

Oddly, there was no pain anymore, just a fleeting feeling of having lost something important. A sensation of floating as if she had drifted from her body and was watching the scene below her.

She lay in a dark cavelike room on a blanket, a slice of moon illuminating her deathly still body. Blood soaked her blouse and chest, her skin was pale white.

Dante was gone. And so was the demon who'd stabbed her. The demon who'd told her that Dante had been sent to kill her.

Was this really death?

The end of her life on Earth?

Shock and anger gripped her as she realized what she would miss. She and Dante would never be together. Her baby would never be born.

She would never finish her work, never find that cure for violent and aberrant behavior.

The darkness beckoned, voices whispering to her to join them. An evil voice promising eternal life if she offered her soul to walk with Satan. Skeletal fingers clawed at her, begging her to join the undead as they defied nature and returned to the land of the living.

But those were the very evil forces who had tortured Dante. The ones he'd fought to save her. The ones in human form that she'd tried to cure with her research.

She would never become one of them.

Then a bright white light broke into the churning tunnel, trying to draw her into its peaceful core, a light so beautiful and alluring that she turned away from that dark tunnel and gravitated toward it.

Heaven... the light she'd heard about, it did exist. Soft, entrancing, soothing, peaceful, it beckoned.

Her mother was there, standing in its midst, her little sister beside her, her hand enfolded in her mother's. Sparkling crystalline lights shimmered around them in a halo, like tiny diamonds glowing against an inky darkness.

She wanted to dive into it, to let the peaceful light wash over her and assuage the pain of her failures and the loss of her future.

Her future lay here now with her mother and sister.

She reached out her hand, stepped toward the light to walk into it and join them.

# Chapter Thirty-two

The light had completely disintegrated in Dante's mind and soul.

It had died with Marlena and his child.

How could he have failed them?

Vengeance hurled him through the storm as he battled the wind and blinding rain on his way toward Eerie. He and his brothers had to formulate a plan, a foolproof plan to destroy Zion.

And not just destroy him but torture him, make him suffer.

Tension knotted his shoulders as he wound up the curves toward Vincent's cabin. Oddly for the home of a powerful demon, the place looked homey. Normal.

Nothing about his life had been normal, though, and it never would be. Their demon blood had cursed him forever.

He parked the SUV, stray limbs pelting him as the vicious wind ripped them from the trees and hurled them across the yard.

He tugged his jacket around him and jogged up to the porch, then climbed the steps. He'd never thought he'd come here for help. But he needed his brothers now to exact his revenge.

And nothing would stop him from doing so.

In spite of the weather, Quinton had already arrived, and the two men met him at the door. Two women stood by a fire, both looking worried and anxious. Again, he wondered if he could trust them, but he had no choice. He needed help.

And vengeance against Zion was worth the chance.

"This is my wife, Annabelle Armstrong," Quinton said as he slid a protective arm around her shoulders.

Dante recognized her from CNN. "You know what we are and you married him anyway?"

She gave a small laugh and pressed a kiss to Quinton's cheek. "You can't help who you fall in love with."

Vincent cleared his throat. "And this is my wife, Clarissa. She is a medium."

Dante studied her serious, pensive face. "You talk to the dead?"

She nodded. "I'm so sorry about Dr. Bender."

He sucked in a painful breath. "Have you seen her spirit?"

She shook her head. "No, but that's not unusual. When a person first passes, some souls go into shock. It takes time for the souls to realize what's happened." She paused and offered a sympathetic smile. "Of course, she has a good soul. There's always the possibility that she's at peace, that she has already crossed into the light."

His chest ached at the thought that she was gone forever. That his child would never be born.

A soul-deep ache hit him, and rage once again heated his blood.

"Tell us what happened," Vincent said. "Who killed Marlena?"

Dante tried to pull himself together. He had to vanquish Zion, then he could mourn his lost family. "Dr. Edmund Raysen."

"Raysen, the doctor who worked with Dr. Bender?" Vincent scrubbed a hand over his chin.

"Yes. Apparently he stole the blood from her research project and used it in his own sick experiment. He even used himself as a subject. Then he showed us a flash drive documenting the experiment that he claimed was Sneed's."

"It wasn't Sneed's?" Quinton asked.

"No."

"What was on the flash drive?" Vincent asked.

"Notes revealing his subjects were experiencing disturbing reactions, including violent behavior, schizophrenia, sexual deviancy, and bloodlust. So he turned those subjects into his hit list."

"Why would he do that?" Annabelle asked.

"I don't know. Either he feared the others would turn violent as well, or he didn't want news of his experiment to be revealed and his reputation to be tainted."

Vincent crossed his arms. "He thought he was doing a noble thing by killing his test subjects?"

"Raysen wasn't noble. In the end, he killed Marlena." Dante stiffened, a coldness seeping through him that he'd lived with for years and battled. A coldness he embraced now. He would need all his demonic strength and power to defeat his father. "Zion was responsible. Raysen confirmed that he ordered him to destroy my child."

Dante studied his brothers' faces. "He also said that you two had joined Zion's side."

Vincent and Quinton exchanged wary looks. "Zion

will do anything to try to divide us, because he knows our powers combined can destroy him."

Dante felt a surge of emotion—of kinship to his blood brothers. He'd been alone his entire life. Had never wanted or needed anyone.

But he would accept their help to end Zion's reign of terror.

His fingers felt tingly, the heat already seeping through him, the need to use his power to turn his father into ashes shooting adrenaline through him.

"Where do we find Zion?" he asked.

Vincent spoke. "The cave of black rock in the Black Forest. It's his palace on Earth and the place where he killed our mother."

Dante gave a clipped nod. "Then let's go to the Black Forest."

⌒

Trees snapped and popped, branches hurling through the air at lightning speed as Dante drove his brothers around the mountain toward the Black Forest. The gray sky had grown darker, bleaker, the wind so ferocious that it bounced the SUV all over the road, and Dante had to fight to keep the vehicle in line.

"We can only go so far, then we'll have to hike through the Black Forest," Vincent said. "We'll have to be prepared to battle the demons and spirits trapped in the Wasteland of the Lost Souls."

An eighteen-wheeler skidded and careened out of control ahead of them, sliding toward the emergency exit ramp to avoid plunging over the mountain. Rain pelted the windshield, a wind tunnel swirling above as if another tornado was chasing them.

Dante glanced up and grimaced. "Get off my tail, Storm," he muttered between clenched teeth. Anger railed through him at the thought that the men he'd once considered family were teaming up with Zion against him.

He speeded up, but the tornado, too, picked up speed, sucked up trees by the roots and tossed them through the air like tiny limbs. The forest on each side screamed with animals scurrying to take cover, and out of nowhere a flock of falcons dove as if to escape the charging storm.

Vincent pointed to the right. "Take that dirt road. It's narrow, but it's a short cut."

A deer skidded across the road in front of him, and Dante braked and slid sideways to avoid hitting it, slowing slightly as he steered the vehicle onto the dirt road. He downshifted, gears grinding as the SUV bounced over gravel, potholes, and broken limbs.

"There's a creek bed up ahead," Vincent pointed out. "Hopefully the bridge is still intact."

Dante accelerated, the giant oaks and pines creating a tunnel that shielded them from some of the downpour. But the tornado chased them, ripping a tree beside them from its roots and flinging it into the road in front of them. Dante slammed on the brakes and skidded to a stop, the SUV's front smashing into the giant oak with a bang.

"Dammit," Dante snarled.

"Turn around and we'll take another side road," Vincent said.

His tires dug into the slushy, icy ground, flinging debris as he shifted into reverse and sped in the other direction.

Another tree cracked and fell in a roar, then a row of pines snapped and toppled like dominos falling.

The earth trembled, the entire mountain shaking, and behind them, the ground divided, the earth literally separating, rocks and dirt collapsing into the sinkhole.

"What the fuck?" Quinton growled.

"He's called out all the forces," Dante said in a hiss.

"Hang a left up there," Vincent said. "We'll meet the river and follow it."

But as they did, another roar sounded, and an avalanche began.

"It's a goddamn landslide," Vincent shouted.

Dante hit the gas and speeded up, dodging falling rocks, ice, and tree limbs as they crashed down around them.

Another giant tree flew toward them, and Vincent lifted his hands and used his power to shatter it. The tree exploded, limbs flying and raining down around them.

Dante swerved, then suddenly the sound of rushing water rent the air, as the swollen river began to rise and overflow the bank. An ancient, rusted steel bridge loomed ahead, their only way across the river. But the water was rising as if a dam had just burst. They weren't going to make it.

"Shit," he barked. "The bridge will be gone in seconds."

"Speed up, " Quinton yelled. "I'll hold it off."

The water surged upward, nearly meeting the bridge bottom, the steel shaking with the force of the winds and trembling earth.

But Quinton focused, ground his teeth, narrowed his eyes, raised his hands to both sides, his body quivering as he focused his power on holding off the flood.

Just as the SUV reached the opposite side, the river

rushed up and swallowed the bridge. Dante continued to fly, outrunning the raging flood as Quinton used his power to hold back the river until they had crossed.

Vincent lifted his hands and flung rocks down from the ridge to form a dam, leaving them on dry ground until they reached the end of the road.

Dante threw the SUV into Park, they grabbed their gear, gloves, and coats, and the three of them strode into the forest.

No one except Vincent had ever set foot in the forest and survived.

Would they make it this time?

They had to.

No light existed inside those woods, no life except for the demons left in the Wasteland of the Lost Souls. Poisonous man-eating plants, snakes, lizards, monsters, werecreatures, and evil spirits roamed the land, hungry and ready to pounce.

Dante clenched his hands into fists, trying to ignore the hideous screech of the monsters, the killer plants, the demons screaming and shouting that fresh food had entered their realm.

Vincent led the way, fending off snakes and flinging his hands like hatchets to tear away the clawing foliage that sucked at their feet and legs. Dante shot a fireball at a monster-faced demon and he exploded, brilliant orange flames lighting the darkness.

Evil eyes glowed ahead, around them, behind them, as if following them, and slimy, vile creatures wound around their feet and ankles. Dante spewed fire at them and sent them screeching for cover while Quinton used his power to ward off an attacking winged creature that swooped from above, its sharp talons bared and ready to pierce them with venom.

It seemed like hours that they hiked, fighting off the monsters and inhuman creatures. The suffocating heat and the foul stench of death and blood and carcasses grew stronger as they neared the cave of Black Rock.

The temperature soared to a suffocating well of heat that seeped through Dante's feet and body, so intense it was if he had stepped through the gates of hell.

Zion must be nearby.

He was the most powerful firestarter of all, and Dante could smell him. The aroma normally would entice him, lure him to the fire, seduce him into using his own ability and flicking flames from his fingertips just to watch them spark.

Tonight it drew him as well. He was finally going to confront his father. He and his brothers would win.

And if he died—what the hell did it matter? He had nothing to live for now, nothing except revenge.

Another creature slithered around his legs and grabbed hold, trying to trap him, but he flung a fireball at it and smiled as the creature burst into flames with an agonizing scream.

Sweat trickled down his jaw as he and his brothers reached the cave of Black Rock.

Vincent and Quinton both looked slightly haggard and were sweating, too, but their faces were chiseled with determination.

The earth rumbled and trembled again, the mountain parting slightly to reveal the entrance to the cave of Black Rock, as if Satan himself had opened the doors and invited them inside.

Dante glanced at his brothers, and they gave a collective

nod, then stepped into their father's lair, ready to vanquish him or die trying.

Dante's heart lurched to his throat as he spotted another Satanic ring of fire, the infinity symbol.

But this time, Marlena's body lay in the middle.

Grief struck him, along with the realization of just how cruel his father could be.

Suddenly the horrific smoky reek of charred ashes, death, and evil swirled through the cave, and Zion's voice echoed low, menacing, taunting.

"Hello, my sons. I've been waiting for you."

Dammit, the demons had found Marlena at his house and transported her here to torture him. What did he plan to do with her body? Feed it to his demons?

# Chapter Thirty-three

Over his dead body.

Dante raised his hands to begin the war, but Zion held up his claws in warning. "Wait."

"Why? You've already killed Marlena and my child," Dante spat.

Zion's evil grin lit the darkness. "I am the most powerful demon in the world, the lord of the underworld. I can bring the woman back to life."

The air collected in Dante's lungs. "What?"

A vile grin twisted Zion's face. "Yes. I can raise her from the dead, and you can spend eternity with her and the child she carries. All you have to do is embrace your dark side, and we will rule the underworld."

Zion's words echoed in Dante's head, tempting him. He could have Marlena and his child. See his own baby grow up.

He could have the family he hadn't even known he'd wanted until he met Marlena.

But the price? Was it worth it?

He'd lived in the darkness for years as a child. He had an appetite for evil, a hunger that once fed only escalated.

But he'd just found his brothers. And they were family, too. They had defied Zion's tests and won.

"Dante, don't give in," Quinton murmured in a low voice.

"Think of Marlena." Vincent's tone resonated with authority. "What would she want you to do?"

Dante whipped his head around to glare at both of them. They had the loves of their lives, their mates, hadn't lost as he had. They had no idea how he felt.

"Marlena fought against evil," Vincent said, reminding him of what Marlena had stood for.

Quinton's tone was hypnotic. "Don't dishonor her by giving in to Zion's demands and becoming the very thing she abhorred and spent her life trying to stop."

"But she's dead," Dante said. "And it's my fault. What honor is there in letting her die because of me?"

Vincent gestured toward Zion. "What honor is there in bringing her back to walk with the very evil souls she tried to save?"

Quinton placed a hand on Dante's shoulder. "Do you think she'll thank you for that, or will she hate you instead?"

"Your brothers have turned soft because of those women," Zion roared in disgust. "But you, Dante, you are like me. You are a firestarter. The dark heat runs through your veins, and you will be my righthand man. One day you can rule the underworld yourself."

Dante pictured himself in the underworld, commanding his minions to carry out heinous deeds, to corrupt lost souls, to tear families and lives apart, to inflict pain, and wreak havoc, and destroy the world.

Then his gaze fixed on Marlena's still body. Marlena, who was kind and good, who had tried to find a way to help those suffering from disorders and violent behavior.

Marlena, who believed in the good in him.

If he agreed to his father's terms, he would have her back, be able to hold her, touch her, taste her. Raise his child.

But he if cut a deal with Zion, he would not only be trading his soul but hers as well. Then Zion would raise his child in the ways the evil demons had raised him.

The ones he had hated and left because he abhorred the fact that they'd lost any trace of humanity.

Then Zion would have won, and he would have failed again.

Pain stabbed his chest, and emotions crowded his throat. He couldn't do that to Marlena or his child, not to the only two people he'd ever loved.

And he did love them.

"Please forgive me, Marlena," he whispered.

Zion walked to the center of the fire and laid a hand above Marlena's heart. "Now, son. Agree and she will live again."

"But she would live in misery," Dante growled. "And you must pay for what you've done."

Every nerve in his body screamed to life, sending fire shooting through his body, an energy that threatened to implode within him if he didn't release it.

He raised his hands and threw a fireball at his father. Zion roared in protest and hurled one back.

The amulet on his chest suddenly burned against his skin, the crystal stone glowing. He glanced at Vincent's, and his glowed a dark red. Quinton's sparkled as well, with a goldish hue.

With a silent nod, the brothers formed a united team.

The war suddenly broke out. Dante and Zion shot

fireball after fireball across the cave of black rock, Vincent shattered rock and sent it tumbling down on Zion, and Quinton used his mental energy and hurled the fireballs back at his father.

"Together we stand," Vincent said.

"Together," Quinton said.

"Brothers." Dante hurled a stream of fire toward Zion, moved his hand in a circular motion until it encased him completely. Their powers seemed to grow stronger, connected, growing as they teamed up.

Vincent flicked out his hands, and suddenly Zion's body started to tremble. Using his mental energy, Quinton focused on vanquishing Zion while Dante made the fire engulf Zion.

A horrific screech echoed in the air, and Zion's human form exploded, shooting sparks off the black walls of the cave as he crumbled into charred ashes and the embers crackled and popped.

A roar rocked the cave floor and walls, black rock tumbled down, the ground opened and swallowed Zion's remains into a burning inferno. Zion's protests resounded through the cave, the horrific sound of monsters and demons screeching from below.

A second later, the hole in the underground closed, the trembling stopped, and a quiet peacefulness descended over the cave. Even the flames shooting up around Marlena died, the oppressive heat tapering off as the stench of their dead father's charred ashes faded.

Then, oddly, a sliver of light seeped into the darkness, then another sliver, as if the storm of evil had been lifted and extinguished, as if light had been restored to the Black Forest, with the death of the evil creatures.

Dante stumbled forward and dropped to the ground beside Marlena, emotions choking him. She lay limp, stiff, on the stone mound, dry blood staining her blouse, her face ashen and cold.

He laid his head on her belly, draped his arm over her, his chest heaving with anguish. "I love you, Marlena. Please forgive me."

Tense seconds passed in the ensuing silence while he mourned her loss.

Suddenly her body jerked, her limbs trembled, and the sound of a choked breath ripped through the air.

"Dante," Vincent whispered.

"My God," Quinton muttered.

Dante lifted his head and stared in shock as Marlena opened her eyes and came back to life.

➤

Marlena gasped for breath, warmth seeping through her, replacing the icy chill of death that had claimed her earlier.

Death—had she really died and come back to life? Or had she been in some near-death state, not alive but not quite dead yet?

Her stomach fluttered, and the whisper of the angel's voice came to her.

*Your son is a great healer. Dante saved him from Zion. Now your son will save you.*

"Marlena?" Dante's voice creaked out a low, anguished croak. "Marlena, are you really alive?"

She nodded slowly, unsure what had happened. But a faint memory like a dream flowed through her head. She'd been stabbed, had seen the white light and reached for her mother's and sister's hands. But a beautiful angel had appeared and whispered that she had earned the right to go back.

That it wasn't her time yet. That she would give birth to one of the greatest, most powerful healers of all time.

Then she'd heard Dante talking. And two other men. And Zion.

She shuddered. He'd wanted Dante to bring her back and walk with him, but Dante had refused.

She looked into Dante's eyes, saw the tortured expression. He hadn't brought her back, because he loved her. Because he knew she wouldn't want to be evil. And he'd wanted to save his son from being possessed by the demons.

"I can't believe it." Dante pressed a hand to her cheek, his look confused but hungry, filled with shock. "How? I don't understand. I refused Zion's agreement."

"I know," Marlena whispered. "Your strength, your unselfishness, your love—that's what saved me." She reached down, took his hand, and placed it on her stomach and felt the fluttering again. "That and our son."

"Our son?"

She smiled through her tears. "Yes. Apparently he's going to be a great healer. And he carries the blood that could cure evil, the cure I've been looking for all along."

~

Hours later, Dante and Marlena left Vincent and Quinton at Vincent's and headed back to his house. He could hardly believe the change that had been wrought by recent events. Raysen had been killed, so the deaths would end. Zion was destroyed, restoring the balance to the underworld.

The elements had pulled back, the flooding, the

tornadoes, the hurricanes, the avalanches—the world had suddenly calmed, as if peace had fallen over the land.

It was temporary, but it was a victory nonetheless.

Other demons had been unleashed upon the Earth, demons who would raise their own kind of evil. Another leader would be named for the underworld and he would have his own plans. He needed to meet with Mortimer and BlackPaw and see if they could form a secret society to protect the town.

But for tonight, he and his brothers, and the women they loved, were safe.

Marlena still seemed weak and had fallen asleep, so he carried her inside. She stirred and glanced at the blood still dotting her clothes. "Let's shower," she whispered.

He nodded, determined to wipe the stench of death, of evil, off them before he carried her to his bed.

As they bathed, he paused to stare at the puncture wound where Marlena had been stabbed, and a curse rolled from his lips.

His hand stilled, his gaze meeting hers. "I can't believe I lost you, and that you came back to me," he said gruffly. "You know part of me will always have that pull toward evil. But I couldn't kill you that day when you were a child." He pressed a kiss to her neck. "I couldn't..."

"I know, you saved me," she whispered.

"No." He traced a finger along her cheek. "You saved me that day, Marlena. You gave me back my soul."

They dried each other off, his movements gentle but hungry, and then he carried her to bed, crawled in beside her, and cradled her in his arms.

"Thank God, it's over, really over," Marlena whispered as he hugged her to him.

He nodded and gazed into her eyes. "The battle with Zion is over, but our life together is just starting, Marlena."

She lay back on the covers, naked and beautiful, his scars and hers a reminder of the evil that had nearly torn them apart, and the hope that brought them together.

He cupped her face in his hands. "I love you," he whispered. "I never knew what that was, Marlena, not until I met you. But I love you and our son."

Marlena feathered his hair from his forehead. "I love you, too, Dante. I always will."

He slid his cock inside her, then kissed her deeply, hotly, a kiss full of promises; then they made love with a passion that would last forever.

CAN SHE DARE TO TRUST
HER HEART . . .
WHEN HIS SOUL BELONGS
TO THE DARK?

Please turn this page
for a preview of

## *Insatiable Desire*

The first book in
*The Demonborn* series.

Available now.

# Chapter One

The first fuck was always the best.

Not that Special Agent Vincent Valtrez ever bedded the same woman twice.

No, twice meant they might misconstrue his intentions. Get involved. Expect something from him.

But he had nothing to give.

Sex was sex. An animal's primal need. The one he fed willingly.

Unlike the evil bubbling inside him that he fought daily.

The motel room's bedsprings squeaked as he ripped open the woman's blouse, and he stared at her breasts spilling over the lace. Heat surged through his loins at the way her nipples puckered, begging for attention. A martini at midnight, and she'd easily become putty in his lust-driven hands.

He straddled her, then released the front clasp of her black bra, his cock twitching as her plump breasts filled his hands. Moaning, she traced a finger along his jaw, then dragged his face toward hers and nibbled at his lips.

Their tongues danced together, and she slid her foot along the back of his calf, driving him crazy with desire.

Clouds shifted outside, moonlight streaking the room with shards of light, illuminating her flushed face and the splay of her fingers as she tore open his shirt and stroked his chest.

Vincent had felt the evil pulling at him for years, ever since his parents had disappeared. That night he'd been found on the edges of the Black Forest, bruised and beaten, and so traumatized he'd lost his memory.

Although he feared his father had killed his mother . . .

The woman's blood-red fingernails clawed his bare skin. A droplet of blood mingled with the sweat, exciting him, blurring the lines in his mind between himself and the killers he hunted.

For an instant the beast inside him reared its head. He imagined sliding his hands around her slender throat, digging his fingers into her larynx until her eyes bulged, watching the life drain from her.

He hissed a breath between clenched teeth, forced himself to pull away. The dark side, the black holes, tugged at him again, trying to take control . . .

He couldn't give in to the darkness. He was an FBI agent. Had sworn to save lives, not take them.

Oblivious to his turmoil, she jerked him back to her, took his hand and slid it between her thighs. She was so hot. Wet. Ready.

Raw need swirled through him. With a groan, he shoved the darkness deep inside, then bent and sucked her budded nipple into his mouth. She purred like a hungry cat, then parted her thighs in invitation, arousing him as she cradled his erection. He cupped her mound, pushing aside the edges of her panties to sink his fingers into her damp flesh. Her sigh of pleasure shattered his resistance, and he tore off her bra and underwear, then shoved her skirt up to her waist. A tight skirt that had drawn his eyes to her ass and made him horny as hell when she'd walked into the bar.

His jeans and boxers fell to the floor, socks into the pile. Then the condom—always the protection. He couldn't chance continuing the Valtrez name with a child.

Growling in anticipation, he shoved her hands above her head, pinning her beneath him as if she was a prisoner of his desires.

She struggled playfully, but her eyes flashed and smoldered as he rubbed his throbbing length against her heat. She licked her lips, then bit his neck, and he groaned again, then flipped her to her stomach. He didn't like to look at their faces, didn't want any emotional connection.

His hands skated over her bare shoulders, slid down to massage her butt; then he lifted her to her knees. She braced herself on her hands and moaned, rocking forward, twitching against him.

"I want you inside me, Vincent," she whispered raggedly. "Take me now."

The flames of lust grew hotter as his cock stroked her ass, and the tip of his sex teased her center. Sliding in her moist channel a fraction of an inch, then retreating, then back again, taunting them both.

"God, sugar, please . . ."

He liked it when they begged.

She spread herself for him, and his control snapped, the vision of her offering setting his body aflame. He thrust inside her, ramming her so hard she cried out his name and dug her hands into the sheets, twisting them between those blood-red fingernails. He gripped her hips and began to pound her, deeper, faster, sweat beading on his body as the blood surged through his penis. Her body tightened around him, squeezing, milking his length, and delicious sensations built inside him. Panting, he increased the tempo, closed his eyes, heard her raspy breathing, his own chest heaving as he fought to hold back his orgasm. Pleasure was not an option, but release was imminent.

Another thrust and he tilted her, pressing her back against his chest as he stroked her nipples between his fingers. That sent her spiraling over the edge, and her body quivered, then spasmed around his. Relentlessly he hammered into her as sweat slid down his brow and the sound of their naked bodies slapping together mingled with the wind.

Vincent never lost control.

Except in the throes of his release, and even then, he held on to his emotions. A guttural groan erupted from deep inside him, and he ground himself deeper, biting back a shout as his orgasm spurted into her.

Outside the moon shifted, slid behind the clouds, vanishing completely. A black emptiness crept over the room, beckoning. The wind suddenly roared, rattling the walls, and he tensed, his senses honed, warning him that the devil had risen again to wreak havoc.

A second later, his cell phone jangled from the nightstand, saving him from the awkwardness after.

He released the woman so abruptly she fell forward, still trembling with the aftermath of her release. He tore off the condom and climbed away from her, hating himself. God, what had happened to him back there? He'd imagined killing her.

She caught his arm and tried to pull him back to her. "Don't answer the phone."

He had to leave. It was the only way she'd be safe. "Duty calls."

Her eyelids fluttered wildly, and she ran a finger over his cock, raking a drop of come off the tip and sucking it into her mouth. "But I want you again already."

"Tell the criminals to take a night off, then," he growled.

She sighed, but he firmly ignored the disappointment in her eyes, the needy look suggesting that she wanted more than a lay, that she wanted to cuddle, to *talk*.

Instead, he reached for the phone, silently relaying what he didn't want to have to say out loud. She was an okay fuck, but anything else was not in the cards. No use telling a lie. She had simply been a momentary reprieve between cases.

She clamped her teeth over her lips, then offered a disappointed smile and reached for that seductive skirt. Still he didn't make excuses; he simply couldn't give what he didn't have.

A heart.

～

The silhouette of the woman's skeletal remains swung from the Devil's Tree in Clarissa King's front yard.

She shuddered, battling the urge to grab an ax and chop it down. She'd tried that before, but the tree was petrified and held some kind of supernatural power. The moment she cut off a branch, it grew back, yet no grass grew beneath it, and in the winter the moment snow touched the branches, it melted. Mindless screams echoed from the limbs, as well, the screams of the dead who'd died there in centuries past.

The screams of Clarissa's mother as she'd choked on her last breath in the same tree mingled with the others.

Forcing herself away from the window, she hugged her arms around herself to gather her composure. Night had long ago stolen the last strains of sun from the Tennessee sky, painting the jagged peaks and ridges of the Smokies with ominous shadows. Wind whistled through the pines and scattered spiny needles, dried and brittle from the relentless scorching heat that drained the rivers and creeks, leaving dead fish floating to the surface of the pebbled beds, muddy wells, and watering holes.

The grass and trees were starved for water, brown and cracking now with their suffering, and animals roamed and howled, searching for a meal in the desolate miles and miles of secluded forests.

There were some areas she'd never been because the infamous legends had kept her away. The Black Forest was one of them. Stories claimed that in the Black Forest, sounds of inhuman creatures reigned, half animal, half human—mandrills with human heads, shapeshifters, the unknown.

The few who'd ventured near had seen sightings of predators without faces, floating eyeballs that glowed in the dark, creatures that weren't human. No light existed inside that forest, no color. And any who entered died a horrific, painful death at the hands of the poisonous plants and mutant creatures that fed on humans.

The whispers of the ghosts imprinted in the land chanted and cried from its depths. And nearby lay the Native American burial ground where screams of lost warriors and war drums reverberated in the death-filled air, where the ground tremored from the force of decades-old stampedes and battle cries.

Clarissa shivered and hurried to latch the screen door of her cabin that jutted over the side of the mountain. Useless, probably. The ratty screen and thin wooden door couldn't protect her should the demons decide to attack.

The year of the eclipse—the year of death—was upon them.

Night and the full moon had brought them, stirring the devil from the ground, the serpents from the hills, the dead from the graves. Granny King—"Crazy Mazie" some had called her, God rest her soul—had taught her to read the signs. The insufferable heat, as if Hades himself had lit a fire beneath the earth, one to honor his kingdom. The blood-red moon that filled the sky and beckoned the predators to roam. The howl of Satan announcing his time for vengeance.

Yes, her once-safe hometown was full of evil, and no one could stop it until the demons fed their hungry souls with the innocents.

Yet the pleas of the women who'd died this week echoed in her head. She'd told the local sheriff her suspicions, that the deaths were connected.

That they were murders.

He'd wanted to know why she thought they were connected, and she'd had to be honest.

The victims had told her.

At least their spirits had when they'd visited.

Thankfully, Sheriff Waller had known her family and hadn't laughed but had listened. Her grandmother had had the "gift" of communing with the dead, and so had her mother. Granny King used to read the obits daily over her morning herbal tea and confer with the deceased as if they were long-lost buddies. Everyone in town had thought she was touched in the head. But she'd been right on so many occasions that most folks believed her.

The rest were scared to death of her.

Clarissa's mother had also been a psychic and an empath, only the constant barrage of needy souls had driven her insane. So insane she'd finally chosen to join them in death . . . instead of living and raising her daughter.

Bitterness swelled inside Clarissa at the loss, eating at her like a virus. She'd been alone, shunned, gossiped about, even called wretched names and cast away from certain families who thought she, too, was evil.

Her mother had visited Clarissa once after her death, ordered Clarissa to suppress her powers. And she had done so most of her life, trying to be normal.

She was anything but normal.

So she'd returned to the one place a few people accepted her. Back to Eerie.

Staying in her granny's house seemed to have unleashed the spirits, as if they'd lain in waiting all these years for their friend to return, and she could no longer fight their visits.

Outside, the wind howled, a tree branch scraped the windowpane, and ominous storm clouds hovered with shadowy hands that obliterated the light. Even with the ceiling fan twirling, the oppressive summer heat robbed the air, stirring cobwebs and dust that sparkled in the dark interior like white ashes.

Wulf, the German shepherd mix she'd rescued last year after he'd been hurt in a collapsed mine, suddenly growled, low and deep as if he sensed a threat, too, then trotted to the window and looked outside in search of an intruder.

Anxiety needled her as she contemplated the meeting she faced tomorrow.

Vincent Valtrez was coming to town.

She'd thought about him over the years, had wondered what had happened to him. Both outcasts, her because of her gift, him because of his violent father, they'd formed an odd friendship as kids.

But when she'd offered to see if his mother had passed, had suggested she could talk to her from the grave, he'd called her crazy and pushed her out the door. He told her he never wanted to see her again.

She couldn't believe he was an FBI agent now. He probably wouldn't be any more open to her psychic powers now than he had been back then.

She had to talk to him anyway. Convince him to listen. She hadn't asked for this gift, but she couldn't deny it, either. Not when others' lives were at stake.

Because this killer wasn't finished. And she didn't want the women's lost souls upon her conscience.

*HE'S EVERYTHING SHE FEARS . . .*
*SHE'S EVERYTHING HE CRAVES*

Please turn this page
for a preview of

# Dark Hunger

The second book in
*The Demonborn* series.

Available now.

# *Chapter One*

Quinton Valtrez was a killer.

A loner. A man without a conscience. A man who roamed the world as a ghostly gun for hire.

He needed no one. Wanted no one to need him.

But it was All Hallows' Eve, and dammit, he was going to get laid.

Still, the Glock inside his jacket rubbed against his chest, taunting him with the fact that he could never relax. That evil never died.

That it was his mission to stop it at all costs. Even if he didn't survive.

And All Hallows' Eve was the time when the veil between the world and the underworld was thinnest, when the spirit world could mingle with the humans and the ghosts of the dead came to life.

A buxom redhead in a pussycat costume smiled at him across the crowded Savannah street, and he put thoughts of the evildoers on hold as she glided toward him.

Even assassins deserved the night off.

"Hey, sexy," she purred. "Where's your costume?"

He cut her a sideways smile, letting his gaze dip to her

ample cleavage. "I am in costume. I'm going as a nice guy."

She threw her head back and laughed. "Want to head over to the party boat?"

"Sure." Despite the lust burning through his body, his heightened senses kicked in as he followed her through the dark, ghostlike alleys along River Street toward the lit-up ship.

The odors of refuse from the late-night partygoers—stale beer, cigarette smoke, and cheap perfume—permeated the air, along with the pungent aromas of fried fish, shrimp, and oysters floating from the pubs.

Suddenly the hairs on the back of his neck rose, and he paused and scanned the crowd, searching for the source of his unease. Kids, teenagers, and adults swarmed the streets in costumes portraying both colorful cartoon characters and the dark and macabre—everything from witches, zombies, pirates, werecreatures, birds of prey, and goblins to demons.

Twinkling orange lights, jack-o'-lanterns carved with scary faces, skeletons, ghosts, spiderwebs, and cardboard tombstones decorated the storefronts, while the sounds of spooky music, ghostly clanging, hooting owls, and moaning zombies added to the atmosphere.

Calling upon his chi, he focused on thumbing through the thoughts of various bystanders, searching for the evil one among them.

It was as natural as breathing, using his gift. He'd honed it when he'd lived with the monks. They'd taught him to access his inner being, drawing on nature and spirituality to strengthen his power. He'd expanded that power to a sharp tool in the military, searching and destroying the enemy on clandestine operations no one would ever admit existed.

His heart picked up its pace in recognition; he could feel the enemy, sense his presence. But an otherworldly sensation inundated the darkness of the enemy's soul.

Was this the demon the monks had warned him about?

Narrowing his eyes, he zeroed in on a stooped old man in a ratty green corduroy coat, his wire-rimmed glasses held together with duct tape. A terrible screeching sound suddenly reverberated from the dark skies.

He glanced up, sweat beading his brow as he spotted a vulture soaring above—not a new-world vulture but an old-world one, black with strong feet and a craving for carrion. And like the raven, this creature's bloodlust was for not only animal flesh but human meat as well.

Just like his own bloodlust.

A feeling of impending doom engulfed him as he connected with the vulture. The black bird was hovering above, ready to swoop down and gather the dead meat of an animal in its sharp talons and bury its bald head inside the carcass and feast on the remains.

Part vulture—part raven? Where had this creature come from?

He glanced through the crowd again, noticing a strange acidic odor emanating from the old homeless man in the green coat. Quinton pressed a finger to his temple, his head throbbing as he struggled to tap into the man's thoughts. His frail body trembled in the stiff wind, his mind a blank slate as if it had been wiped clean, all thoughts erased.

The old man's skin held a dull gray-black pallor, as if he'd already met death; his eyes were glassy and vacant, dazed, a shell of a human.

The redhead tugged at his elbow. "Aren't you coming, sugar?"

But a different woman's scent assaulted him. Delicious. Sultry. Enticing. "Go ahead, honey. I'll catch up," he murmured.

She raked her sharp nails down his arm. "All right, but don't make me wait long. I promise I'll destroy that nice-guy image of yours."

He chuckled. As if he'd ever had one.

She pranced toward the ship, and the enticing scent of the other woman quickly obliterated the redhead's cheap, flowery perfume.

Then his gaze fell upon the source.

Shiny, straight long blonde hair cascaded over slender shoulders. Intrigued, he forced his mind to drown out the sounds of the night. The party whistles and noisemakers prepared to ring in the celebration of the supernatural with witchcraft, séances, and pagan rituals that transcended time and worlds.

His body tingled with arousal, the fierce need he had to hunt stirring primal instincts he couldn't extinguish. He could almost smell the scent of her sex.

As if she sensed him watching her, she slowly turned, her gaze shifting through the crowd toward him.

His stomach clenched as their gazes locked. Shit.

It was *her*. CNN reporter Annabelle Armstrong. He'd watched her newsclips on TV, her do-gooder pieces on the homeless, her stories behind the stories.

A sliver of moonlight played across her face, her hair shimmering beneath the spilled light. He couldn't tear himself away. Her big blue eyes were hypnotic. Her pale creamy skin, exotic. And her rosy lips made him ache for a sinful taste.

A taste he could never have.

Because she was a damn reporter. A beautiful one, but falcons were beautiful, too. Still, they were birds of prey.

A bead of sweat slid down his neck. Had she discovered who he was?

Had she come to Savannah to expose him?

Annabelle Armstrong's gaze locked with Quinton Valtrez's. Damn. She'd come here to find him but hadn't expected to see him tonight. Not in the midst of a party in town.

And she certainly hadn't expected his penetrating gaze to rattle her. Or make her tingle with desire.

"Annabelle, are you listening?" Roland, her boss from CNN, barked over the phone. "Do you think you can get this story?"

"Yes," she said into her cell phone. "If Valtrez is this Ghost assassin working for some secret government unit, I'll find out."

She sucked in a sharp breath, well aware that the man hadn't moved since he'd spotted her. That his cold eyes and tightly set mouth screamed of danger. That every bone in her body warned her to run.

To forget this story—or she might end up dead.

"Annabelle?" her boss shouted.

"Yes, Roland, I'll do whatever I have to do to find out the truth."

She snapped the phone shut, smoothed down her skirt, and desperately struggled for a playful, flirty smile.

Quinton Valtrez was devastatingly and darkly handsome. Bigger than she'd imagined. His features were chiseled in stone, and his five o'clock shadow painted his bronzed stoic jaw with a hint of menace.

Her body tingled. Still, he was just a man.

And she was damn well tired of being at the bottom of the food chain at the station. Of being assigned human-interest pieces instead of the big stories.

She'd do whatever was necessary to get the scoop this time.

Even if it meant cozying up to a killer.

Suddenly a loud explosion rent the air, and the outer deck of the party ship exploded. Annabelle stumbled, the earth trembling below her feet as flames shot into the air. Wood and fiberglass shattered and spewed across the sidewalk as bodies collapsed into the burning rubble.

Quinton threw himself over Annabelle Armstrong, his heart hammering. What in the hell was happening? Were they under a terrorist attack?

And why in the hell had he tried to save her?

*Pure instinct*, he thought quickly.

A bloody arm landed beside them, its charred fingers reaching toward him as if begging for help.

Then a vulture swooped down and snapped up the arm, crunching it between its jagged teeth. A sinister look lit the bird's beady eyes, and in that split second, Quinton could have sworn the vulture smiled.

The rumble of the blazing fire continued as heat pelted him, and Annabelle's soft body trembled beneath his.

In the midst of the chaos and acrid odors of charred

flesh and burning wood, the horrific scent of evil splintered the air.

He had to do something.

He lifted his head slightly. "Are you okay?" he growled.

She moved slightly as if to push him off. "Yes, I think so."

Forcing himself onto his hands and knees, he stood, studying her. "Are you sure?"

"Yes," she said, her voice strained as she looked around at the mad chaos and dead bodies floating in the river.

Panicked screams jerked him into action. He dashed toward the burning ship, leaving Annabelle alone.

He needed to sniff out this killer. As he ran, he sent a text to his contact at Homeland Security to alert them of the attack.

---

The Death Angel flapped his black wings and bowed his bald head to Zion, paying umbrage to the new leader of the underworld. His belly was swollen from his recent meal, yet he still craved more tasty carrion.

The human bones and meat were especially delicious. The vulture-raven hybrid that was his demonic form for eternity had at first been punishment at its worst, but over the past century, he had embraced the predator's needs and urges, and now savored the agility of the bird's keen eyesight, flight patterns, and sharp talons.

Demons, shape-shifters, werecreatures, vampires, fallen angels, and other soldiers of Satan gathered in the underground cave of black rock lit by fiery torches.

Zion entered, his black cape billowing around his demonic form, his orange eyes lighting up the darkness.

The mortals would run in terror if they saw him now, complete with sharp fangs like claws, the devil's horns, flaming red scales, and cloven feet.

"The death toll?" Zion asked.

"In the hundreds."

Striking on All Hallows' Eve, the night of the dead, had been genius. All the Death Angel had to do was slide past the Twilight Guards, those with powers who guarded the portal between the mortals and demons, then he'd crossed into the mortals' world. Thousands of other demons had unleashed themselves tonight, their screeches unrecognizable to the humans but calling out to the others to announce their presence. The pagan holiday had also afforded him the opportunity to possess a human's body and walk among the masses unnoticed—the one he had chosen would serve him well.

And now that same one lay in a sleep-induced state awaiting his return. The bastard had been an easy mark, had been too weak to fight, his soul already black.

The Death Angel's power allowed him to crawl into the feeble minds of the weak on earth, put their minds to sleep, then bend them to his will. One touch and they became marionettes dancing on his string.

"I commend you." Zion's fiery breath rippled out in pleasure. "When I said spread evil and create chaos, you embraced the challenge."

The Death Angel flapped his wings with pride.

"And my sons?" Zion asked.

"The Seer found one of the twins, Quinton. He lives in the place they call Savannah, Georgia. This attack should capture the demonborn's attention."

Zion's red eyes flared, shooting sparks of crisp yellow

flames across the black rock in jagged lightning-bolt-like lines. "Quinton should be easy. He has succumbed to his destiny already by choosing to be a killer."

The Death Angel refrained from comment. That was true, although technically the Dark Lord targeted only sinners.

But the fact that Quinton had no regrets, felt no remorse over his kills, worked in their favor and would ultimately be his downfall.

Unfortunately, the Dark Lord's cause also kept the balance of good and evil alive within him.

That balance had to be destroyed.

The Dark Lord had a weakness for that reporter. They could use her to trap him.

She would also bring attention to the Death Angel's victories with the mortals, keep a tally of the dead and create pain and misery with her stories.

He'd use her until she became dispensable, then he'd dispose of her. He might even be able to twist Quinton to the point that he killed the woman.

That would definitely earn Quinton his place in the kingdom of evil.

# THE DISH

*Where authors give you the inside scoop!*

♥ ♥ ♥ ♥ ♥ ♥ ♥ ♥ ♥ ♥ ♥ ♥ ♥ ♥ ♥ ♥

*From the desk of Dee Davis*

Dear Reader,

The American Tactical Intelligence Command (A-Tac) is an off-the-books black ops division of the CIA. Hiring only the best and the brightest, A-Tac is made up of academicians with a talent for espionage. Working under the cover of one of the United States' most renowned think tanks as a part of Sunderland College, A-Tac uses its collegiate status to keep its activities "eyes only."

I suppose my love of academia is in part responsible for the creation of A-Tac. I graduated from Hendrix College in Arkansas. A small liberal arts school, the campus is dotted with ivy-shrouded buildings and tree-covered grounds. So although I moved my fictional Sunderland to upstate New York, it's still very much Hendrix that I see as I write. And like Nash Brennon (the hero of DARK DECEPTIONS), my degree is in political science. Although, unlike Nash, I have never worked for the CIA or taught in the social sciences.

But I have been in love. And I know how easy it is to let things get in the way. To let fear and distrust rule the day. To let a twist of fate stack the cards against finding happily-ever-after. Thankfully my situation was never quite so dire, but I can understand how Annie Gallagher feels when her path crosses Nash Brennon's again. Eight years ago, he betrayed her in the most basic of ways, and now they find themselves on opposite sides of a dangerous game. Annie with a desperate mission to rescue someone she loves, and Nash charged with stopping her—no matter the cost.

To get some insight into my world as a writer—particularly as the writer of DARK DECEPTIONS—check out the following songs:

"When I'm Gone"—3 Doors Down
"Into the Night"—Santana (featuring Chad Kroeger)
"Fields of Gold"—Sting

And as always, check out www.deedavis.com for more inside info about my writing and my books.

Happy Reading!

*Dee Davis*

♥ ♥ ♥ ♥ ♥ ♥ ♥ ♥ ♥ ♥ ♥ ♥ ♥ ♥ ♥

*From the desk of Jennifer Haymore*

Dear Reader,

When Katherine Fisk, the heroine of A TOUCH OF SCANDAL (on sale now), entered my office for the first time to ask me to write her story, I realized right away that she wasn't like one of my normal heroines. She was obviously of the lower orders, dressed in plain brown wool and twisting her hands nervously in her lap. Still, there was something about her dancing brown eyes that intrigued me, and I asked her why she had come.

"I'm in love," she said simply.

I laughed. "Well, that *is* what I write about. But tell me about this man you love."

"Well—" She swallowed hard. "He's a duke."

"Hmm." I studied the calluses on her hands, evidence of a life of hard work. "That makes it...difficult."

"I know," she sighed. "But there's more—much more."

"All right," I said. "Tell me."

I was already feeling doubtful, and I hesitated to encourage her. Don't get me wrong. I mean, I love Cinderella stories—but this girl really didn't look like a match for a duke. Plus, she didn't look like she could pay me what my last client had (my last client was a duchess, and she was loaded).

"Well...I think he wants to kill my brother."

I tapped my pen against my desk. A servant girl besotted with a duke intent on killing her beloved brother? Impossible, but also..."Intriguing," I said, "but you're making this difficult, you know."

"I know." She clasped those calloused fingers tightly together. "There's still more. There's the matter of the duke's wife..."

Well, that was that. I rose, intending to politely show her out. "I'm so sorry, Miss...Fisk, was it?"

She nodded.

"Miss Fisk, I'm sorry. If the man is already married, there's nothing I can do for you—"

"Oh, he isn't married!" Her brow furrowed. "Well, I don't think he's married...But he has a wife." Her frown deepened. "At least...he had a wife, but..."

I lowered myself back into my chair. "Okay. You're

going to have to start from the beginning. Tell me everything. Don't skip any detail."

She nodded, took a breath, and began. "When I first saw him, he was naked…"

And that was how it began. With a servant and a naked, married (or not!) duke seeking retribution from her brother. By the time Miss Fisk finished telling me her story, I was so hooked, I had to put pen to paper and write the entire, wild tale, and, believe it or not, I offered to do it pro bono. I'm usually pretty mercenary about these things, you see, but I figured if I pulled it off, at the end Miss Fisk would be more than capable of paying me, and quite handsomely, too.

I truly hope you enjoy reading Katherine Fisk's story as much as I enjoyed writing it! Please come visit me at my website, www.jenniferhaymore.com, where you can share your thoughts about my books, learn some strange and fascinating historical facts, and read more about the characters from A TOUCH OF SCANDAL.

Sincerely,

*Jennif Haymore*

♥ ♥ ♥ ♥ ♥ ♥ ♥ ♥ ♥ ♥ ♥ ♥ ♥ ♥

### From the desk of Rita Herron

Dear Reader,

I've always loved small towns. They feel homey and friendly. Everyone knows everyone else, trades recipes, and watches over one another's children. A small town is a safe place to raise a family.

But have you ever noticed that there seems to be one news story after another about the man or woman next door in those small towns who turned out to be a serial killer? Then there's the soccer mom who killed her husband. Or the man who slaughtered his family.

I've always been fascinated by this idea and it occurred to me one day, what if I took it one step further? What if brutal killers are living among trusting people in small towns...and they're not the scariest and most dangerous hidden element? What if there are demons, too? An entire world of them who live underground and mingle with the normal citizens.

And nobody in town knows about those demons... except, of course, for the local sheriff, Dante Valtrez... who is one of them!

There, I had my setup. But that wasn't enough. I needed to get into the heart of my hero and heroine.

Having a degree in Early Childhood Education, I've always been intrigued by the effects of parenting and society on young children. Our parents teach us to be nice, to follow the rules, to respect others and not to be naughty. But what if my hero wasn't taught that behavior as a child? What if he was taught to be naughty, to be evil? What if Dante Valtrez was raised by demons?

But even if Dante was a demon, I wanted him to be a hero. Like his brothers Vincent in INSATIABLE DESIRE and Quinton in DARK HUNGER, he has both good and bad in him (don't we all?), so he struggles with his own evil side throughout his entire life.

But how to showcase this struggle between good and evil? And then it occurred to me—what if he had to choose between killing a little girl to earn the acceptance of his fellow demons and doing what he knew was right and being forced out of the only community he ever knew? I chose to have Dante put to the ultimate test at age thirteen because that's the beginning of adolescence, a confusing time when a boy changes from a child to a man. This is a pivotal moment for Dante, because he's so torn at the sight of the little girl and her happy family, something he secretly craves, that he can't kill her. He fails the demon test because his humanity surfaces.

From that point on, Dante can't go back. But he doesn't fit into the mortal world either or think he deserves love. Still, he becomes determined to protect innocents from the monsters who raised him.

But Dante has suffered a painful childhood and has been tortured, He does deserve love, and the romantic in me had to find the perfect woman to give him that love. And who else could possibly save Dante but the one he was supposed to kill? The little girl he saved as a child who becomes the woman who wants to destroy all evil through her work?

Romance, suspense, murder, demons, family issues, secrets—this story is chock-full of them all. I hope you'll enjoy the surprise twist at the end and the final installment in *The Demonborn* series, FORBIDDEN PASSION—out now!

Rita Herron